VIBING

FRIENDSHIP & LYRICS BOOK ONE

KRIS BUTLER

Vibing
By Kris Butler

Second Edition: July 2024

Proofreading: © 2021 by Dee's Notes Proofreading Services
Formatting: © 2022 by Incognito Scribe Productions LLC
Cover Design: © 2022 by Incognito Scribe Productions LLC

❀ Created with Vellum

BLURB

When my bestie dragged me to the Caribbean after an ill-fated karaoke incident went viral, flushing my carefully laid plains down the drain, I jumped at the opportunity to run away for two weeks. Poppy had always been my rock, so following her here was a no-brainer. But as usual on the Penny & Poppy show, she failed to mention a few tiny details. Or in this case, a pretty big one.

DIYing, teaching, and having a spreadsheet for every occasion were so my jam.

Social media management, engagement, and loving the limelight, on the other hand, were definitely *not* in my wheelhouse.

So, finding myself on an island as part of some social media experiment, not my idea of a vacation! But as usual, Poppy landed me in a cluster and I had to make do. It helped that there were three guys who made my insides turn to goo.

Aspen-the thoughtful and caring musician.

Cooper-the friendly and playful athlete.

Rafe-the sensitive and charming stranger.

Sunscreen, contests, and a legendary DIY list, turned this two-week getaway into a vacation of a lifetime—tan lines not included.

And to think, it all started because of a vibe.

FOREWORD

CONTENT

- No third act breakup
- Threesome
- Mental Health Rep
- Finding yourself
- HFN ending-no cliffy!

SENSITIVE TOPICS

- Self doubt
- Feelings of Insecurity
- Morality Judgments
- Death of parents (in past)
- Family pressure
- Accidental drug use

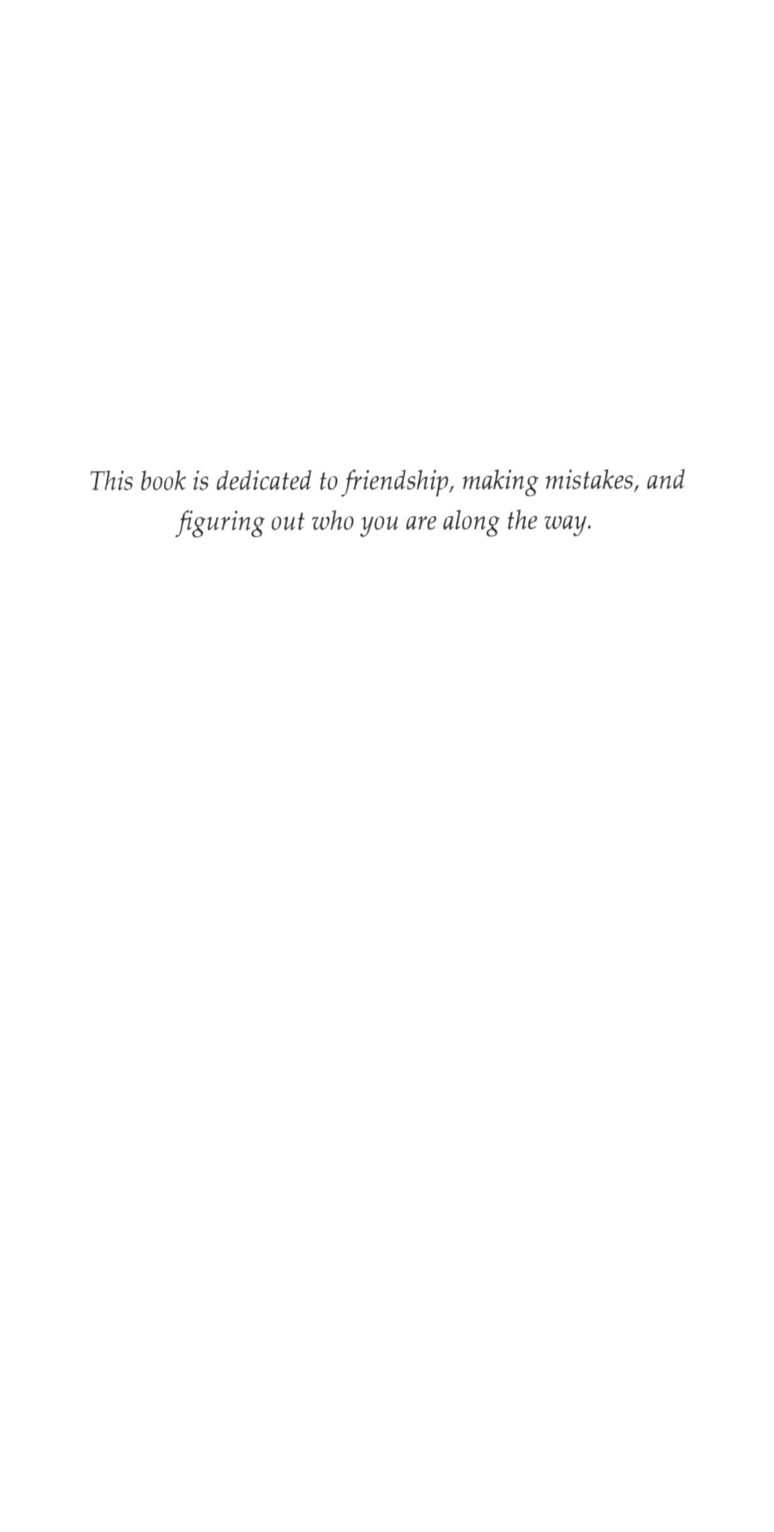

This book is dedicated to friendship, making mistakes, and figuring out who you are along the way.

CHAPTER
ONE

PENNY

Buzzzz. Buzzzz. Buzzzz.

Rolling over, I shifted my pillow again, trying to find a comfortable spot. The strange sound I'd heard for the past half hour vibrated again, and I peeked my head up, wondering what it was. My phone was dark, with no incoming message, so I ruled that out. Flopping back down, I narrowed my gaze at the snoring man next to me, counting all the ways I wanted to smother him with a pillow. Sleep was a precious commodity, and I was getting little of it nowadays.

Huffing, I rolled over again, and the noise sounded again. This time the vibration was louder, and I leaned up, braced on my elbows to see what it was. Moving my pillow, I waited to see if I could hear it again.

Buzzzz. Buzzz. Buzzzzz.

The realization of what it was hit me, my pulse skyrocketing as my face heated, as a laugh bubbled up. I jerked my arm out to grab it, wrapping my hands around my vibrator, and twisted it, turning it off this time before I shoved it back in its hidey-hole. Now that the noise was gone, I peered through the hair that had fallen in front of my face at the sleeping man who'd quieted. When a raucous snore rang out again, I relaxed, relieved he hadn't noticed. Grabbing my phone, I rolled out of bed and tiptoed into the bathroom. Walter's cat, Dusty, peeked her head up at my movements but decided I wasn't interesting enough and laid back down.

Sticking my tongue out at the snooty cat, I realized what I was doing and quickly, but quietly, shut the door behind me. I didn't know why I bothered, it was unlikely he'd wake from anything with the sounds he emitted, but politeness was a habit, I suppose. I wouldn't be me if I didn't consider others' feelings first.

Sitting on the toilet lid, I unlocked my phone to send a message to my best friend, knowing she'd be up. Poppy was a night owl, and her job as a singer had her out late at night, sleeping most of the day away. Unfortunately, my job as a teacher didn't lean toward that schedule, but it was nice when I needed her late at night. By the light of my phone, I opened my messages and sent her one.

ME: You'll never guess what I just did.
Poppy: You broke up with Walter?
ME: No. Why is that always your first guess?
Poppy: Because he doesn't deserve you. He's boring, and you'll live a perfect but miserable life if you stay with him.
ME: He's not that dull.

Poppy: Oh, is this backward Wednesday? My bad. You're right. He's soooo not boring.

ME: Haha. Why are we friends again?

Poppy: Because I'm awesome, and you couldn't resist my charm after I saved you on the school playground.

ME: Hmm, I seem to remember it differently.

Poppy: Nope, I'm pretty sure I was the one who pushed Samantha down into the dirt for saying redheads had no souls.

ME: That was epic. I'd never seen such a heroic thing from a 5-year-old.

Poppy: That's me, babe, epic. Now, what did you just do if it wasn't to break up with Walter?

ME: I masturbated while he was sleeping and then left my vibrator on for the past 30 minutes. I kept rolling over and hearing a sound, and I couldn't figure out what it was until just now.

The notification for an incoming video call popped up, and it didn't surprise me in the least. Hitting accept, I waited until her screen focused on a laughing face. She wiped her eyes a moment later, her laughter dying down.

"I think you broke me, Pen. That's the funniest and saddest shit I've ever heard. Fuck. I'm sorry you have to paddle the pink canoe while he sleeps. That's some messed-up shit. Though, imagining you trying to figure out the noise makes me laugh so hard. I almost wish I could've been there for that part."

"You done laughing at me?" I sighed playfully, rolling my eyes. I wasn't upset with her, it felt nice to laugh about it actually.

"Never. I'm your bestie. I get to laugh at you and beat up others that try to. That's how it works."

"Hmm, I don't remember that being part of the creed." I smiled, Poppy already making me feel better.

Blowing a kiss, Poppy shook her head at me, knowing I wasn't upset. "So, did he wake up and find out?"

"Nope. Thank God. I would've been mortified."

"You know, if you're that embarrassed to talk to your boyfriend about touching yourself, I'm scared to ask how your sex life is. Not to mention the fact you were *DIYing* yourself, which is funny because you're you." Poppy gave me a pointed look before bursting into giggles at her pun.

"I'm not even going to acknowledge what you just said there. How's your night going?"

Blowing out a breath, the front part of her hair fluttered as she looked upward for a few seconds. "Eh, it's okay. I've got one more song to sing. There haven't been too many people out tonight. I'm just feeling blah today, but your call definitely perked me right up. So, thanks for that."

"Hey, what are friends for if not to provide fodder for one another? At least my blunder is good for something." I smiled, wanting to pick up her mood. Poppy was the type of person who was the life of the party with her infectious attitude and personality 98% of the time. It was the other 2% that worried me when she got into her head too much, her moods spilling over into all the areas of her life like a dark blanket.

Poppy and I had been friends since the infamous playground battle in kindergarten when she'd tackled my bully, effectively scaring herself to my side ever since. It helped that we were both redheads whose names started with a P, and when we discovered our last initials were B & J, it secured our friendship as PB&J for a lifetime. She was the sister I wish I had instead of the one I did and the best friend anyone could ask for. My life wouldn't be half as fun without Poppy.

"This is true," she said, nodding. "You do provide excellent comedic relief. It's one of your best features."

"Who knew all those years of failing summer theater camp would pay off?" Laughing together, we both smiled as we remembered our childhood summers spent together at all the various camps we attended throughout the years.

"Speaking of," she started but was interrupted by a knock. "One sec, babe." She set her phone down, the angle giving me a side view of her walking to answer the door. Poppy was backstage in a dressing room of one of the venues she regularly sang at. She opened the door, a stage-hand in a headset appearing on the other side.

"Five-minute warning, Poppy."

"Thanks, Mark. I'll be right up."

Sauntering back to me, she lifted the phone, and I watched as she checked herself out in the camera. "I'm still rocking it."

"Yeah, you are. You'll do great. We can talk about our summer plans on Friday. I've got two more days of school left. I can't fucking wait. This year has been rough."

"Sounds good, Pen. Now, go and ménage a moi. Just keep it quiet. No vibing interruptus needed." She winked, the camera going dark before it blinked off. A delayed chuckle left me at her euphemism, and like always, I felt lighter after talking to her. Standing, I tiptoed to the door and opened it a crack to peek out. The lumbering man snored on, and I sighed, stepping out into the room.

As much grief as I gave Poppy about her countless quips to break up with Walter, as I stared at the sleeping man, the realization she wasn't wrong sat heavily on my chest. She was right and had been for a while if I was honest with myself. Tonight only proved it. Walter was not the guy for me.

He was a nice guy. The type you took home to your parents and would help little old ladies cross the street. He was moderately attractive and had a steady job. He didn't excessively drink, smoke, or cheat on me. Walter followed all the rules and was as straight-laced as they came. There was no doubt he'd provide me with a good life, a decent life.

On paper, Walter and I made sense—elementary school teacher and an accountant. We were close in age, had similar goals, and I thought we wanted the same things in life—marriage, our own home, and someday, kids.

But as I stood at the foot of the bed, listening to his snores, I knew I couldn't do *this* for the rest of my life. Hell, I loved sleeping too much to never get any ever again.

My emotions warred inside me with the realization I had to break up with him. I'd never dumped someone before, typically we either both came to a conclusion we wouldn't work, or I was ghosted, only later to discover they'd used me to get to Poppy. This was new territory for me, and as I contemplated it, sweat began to drip down my back at the thought of disappointing him, of disappointing my parents.

I was, after all, the girl who always did the right thing, who never wanted to hurt anyone's feelings, and was always described as 'you're just so nice.' My parents, and even Walter, assumed we'd be tying the knot within the following year. The thought of that gave me hives. A proposal and marriage shouldn't give you hives. At least, I didn't think so.

A sense of adrenaline surged through me at my conclusion, and I hurriedly ran around the room, picking up my belongings as I tossed them into a bag. Thankfully, we didn't live together, only having 'sleepovers' at one another's places on scheduled nights throughout the week. A laugh bubbled up at the insanity of that realization.

Stuffing the last of my clothes, a few books, a hairbrush, and my toiletries into the bag, I slung it over my shoulder before grabbing my pillow and the blanket I'd brought with me. Did I delight in yanking it off the man who slept? Maybe. Would I admit it? Never.

The snoozing beast didn't even budge, and I realized how idiotic I'd been tiptoeing around all this time like I might wake him. Walking over to his dresser, I picked up a thick graphic novel he had lying there. At one time, I thought it gave him substance to be interested in these. That was until I discovered he'd been gifted it by his brother and didn't have anywhere else to put them. Walter actually turned his nose up at the hefty tome.

Picking it up, I dropped it, the large mass slamming into the wooden surface with a nice thud and scattering his change across the surface.

Walter startled, sitting upright and twisted from side to side until he found me standing near his dresser. "Honey, everything okay? What are you doing over there?" He rubbed his eyes, peering at me in annoyance.

"Walter, I hate that you call me honey, so I think we should break up."

It wasn't the most eloquent breakup speech, but it would do.

"What?" he sputtered, twisting to reach for me. Stepping back, I kept my hands full of my pillow and blanket out so he couldn't touch me. I didn't want him to try to convince me I was making the wrong choice. Because I knew with every part of my being that I wasn't.

"It's time, Walter. I'm not happy, and if you think about it, I doubt you are either."

"Penelope, what's this about? Has Poppy been getting into your head again? Come to bed. We can talk about this in the morning."

"Sorry, no can do. I'm leaving and felt I owed it to you to say goodbye. So, bye." I turned to walk to the door, but he couldn't leave it at that, and the Walter no one saw behind closed doors emerged.

"For fuck's sake, Penelope. Get your ass into bed, and stop this bullshit."

"Ha! The answer is still no."

"Fine. Go and be a little bitch with your slut friend. You can be the one to break it to your parents why they won't be getting the summer wedding next year they wanted."

"Funny, we'd have to be engaged for that to happen. But yeah, I will, and they'll deal. But watch your mouth with how you talk about Poppy."

"Whatever. Go fuck yourself."

"Already done that tonight, in fact." I stopped, pivoting to turn toward my hidey-hole to pull out my vibrator. "I can't forget my best friend here. Lord knows I've had to use him a lot over the past few months. Have a nice life, Walter."

I was almost at the door when he tried to hurl another

insult at me, clearly grasping for straws. "It wasn't like sex with you was all that great to begin with!"

"Have fun using your hand!"

Waving, I flipped him off before I shut the bedroom door and hurried out of his apartment. Adrenaline pumped through me as I practically skipped to my car, and I quickly shoved my stuff to the passenger seat as I climbed in. I wouldn't put it past him to run out after me once he realized I wasn't joking. This wasn't a manipulative tactic on my part, this was freedom and I was taking it.

The car pinged once the Bluetooth had connected, and I turned out of the complex, practically bouncing in my seat. "Call, Poppy."

"*Calling, Poppy,*" my speakers announced, and I tapped my fingers on the steering wheel, urging her to answer.

The phone rang three times before she did, and I wanted to slap myself for forgetting. Cringing, I turned, the clicker sounding into the night as I waited for Poppy to catch her breath.

"Sorry."

"It's fine, Pen, what's up?" she asked, but I could clearly hear 'my dick' in the background, her after-show hookup having been interrupted by me.

"I did it. I broke up with Walter, and I'm currently fleeing the premises."

"Shut up! Are you fucking with me? Please say you're not fucking with me?"

"I'm not. I'm a free woman, Pop. I just couldn't take the snoring anymore. It was the last straw, and I knew I had to get out of there before I talked myself into doing what everyone else wanted me to do."

"Hell to the fucking yes, girl! We need to celebrate. I don't care that you have school in the morning. Get your ass here to the Flying Pig, pronto. I owe my girl a drink!"

"I'm on my way, but what about…" I trailed off, a little uncertainty filling me. Poppy wasn't shy about her sexual escapades, but I didn't want to ruin her fun.

"Him? He's a dime a dozen. You and me, we're forever, babe. I'll have a spot at the bar waiting for you."

"Oh shit, I'm still in my PJ's."

A cackle rang out over my speakers, and it took her a few seconds to recover. "Shit, Pen. I think you're trying to kill me tonight. Okay, new plan. I'll meet you in the parking lot. Then shots."

"Okay, that I can do. I'll be there in about five minutes."

"Wahoo!" I heard her walking and the music getting louder as she neared the main bar area. "Hey everyone, Penny's on her way here, and she just dumped Walter's ass!" Shouts rang out through the bar, and I inwardly groaned.

"Thanks so much for that. I'm sure my mother will know before sunrise now."

"Why do you think I did it? Now you can't change your mind later."

"Ugh, bish, fine. See you in a bit."

"Hey, Pen?"

"Yeah?"

"I'm so fucking proud of you."

"Thanks, Pop." The call ended, and I found myself smiling the rest of the way to the bar, her praise feeling nice. I knew there would be backlash later, but for tonight, I'd enjoy my decision. I had school in the morning, but it was almost summer break and everything had been completed. The last two days were primarily make-up ones anyway. It wouldn't be anything significant to do, and while trying to wrangle eight-year-olds with a hang-over wasn't ideal, I'd manage if it meant I got to celebrate this tonight.

It felt weird being happy because I broke up with my boyfriend. I should be sad or something. But the reality of the situation was, I'd stood up for myself and what I wanted out of life instead of what others wanted for me. It was small, but I'd pushed that people-pleasing need aside for one moment and won.

So, I'd go and get dressed up into something other than Hello Kitty pajamas, and I'd share a shot or two with my friend, relishing in the fact that it was my vibrator who'd finally convinced me to do what I wanted for a change.

CHAPTER
TWO

My head pounded as I waited in line for a coffee. I wanted to be angry with Poppy, to blame her for my current state, but my current state had been all me. I'd known full well when I stepped into that bar I wouldn't be leaving after one shot. I never did, and like the grown-up I was learning to be, I pulled up my sassy underpants and accepted responsibility for it. Hangover and all.

Though, in hindsight, I might've wanted to wait until after the school year had ended. The hangover I was fighting, wholeheartedly agreed.

"What can I get you?"

"Coffee. Big. Black."

The barista snickered at my obvious pain, the sunglasses and raised hood of my jacket doing nothing to hide my sorry state. Smiling sardonically, I shuffled to the side after paying and waited for the hopeful cure to the maracas in my head. The lack of sleep had me zoning out, and I almost missed the whispers behind me.

"I heard she slept with his best friend."

"No way! I heard she told him she was in love with her slutty friend."

"Nothing but trouble, those two."

"Walter's too good for her."

It was the last one that had me snapping my head up, the force sending the hood back, off my head, and I heard the whispers stop. I didn't turn, though. The thing about small towns, it was never short on gossip and limited on the number of redheads. And my mop of red hair was pretty distinct. The barista walked over, handing me my giant cup of coffee, and I smiled gratefully, taking it from her.

Taking a big sip, I steeled myself to face whoever it was behind me, having a good guess on just who. Once the coffee had traveled through my system, I turned and laid eyes on a few of my high school classmates sitting at a round table. They were all purposefully avoiding eye contact, only adding to their guilt. Figures.

"Good morning, ladies. How are we doing today?" I asked, addressing them, not hiding the fact I'd heard them. I'd found over the years that I could fight bullies in a different way than Poppy.

I hadn't been joking when I said I'd failed out of theater camp, but it had taught me how to fake it with the best of them. Nothing like a camp full of middle schoolers to help you strengthen your backbone. Those kids were ruthless!

Of course, my grit was only limited to humiliation, but

we all had to start somewhere. At least the bonus was how much it irritated the popular girls when I didn't get embarrassed, and in the end, it became my strength.

Smiling down at the table, I waited for them to say something, their unease making me feel loads better. When they only shuffled their plates around and didn't have anything to add, I took another big gulp. The scalding liquid burned its way down my esophagus, but it helped me focus on the three of them instead of the two-man band in my head.

"Well, good talk. See you at the next PTA meeting!" Walking around the table, I was at the door when nasty Samantha finally decided to say something.

"I wouldn't be so sure about that."

The other two tittered at her comment, finding their friend hilarious. I stopped halfway through the door, half my body in the shop and the other out, as I debated on saying something. In the end, the person coming into the store had me moving, leaving them to their nonsense. When I pulled into the school parking lot five minutes later, I wished I'd taken their comments more seriously.

Standing at the front of the school with grim faces were the principal and school counselor. They eyed me with unease as I approached, and I swallowed, not liking how this felt all of a sudden. The wind whipped around me, tossing up my hair, I grimaced when I pulled the sunglasses off, attempting to appear professional as I greeted them.

"Good morning, I didn't miss a special announcement to be early today or something, did I?"

"No, Ms. Baxter. Can you join us in my office, though?"

the stodgy older man asked, without really asking. It was a command if I ever heard one.

"Um, sure."

I followed behind them, dread rising up in my throat as I attempted to smooth down the flyaway hair. This wasn't something I'd anticipated this morning. In fact, I'd never been called to the principal's office before.

Well, actually, that wasn't true. Being friends with Poppy lent to a certain amount of trouble. But, never like *this*. Not when I didn't have any clue what it was about. I couldn't even formulate a strong argument since I had no clue what was going on. Maybe I was overreacting and it was something good. Wasn't that a statistic? We jumped to the worst-case scenario when typically it wasn't a bad thing?

Yeah, let's go with that.

I conveniently ignored the pitying looks the counselor kept shooting me over her shoulder.

Following them into the front office, I found myself facing the firing squad a moment later once we squeezed into the space. Principal Allen motioned for me to take a seat, so I did, setting the multitude of things I carried down at my feet. I'd made cupcakes before I'd gone over to Walter's last night for the end of the year party, as well as having all the supplies for the craft projects I had planned today. Yarn, popsicle sticks, and glue bulged at the top, daring to spill out onto the floor. Clearing my throat, I sat up straight, staring at the man who'd been my boss for the past five years.

"It's come to my attention, Ms. Baxter, that there was a lapse in judgment on your part last night."

I blinked, trying to understand what he was saying, but

nothing came to mind. "I'm sorry, I don't know what you're referring to."

He shuffled, a little uncomfortable by my question. Principal Allen looked over to Mrs. Jeffries, and she stepped forward, taking over.

"We're referring to your break-up with Walter."

"Okay, what does that have to do with the school?"

"Well," she started, fidgeting, "it's come to our attention that you might not be in the best state of mind. That perhaps, the stress of the school year is getting to you, and maybe it would be better for you to start your summer vacation today."

"Today?" I asked, blinking.

"Yes. I'm so glad you understand."

Shaking my head, I fumbled for the words. "But I don't. You heard I broke up with Walter, and now you think I need to take time off? I'm still struggling to understand how my personal life connects to my job."

"Well, you see," the principal interrupted, taking over, "it became our business when you made a *spectacle* of yourself." He practically spat the last part, the force hitting me like a slap, so similar to my own mother's words, I had to focus for a second on where I was.

"I'm sorry, wh-at?" I stuttered, blinking back the tears that wanted to form.

"Ms. Baxter, did you happen to go to the Flying Pig last night?" Nodding, I stared at her wide-eyed.

"It seems that in your, um, celebration of the end of your relationship, you sang karaoke and took a video. I believe you intended to send it to your ex, Walter, but instead, it, *unfortunately*, was sent out to the entire school."

"The entire school," I whispered as the color drained

from my face, and I struggled to swallow, my throat becoming thick with unshed tears rising up. She nodded, her uncomfortableness turning to pity once again as I tried to recall what I'd done.

"Yes, and well, that includes every teacher, the school board, and…"

"Parents," I finished for her.

She dipped her head, the sympathy in full force, and I wanted to be sick. This was beyond humiliating; this was a fucking disaster.

Of course, the smug principal had to pull the video up and turn his phone around for me to see my epic shame. Sure enough, there I was, the camera angle wobbly and the lens a little blurry as I held it up. At first, it was just the bar, but then Poppy and I came into focus. I had no clue what time it was, but the blank in my memory made me fear how many shots I'd had.

"Walter," I slurred, "in case you didn't understand earlier. You're a horrid lover, *horrid*. Tonight wasn't the first time I had to finger paint by myself after you fell asleep. It's been practically every time. Every. Time. You might want to think about that and up your game. Just saying."

I shrugged, placing the phone on the bar and then jumped up on the stage. The person singing wouldn't give me the microphone, so I grabbed my purse, shouting I'd use something better. Poppy stood off to the side, laughing with me. When I pulled out the hot pink vibrator and began to sing into it—I wanted to die. Fuck. I didn't think I could be embarrassed by anything anymore, but apparently, I hadn't met myself.

Kind of a slap to your face when you were the cause of your own humiliation.

The video kept playing, the song ringing out as I tried to sing along, albeit off-key. A songbird, I was not. Lifting my hand, I pushed the phone down, no longer able to watch. Remembering my commitment to myself earlier to have a stronger backbone, I raised my head, prepared to own my blunder.

"So, yeah, what do you need me to do? Just leave school early and hope it blows over during the summer?"

"Well," Mrs. Jefferies began, shuffling awkwardly, "that's a start. We do appreciate you not making a fuss about this."

"Of course. I'm not going to deny it. It's obviously me. Clearly, I didn't use good judgment last night and things got a little out of hand. If you need me to make a statement, then I'm willing to do that."

"Thank you for taking this seriously, Ms. Baxter. For starters, finishing your school year today, and then the school board would like to reevaluate your employment over the summer and whether or not you're still a good fit for Maple Ridge Elementary."

Gulping, I nodded slowly, trying to keep the tears back at that statement. Shit. "Of course. I'll just go and clean out my classroom."

"Actually, we had a staff member grab the things we felt were important, and the rest you can gather after school is out."

Standing, I grabbed my stuff in shock. When I noticed the cupcakes, I passed them off to Mrs. Jeffries in a stiff motion. "Could you make sure my class gets these?

They're labeled which are gluten-free, peanut-free, sugar-free, and vegan."

"Of course, honey."

Nodding, I couldn't quit agreeing, afraid I'd start sobbing in the office if I opened my mouth to say anything else. When I walked out, a box with the items from my desk waited for me. Gathering it up into my arms, I hurriedly exited out of the front of the school. As soon as I hit the fresh air, the tears started to fall. When I made it to my car, I shoved the box into the seat and turned on the vehicle, debating what to do. The song I'd sang in the video came on, blaring through my speakers, mocking me.

Shutting it off, I turned out of the parking lot. "Call, Poppy."

"Calling, Poppy."

The ringing trilled through the speakers, and I begged her to answer despite knowing it was early and I'd been barely functional.

"Somebody had better be dead," she answered on the last ring before voicemail.

"P…" I swallowed, the tears clogging my voice. "I think I screwed up."

I heard the sheets moving as she sat up, drawing the phone closer to her face. "I'm here. What happened?"

"Apparently, I basically live-streamed me signing into a vibrator to the entire school, parents included."

"Oh, shit, babe. Though, I bet that's the most fun most of the bitches have seen in ages."

"This is serious, Poppy. I might lose my job."

"What? That's stupid. You weren't saying anything about the school! How can they do that? Alright, who do I need to kill, and what's their address?"

"I love you, P, but I don't think you can make this go away by threatening anyone. I have to own up to it and hope the past five years mean more than one drunken mistake."

I heard her blow out a breath. "I know. I'm sorry. I'm not trying to make light of it. It's just my comfort zone, you know. Someone messes with you, and I fix it with my death stare. I can't do that here, so I'm feeling helpless. I'm sorry this is happening to you. I guess we shouldn't have had those last shots, huh?"

"No, definitely not. And Pop, I love you for who you are. You're my girl, and if I ever did need to hide a body, I know you'd be there to show me how."

"Damn straight." I could hear her smile through the phone, helping me smile in return, the tears receding for the time being. "Have your parents heard?" she asked.

"Honestly, I don't know. Though, now that I think about it, probably. The three amigos were already gossiping about it at the coffee shop this morning."

"Damn, those bitches don't waste time. How was Samantha doing? Her nose still crooked?" Poppy chortled through the phone, and I couldn't help but laugh with her.

"Yeah, I think she's too stubborn to get a nose job." Poppy had given her a broken nose and two black eyes before senior prom for stealing my date and saying she was doing me a favor by not having to break his heart when he discovered I really only loved vaginas. Ever since Poppy and I became friends, Samantha has been threatened by our closeness and relationship.

"So, are you off work now? What's going to happen?"

Blowing out a breath, I took a turn toward my apartment, the blinker sounding in the background. "They suggested I take these two days off and start my summer vacation early. They had someone clear out my desk and said they'd let me come back over the summer to grab anything else; the school board will meet and determine if I'm redeemable and capable of continuing teaching second graders."

"Well, as much as that sucks, it might be the perfect silver lining."

"How so?" I asked, apprehension in my voice.

"Don't hate me," she started before I cut in.

"Never," I affirmed, not even having to consider it.

"Fine, wrong choice of words. Don't be mad," she cringed, "but I sorta signed us up for something a few months back. I didn't tell you because I wasn't sure if I'd get it, or well if *we'd* get it."

"Uh-huh. Classic Poppy thinking... go on," I encouraged.

"Listen here, girl, just because you know me better than anyone doesn't mean I deserve your sass before coffee."

"Keep telling yourself that. Now, spit it out. I'm almost to my apartment."

"Well, start packing your bags, Pen! Because you and me, we're headed to the Caribbean!"

"Say what, now?"

"You heard me. Bikinis, flip flops, and summer flings are about to be our whole agenda. Let me kick this guy out of bed, and I'll be over to help. My bags are already packed. I've been trying to figure out how to get you to either miss school tomorrow or pack your bags for you so I could kidnap you once the bell rang and hide you away from Walter. So thanks to your indiscretion, now I don't have to think more than I need to."

"I'm so glad my public shame can help you avoid doing extra work, slob."

"Call it whatever you want, but tomorrow we'll be on the beach, and nothing bad happens there."

"Um, yeah, it does. Did you forget we both burn just thinking of the sun? Or how about ocean pollution? Or—"

"Pen! Stop the hysterics and just say, '*Yes, Poppy, you're brilliant and the bestest friend a girl could ask for. I would love to spend two weeks this summer on a beach for free. What would I do without you?*'"

"Yeah, all that," I grumbled.

"You're no fun when you get halfway fired."

"Hey!"

"What? You're not. Now, start packing, or when I get there, I'm doing it. And I'll just throw in the sluttiest things you own. Wait, you don't own anything an eighty-year-old wouldn't wear. So basically, I'll grab your toothbrush, phone charger, and sunscreen. Your choice."

"I feel like we need to talk about this. I mean, I need a wax, and I'm not sure I have a bathing suit that isn't five years old."

"Even better. Buy all new things there. This isn't as complicated as you're making it."

"But I have my plants and my gerbil."

"Already covered. Liam said he'd do it."

"Oh, *Liam*, was it?"

"Shut it. Nothing going on there. He's my brother's best friend. He sees me as a little sister. Always has. So, this is your ten-minute warning. See you soon, best bish."

"Okay, okay. Bye, you crazy girl."

The phone call ended as I pulled into my parking lot, thankfully finding a close spot. As I walked to my door, I found several messages from my parents and sister telling me how disappointed they were in me. Suddenly, this trip seemed like the best idea ever. Getting away from this town and the gossip wouldn't be bad.

Besides, Poppy might be crazy, but we always had fun. Even if it ended with me singing bad karaoke into a vibrator, I couldn't deny I hadn't enjoyed it.

CHAPTER
THREE

ASPEN

My ears were still ringing from the concert last night; the last band had given a new meaning to screamo. I'd been shocked they could still talk afterward; their vocal cords had to be torched. Laughing at a memory, I nudged Jett next to me.

"Do you remember Coop telling us that story about how the voice actor for that anime he watched screamed so loud he passed out? I wonder if the guys from last night's concert have ever done that?"

Jett pulled his dark sunglasses down, narrowing his eyes at me. "Really? That's what you're thinking about right now?"

Shrugging, I turned back to the conveyor belt, waiting for it to turn on. "It's better than whatever you're stressing over."

"Hmph," he grunted, not acknowledging my brilliance. Jett was one of my oldest friends and bandmates, but the dude was broody. It worked well in our band, Shadows of Mayhem, but he sometimes needed to lighten up in real life.

Jett and I had grown up together, forming the band in high school. Our other two members had joined later, after a few transitions, and we'd created Shadows of Mayhem or S.O.M for short. We'd just finished a ten-city tour, and Jett and I had jumped on a plane for our next adventure. Our agent thought it would be great coverage and a way to get our name out there more. Jett didn't necessarily disagree with the logic, but he wasn't happy about it either.

Sun, beaches, and pretty girls would be my environment for the next two weeks. I didn't get what there wasn't to like. He only caved when Trinity convinced him to use it as a writer's retreat.

The whirling started, and I sighed, stepping forward to grab my bags. It'd been a long flight from Pennsylvania, and I was looking forward to a shower, some food, and sleep. Preferably in that order.

When I spotted my suitcase, I leaned forward to grab it but was intercepted by a cute redhead. Smiling, I crossed my arms and watched as she lugged the heavy bag off the conveyor belt. When she turned, I winked, stopping her.

"Oh, hi, sorry, did I cut in front of you?" she asked, her cheeks heating with the question.

"You did, but I don't mind."

"Great, sorry about that." She started to walk away with my bag in tow.

"You know, I've never had a girl try to steal my luggage before to get my attention. Well, you got it, suitcase bandit."

"I didn't steal your luggage," she huffed, turning to defend herself.

"Hmm." I cupped my jaw, covering my smile at her cuteness. "Is that a fact?"

"Yes, I'm not, you know, flirting. I'm anti-boy on this trip." She waved her hand around, pointing in my direction in a frenzied gesture.

"That's too bad, bandit, because I think you're adorable."

"Well, deal with it. I'm not flirting, so bye." She lifted her chin and turned to go. Reaching out, I softly placed my hand on her arm.

"Okay, fair, but *that* is still my luggage."

She whirled, some of her fire peeking through, and I found my blood rushing to my cock in excitement. "This is *my* bag! I'll prove it." She bent down to unzip the suitcase in the middle of the airport, determined to prove her point.

"I wouldn't do that if I were you," I warned.

"Why, embarrassed to be wrong?" she teased, looking up from the ground. Her blue eyes sparkled, and I noticed the freckles across her nose and cheeks. Her hair was long, with a slight curl at the end. She had part of it pulled back, sunglasses perched on her head. She was dressed simply in jean shorts, converse, and a tank top, but I found her undeniably sexy. Crossing my arms, I braced my chin and smirked as I waited, wanting to see how she handled it when my boxers spilled out.

Accepting the challenge, her eyes sparkled and she returned to the zipper, pulling it hard and flinging the lid up. My sorry packing job became evident immediately as dirty clothes mixed with a few clean ones fell out, tumbling to the floor. Squatting down, I picked up the polka-dotted boxers, holding them out between us.

"I dunno, but I think I pull them off better."

She turned slowly, her face reddening more with each second, and she covered her mouth. "I'm so sorry. I honestly thought this was my suitcase, and *you* were trying to flirt with me or something. I can't believe you just let me show your underwear to an airport full of people, though." She slapped my shoulder, and I laughed, liking she wasn't too upset with me.

"It was worth it if I got to talk to you more."

"Wow, okay, you're good." She stuck out her hand, her smiling hitting me straight in the heart. "I'm Penelope, but everyone calls me Penny."

I reached across, making sure to use the one not holding my underwear to grasp hers. "It's a pleasure to meet you, Penelope. I'm Aspen."

"Well, Aspen, how can I help make this suitcase snafu better?"

"Hmm, that's a great question. Let's first get all my clothes off the floor and shoved back in, and then maybe I'll have an idea."

"Okay, I can accept that." She giggled, the sound light and airy. "Though, there's a part of me that is itching to organize this for you. I have kind of an obsession with folding things."

"As kinky as that sounds, Penelope, I'd prefer you touching my underwear without an audience."

"That was a sex joke, wasn't it?" she asked, turning toward me.

"Apparently a bad one."

"Nah, it was cute but could use some work." She

shrugged one shoulder as she kept stuffing my boxers, socks, and t-shirts into the luggage without a care in the world.

"You're very unexpected, Penelope. I like that." I smiled wide, my cheeks hurting from the gesture as I beamed at her.

"Penny! There you are. I swear, I always forget how crazy you are in airports. I think I block it out, so I don't have to remember running. God, I fucking hate running," a statuesque woman with a lighter shade of red hair panted as she pulled two suitcases to a stop next to Penny. I almost snorted when I read her shirt, *"I hate running, but I love pizza."* She eventually looked down at her friend kneeling on the ground and noticed me.

"Oh, well, hello. I see you work fast, Pen."

"Ha! No, just a case of mistaken luggage."

She finished putting the last sock in, and we both zipped it up. My hand brushed hers for a brief second causing goosebumps to flood me at the touch. It felt like something out of a book, and I looked up to see if she'd experienced it too. Penelope stood, placing her hands in her pocket, rocking on her heels suddenly, appearing awkward.

Jett walked over, his nose in his phone, not having noticed the two girls. "Aspen, are you ready yet? I need to —" He stopped, looking up, and his eyes landed on Penny's friend.

She was gorgeous in an entirely different way from Penny, but women like her typically intimidated the crap out of me. I'd always found myself drawn more to the cute girls, the ones who got my lame sex jokes and didn't make me feel like a fool. Who were comfortable to be around and didn't make me doubt myself. Penny had that quality about her.

"Um, *hello*. Aspen, introduce me to your friends." He shoved his phone into his back pocket, making sure to flex his forearm for good measure.

"Sure. Jett, this is Penny and her friend… ?"

"Poppy," she offered, sticking her hand out for Jett. He took it, bringing it to his lips to kiss. Jett was a broody fucker at times, but the guy had swagger in spades. It was why he was the lead singer, after all, and I was the lead guitarist. I played better than him and could rival his voice when I wanted, but I didn't have that performer's charisma like he did.

Penny nudged me, and I startled, forgetting she was there for a second as I'd gotten lost in my thoughts. "It looks like I might get to teach you a thing or two about organization after all."

"Oh?" I smiled, turning to look down at her. I found myself liking how her eyes sparkled up at me and the easy way we seemed to fall into conversation. "I think I'll be okay with that. First, let's get your real suitcase."

"Good idea. I'm sure it's the only one left at this point."

We left Poppy and Jett to their flirting and walked a few steps to the belt. She wasn't far off. Two suitcases remained, both looking sad as they traveled around the belt forlornly. "I'm guessing, this one?" I asked, pointing to the one very similar to mine.

"Yep, how did you guess?" She giggled, and I knew I wanted to hear it again.

Lugging it up, I was impressed when it wasn't heavy; in fact, I'd say it was lighter than mine. "Hmm, now I think you intentionally took mine to flirt with me. There's no way you thought my heavy one was yours?" I lifted an eyebrow as I stared, my smile covering my face.

"I plead the fifth. Besides, what do you take me for? I'm a lady!"

Chuckling with her, I passed the suitcase over, our hands touching again, and I sucked in yet another breath.

"So, Penny who organizes, where are you staying?"

"I feel like that's the first thing they teach in Stranger Danger 101. How do I know you're not going to follow me there and murder me?"

"Well, unless there's a weapon hiding under all my clothes, I doubt that would be my play."

"True, unless you suffocate people with your stinky socks."

Cringing, my face tinted, and I pulled my hat down, rubbing the back of my head. "Yikes, you noticed that, huh?"

"I mean." She smiled, doing that one shoulder shrug again, killing me softly with how cute it was.

"How about this, we're staying at *The Palm Oceanfront*, so if you're close or in the area, you could look me up? For those lessons, of course." I nodded sagely.

"Aspen, I think it's your lucky day."

"How so, Penny? Meeting you has been pretty lucky. Maybe you're my lucky Penny?"

"Oh, so close." She grimaced, scrunching up her nose, and I was entranced by how the freckles moved with the action.

"Ah, get that a lot?" I sighed.

"Yeah, it's okay, though. I'll give you a chance to redeem yourself. Especially since it seems we're staying at the same place."

She winked, walking backward, and I found myself grinning wide again. Grabbing the handle of my suitcase, I jogged to catch up, the other two already having walked off. She turned forward when I caught up, and I bumped her shoulder. I kept my face straight, determined to get this girl to like me.

"So, curious minds would like to know what these organizational courses cost?"

"Hmm, good question. Let's say, a pizza?"

"That's a fair price that I think I can agree to."

"Perfect. It's a date."

"Oh, a date?"

She blushed again. "I mean, an organizational class. Don't read into it. I'm clearly helping you because you desperately need it."

"Sure, sure. If that's what you need to tell yourself, suitcase bandit." I kept my face forward, enjoying how red hers was getting.

Jett and Poppy were ahead, leaning close to one another. She handed him his phone and turned, swaying her hips as she walked off.

"I have a feeling your friend might be a bit of a heartbreaker," I said as I watched her walk away. Penny looked over at me, and I saw her whole posture change, and I tried to figure out if I said something terrible.

"Oh. You like Poppy. I can pass your number on to her if you'd like. You don't have to get pizza with me to get it." She started walking faster, and I stopped, confused. Picking up my speed, I gently touched her elbow again, stopping her.

"Penny, I think I need to trade insurance information

with you. You side-swiped me out of nowhere back there, and I'm a little bent."

She giggled, and I relaxed as she sighed. "Sorry, habit. Most guys see Poppy and go all goo-goo-eyed for her, I just assumed." She shrugged again, but the energy was off, her face dropping as she did.

Lifting her chin with my finger, I brought her face up. "The only girl I'm going goo-goo-eyed for is standing right in front of me."

"Yeah?"

"Yeah. So, are we still on for pizza? Because I'm really looking forward to this course you teach."

She smiled, nodding her head. "Yeah, me too." She blew out a breath, her shoulders relaxing.

"Come on, let's figure out how we're getting there. I'm not sure if our agent set up a ride or not."

"Agent?" She asked, looking over at me, trying to figure it out.

"Yeah, um, we're kind of in a band."

"Oh, really? That's cool. Poppy's a singer too. I'm horrible. Not one of my skills."

I saw her swallow, some nerves returning. "I feel like there's a story there."

"Uh, yeah. But I don't want to talk about it. So, what do you play?" she asked quickly, changing the subject.

"Guitar. We had them sent ahead to the hotel, hoping to get some writing in while we're here. Our other two bandmates, Roscoe and Zion, are back stateside."

"Wow, you sound legit. Not just something guys say to impress a girl."

Chuckling, I bumped her shoulder again. "I have a feeling that being in a band doesn't impress you. I'd be more likely to impress you by telling you I actually have a Bachelors in Geology."

She giggled, agreeing as she nodded her head. "Yeah, you'd be right. That sounds more up my alley. Sorry." She grimaced.

"It's refreshing, actually. Not that we're super famous or anything, but we do have groupies from time to time. It's hard to know if a girl likes you for you or only because you're in the band, you know."

"Yeah, I can see you're really torn up about it."

"Hey! I'm a sensitive soul," I argued.

I watched as she peered at me from the corner of her eye. "That might be true, but nowhere in any universe do I think you struggle to get girls with all that." She turned, waving her hand in front of me.

"Oh? Do you find me attractive, Penny?"

She rolled her eyes. "Don't play dumb. It's not a cute look. You have tattoos, a scruffy beard, and a backward cap on. Your eyes are like mystical gems, pulling me into the depths of their soothing water, and your voice makes me shiver every time you say my name. You, sir, are a trap that I can't seem to keep from falling into."

Stunned, I stared at her. "You really think I'm trying to trap you?"

She shrugged one shoulder, her arms crossed, and I found myself noticing the slight differences in her body language. This wasn't the carefree Penny or even the under-appreciated one, this was a girl who'd been hurt by some jackass, and it was my job to redeem men for her.

Okay, not really, but at that moment, I wanted it to be.

Stepping closer, I found myself being more forward than I typically was and cupped her cheek, tracing my thumb across it. "Penelope, I'm sorry for whoever hurt you. But I hope you see me for who I am and not who I might represent. If you give me a chance, I'd like to show you that not all men are scumbags."

Her eyes searched mine for a moment, and I felt her lean into my touch with a wistful sigh before she answered me. "Okay."

"Okay." I smiled wide. "I'll take it."

Stepping back, I grabbed her free hand with mine, determined not to let her go until she shrugged that shoulder with a smile on her face, all the confidence in the world was in that one shoulder.

Was I crazy? Maybe.

But sometimes, the simplest things meant the most.

CHAPTER
FOUR

PENNY

I WAS HOLDING HANDS WITH A BOY.

I was holding hands with a boy who wasn't Walter.

I was holding hands with a boy, and I liked it.

I liked it.

Fuck. What was I doing?

Dropping his hand, I made it appear like I needed to reach for my phone. I avoided eye contact but kept a lookout from my periphery. Aspen frowned, glancing over at me. I fiddled with my screen, absently hitting a call button. When the person answered, I almost wished I'd just kept hold of his hand.

"Penny! It's about time you called."

"Hello, Mom. I just wanted to let you know I landed and made it here safely." Inwardly, I cringed. I hadn't told my parents, or *anyone* for that matter, I'd left the country. And now, I would get her lecture and have to explain my reasoning for wanting to live my own life and make my own choices. You know, because apparently at twenty-six years old that was unheard of.

"*Landed?* Where are you? Is Poppy behind this?"

"Love you too. I'll talk later." Hanging up, I stuffed my phone back into my pocket as we reached a van with the name of the hotel on the side.

Clearing my throat, I peered up at Aspen. "Parents." I frowned. He nodded, but I noticed some of his earlier openness had disappeared. We found Poppy and his friend already in the van… making out. It didn't surprise me that Poppy had already met someone. She was the 'love 'em and leave 'em' type to a T.

"Poppy!" She jumped, turning to look at me with a glare. "Deb sends her regards." I rolled my eyes, handing my suitcase to the attendant, assuming this was how we were getting to the hotel. Poppy cackled at my statement, pulling away from the sexy guy she'd been attached to at the lips.

"Oh, I bet she's already called my parents and is lamenting how much of a bad influence I am for you."

"Hmph, yeah, probably." I scooted in, my mood souring with each passing minute. Sometimes I fought so hard to do the right thing, I inevitably made it worse. Leaning against the window, a battle for supremacy took place in my head as my thoughts fought it out.

You're such a screw-up.

This is why your only friend is Poppy. You push everyone else away.

Walter was safe because he didn't make you nervous. Poppy was right; he was boring, and deep down, so are you.

Quit being scared.

No, seriously, quit it.

A shoulder nudged into me, breaking me from my spin cycle. I expected it to be Poppy but instead found Aspen, his hazel eyes staring into mine. His smell was intoxicating, a citrus and ocean combination, and I didn't know if it was him or the air, but I liked it.

"You okay?" he whispered.

The simple question made me want to tear up, but instead, I forced a smile, nodding. Slouching back into the seat, I took a deep breath. I could do this. Casually, I reached over, brushing his pinky with mine. Peeking out of the corner of my eye, I relaxed when I noticed his smile, and his pinky reached out, wrapping around mine.

The smile that broke out this time was genuine, and I could feel my mood lifting as a few more people joined us in the van. I didn't want to know if Poppy had gone back to making out and instead decided to enjoy this bliss-filled moment and just be.

When Poppy had told me about the trip, I'd been excited. That was until she told me what she'd done and I'd wanted to strangle her. Signing us up for a free trip to the Caribbean sounded great until she told me the catch. Twenty-five accounts from the popular streaming app, LiveIt, had been selected to spend two weeks as a social experiment.

Among the many things Poppy did, one of them was being a social media influencer. She had a large following and did videos of her performances, song parodies, and make-up tutorials when she felt like it. Her song remakes were her most popular and what she was best known for. She would take a song or lyric and sing back a response. So if the song said something like, "Girl, I want your body." Poppy would sing back, "But it doesn't want you" or "Is that all you want?"

The level of genius she had at doing it on the spot was legendary, and I was always amazed at her wit and ability to express herself. She'd gone viral with them so many times now, creating a lot of success for her in securing gigs.

So, how did I fall into being eligible? I was here as her assistant, LiveIt had apparently agreed to it. Which was fortunate because while Poppy was a wiz at the online stuff, I was not. She'd talked me into doing DIY videos a few years back when it had started. I had no clue how to operate it, though, so I left it up to her after a few weeks of feeling frustrated with the whole thing. I'd record myself doing a new project and send it on, and then she'd make it into something trendy. I only had a handful of followers and views the last time I'd checked a year ago, but it was fun to combine my artsy and teaching sides together.

Walter had hated it, though, so I hadn't gotten on to my account for a while to check it. Which reminded me of something else I wanted to work on myself. I had decided to do a DIY of myself and started a list after my disastrous break-up and semi-firing.

1) Stop changing yourself to fit what others needed—no more chameleoning
2) Figure out what makes your soul catch fire and do that, even if it was no longer teaching
3) Do something purely for you

It wasn't long yet, but I'd keep adding to it and see if I could get myself back on track. The scary part—I didn't know what that track was anymore.

Looking out the window, I watched the scenery pass by in a blur, the palm trees giving way to a few peeks of sand and ocean. Breathing deep, I relaxed, the ocean air reminding me it was a summer of fun, and hopefully, if I didn't get too much in my own way, a fling as well.

The van turned down a long road, weaving itself through the natural surroundings as it found its way to the hotel. When we came out through a copse of trees, I sucked in a breath at the beautiful hotel in front of us. It was breathtaking, and a giddy sense of excitement rose up in me at the thought of being here for two weeks.

"Wow, this place is incredible," Aspen said next to me. I nodded in agreement as I kept looking around as we drove.

Trees and tropical flowers decorated the front. A large stone fountain was in the middle, and the all-glass front offered incredible views of the place as it opened out onto the beach. Pools and little huts branched off, docks leading to them, the water so blue, it looked fake.

"I don't think I ever want to leave," I whispered. Smiling, I turned and looked at Aspen. He appeared as excited as me, his eyes twinkling. The backward cap had me drooling a little, and I hoped it wasn't what Poppy called the guy catfish—making them hot until they took it off. The van rolled to a stop, and Poppy leaned forward on the seat, putting her head between us.

"What do you think, Pen? It's awesome, right? I did good."

"Yeah, you did." I grinned, turning to my best friend. "I'm looking forward to watching you kick some butt."

Poppy grimaced, and my stomach sank. "What?" I asked.

"Well." She cringed deeper before ducking back and hopping out of the van. I looked to Aspen, and he had a confused look on his face.

"Are you here for the LiveIt competition?" he asked.

"Com-petition?" I stuttered, my head going fuzzy at what it could imply and what else Poppy hadn't told me.

Aspen grabbed my hand, pulling me out of the van, and I followed in a daze. I was going to murder Poppy. There would be one less ginger walking the streets of Somerville when we returned. I could push her off a cliff, and that would take care of the body. Or maybe go on a shark watching expedition, and she'd fall overboard. Oops, faulty life jacket. Or even put tanning oil in her sunscreen, and she burned to a crisp!

"What's she doing?"

"Plotting my murder more than likely."

"Should you be worried?"

"Nah, it happens at least once a month, sometimes more."

"Penelope, it will be fine. Jett and I are doing it too."

Blinking, I looked up and found Aspen staring down at me, his hand cupping my cheek. I found myself naturally falling into his hold before I realized he was practically a stranger despite the fact he didn't feel like one.

I stepped back, and Poppy grabbed me, pulling me over to the side. "So, I might've fibbed a little about how I got you here."

"How little, P?"

As she started to open her mouth, she was cut off by some girls shouting. At first, I assumed it was for the guys, but when I heard, "Pen Can! It's *DIYing Girl* and *Poppy Rocks*!", the panic returned.

Wide-eyed, I grasped both of Poppy's hands, pleading with her. "Please tell me there's another person here who goes by *DIYing Girl* with the catchphrase Pen Can? Please!"

"Nope, that's all you, babe! I know you don't care, but your account is quite popular."

"How is that even possible? I'm just *me*."

"And you're awesome. Embrace your weird fandom and come kick butt with me. Everything I told you is true, except the assistant part and the fact the social experiment is a competition of sorts."

"So, basically, *everything*."

"Semantics," she said, brushing it off. I looked over my shoulder and saw Aspen and his friend watching us. He smiled when he spotted me, and I waved awkwardly over my shoulder as Poppy dragged me toward the entrance.

An intimidating woman with a clipboard stood in the lobby, directing people in different directions. LiveIt signs with their slogan, "If you didn't LiveIt, then you're dead," covered banners and posters in purple and blue.

"Ladies, this way, and I'll get you signed in and your room keys." Poppy tugged me toward her, Aspen and Jett following until they were intercepted by another clipboard carrying entity and sent in the opposite direction.

"Poppy Jackson and Penelope Baxter, you'll be in hut 240. You're rooming with Jemma Haunt. All the rules and information you'll need while you're here can be found in these info packets." She handed us thick, purple folders, along with a gift bag. "Is there anything else I can help you with?" she asked, but I had a feeling she really didn't want to assist us in anything, just asking out of obligation.

I shook my head, and we started to walk off when I

remembered our luggage was still in the van. But when I turned back, the van was no longer where we'd left it. "Wait!" I shouted, stunning the woman. "Where's our suitcases?"

She sighed, turning back to us, and I could've sworn she rolled her eyes. "They've already been taken to your rooms." The lady turned back around, dismissing us.

I looked around, but didn't see Aspen or his friend, so I allowed Poppy to drag me off, hoping she knew which way to go.

When we got outside, the view was even more incredible. Infinity pools, filled with attractive coeds, greeted us along with swim-up bars adding to the ambiance. Beaches were just a few yards in front, the sound of the ocean filling my ears. As we walked by one pool toward the dock area, whistles rang out, a group of guys playing volleyball stopped to gape at Poppy. She waved, blowing a kiss, but didn't stop as we continued on our trek.

"I'm still mad at you," I grumbled.

"I know. But you'll forgive me eventually. Especially once you hear me out."

"I don't know. This is pretty extreme."

She stopped, pulling me into the shade, and my eyes thanked her, along with the skin I could already feel burning.

"Listen, I know it was wrong not to tell you the full scoop. At first, I didn't think you'd come because of Walter if you knew the full details. Then, things were so messed up, and you were feeling down on yourself. I figured you just needed to get here and it would be better. If you really don't want to do it, though, I'll talk to them."

"I don't even know what *this* is." I gestured.

Poppy smiled wide, and her excitement started to bleed into me. It was hard not to have fun when she had her big, infectious smile.

"It's going to be a blast, Pen. It will be a new adventure we get to do together. No responsibilities; just sun, fun, and cute boys."

Sighing, I nodded. When she put it that way, it didn't sound so bad. "Just no more surprises, okay? I think I've hit my quota."

"I promise. PB&J forever." She held up her pinky finger, and I hooked mine with hers.

"PB&J."

"Alright, let's find this hut, so we can scope out all the hot guys and competition."

"What about the one you were lip-locking with earlier?"

"Ah, Jett. He's a great kisser, but I can't let him think he's the only one."

"One of these days, you're gonna meet someone you want to settle down with, you know?"

"Ew, gross, stop that! Don't put your ideas of monogamy on me."

Rolling my eyes, I huffed out a laugh. "Fine. I'm not saying you have to marry the guy, but, I don't know, maybe spend more than one night with him?"

"We'll see. There are just too many flavors of cocksicles for me to try to settle on one."

Spluttering, I stumbled, and I reached out to steady myself on the nearest object. When I looked up, I found the thing I'd grabbed happened to be the arm of a guy. A *really* hot guy.

If the Greek Gods existed, this guy was a descendant of

them. He dripped in gold attributes. Golden honey hair, champagne eyes with golden flecks, and golden skin on full display. He only wore board shorts and flip flops. His hair was damp, and he held a pineapple that had a fruit smiley face with a colorful straw and a little umbrella poking out the top of it. He grinned at me, and I felt a girly giggle rise up.

"So sorry." I let go of his arm, patting it to make sure it was real. My hand happened to keep patting him, feeling all over his gorgeous skin. When I realized I was petting his abs, I stepped back to stop myself. "Again, so sorry. It seems my hand has a mind of its own and it wants to touch your abs. They're great, by the way. Top-notch." I'd say I was embarrassed, but I wasn't. He really did have great abs.

"Feel free to check them whenever you want, Red."

I grimaced, and Poppy laughed. His eyes flicked over to her briefly but returned to me, and I decided to ignore his minor transgression. After all, I *had* groped him without consent; I could let the cringe-worthy nickname go.

"Oof, bad luck, pal. Penny here, she hates nicknames that don't have any real thought behind them. Red? Too obvious, not even trying in her book. You'll have to try a little harder. Now, me, on the other hand? I love it when a guy calls me Red." She winked, and I elbowed her. We didn't typically go after the same guy, both having different types. I had to guess she was either testing him or trying to help me by giving him that bit of info, her natural flirtiness coming through even when she didn't try.

"Well, Penny." He paused, searing me with his eyes. I didn't miss the way my name rolled off his tongue either.

"I shall look forward to christening you with one. I'm Cooper, in case you wondered." That time he winked, and I found my head going light again. I grabbed hold of Poppy as she turned us around, leading us away from the hot, pineapple, golden guy.

"I think pineapple is now my favorite fruit," I mumbled. Looking at Poppy, we both burst out laughing, and I knew that despite the secretive nature on Poppy's part, it'd been a good idea, and this would be a memorable vacation. Who knew, maybe my vibrator would get a break too?

CHAPTER
FIVE

COOPER

MY BODY TINGLED FROM HEAD TO TOE AS I WALKED AWAY from the beautiful redhead. I quickened my pace as I weaved through the hotel guests, a few shouting out hellos as I passed. I knew if I stayed too long, I'd inevitably stick my foot in my mouth and make a fool of myself in front of Penny. While that typically was my whole personality, I wanted to remain in the cool category for as long as possible with the cutest girl with freckles I'd ever seen.

Penny seemed like the type of girl I could have fun with. The fact she hadn't gotten embarrassed about touching me and laughed it off told me she'd be someone I'd have a good time with and appreciate my corny jokes. That, in itself, was a big plus for me.

Most of the time with girls, I felt too constricted to be myself, worried that my joking nature would be taken the wrong way. And so, inevitably, I held back, which then made me look constipated or come across as boring. Finding that line with girls was hard for me since I hadn't grown up around that many.

"Hey, Coop! How are you?" The shout pulled my attention and I stopped, spotting Drew.

"What's up! How are you?"

As he talked about his latest nerd video where he played with a lightsaber while shirtless, I couldn't help but wonder if this was my fate.

When I was younger, my mom moved around a lot for her job, meaning I never really developed deep connections with my peers. When I was sixteen, she remarried, and we found ourselves finally settled. It meant I got to attend high school for longer than a year. But by then, I was training nonstop and had very little free time to go on dates. And considering most of my time was spent jumping rope, and there were very few girls who did the sport, I spent my formative teen years with mostly male friends like Drew.

"Wow, that's awesome. Hey, let's catch up more later, okay? My brother should be here soon and I want to make sure I don't miss him."

"Of course! I'll shout at ya later."

Walking off, I recalled my dating life and while it wasn't hopeless, it wasn't stellar either. I never had a steady girlfriend, as most of my relationships ended after a couple of dates and kisses. As I got older, it transformed into a couple of hookups, and then they'd move on. Somehow, I became known as the in-between guy, the nice guy —the one you could mend your broken heart with, but not settle down with.

And while it had its perks, it eventually began to feel

like I was used. Wow, I never realized how empty it all felt until now.

A few more people I'd met waved as they passed, calling out greetings as I kept making my way down the long, wooden deck, pineapple drink in my hand. I never realized how much my easy-going nature had hindered me. It allowed girls to trust me quickly, which was nice, but they only trusted me to be their friend, not the one they fell in love with.

Worse, from the outside, it looked like I was a player; even though girls were the ones who left me, it didn't seem that way to everyone else. When I thought about it, my whole dating life, I'd fallen somewhere between the player and the friend. Suitable for a fuck, or to take you to the airport, but never the boyfriend.

And I really wanted to be that person, badly. I knew I could be a good boyfriend for the right person.

My thoughts had me feeling down, so I shook them off, wanting to think positively. Penny was my chance to do things differently.

The rest of the people faded away as I neared the hut, the sounds of the ocean the soundtrack to my thoughts. I hoped my roommates had arrived by now. I was looking forward to spending the next two weeks with my brother. It had been a while since I'd seen him due to his tour coinciding with my training schedule. So I was looking forward to catching up with him.

Our parents had gotten married when we were in high school, and at first, I wasn't sure about having a brother, much less one the same age as me. In the end, we became best friends. He'd been there for me through a lot, and after I was injured a few years back, I realized the importance of that even more.

A lot of my so-called friends had abandoned ship when I was laid up. They'd been coat tail friends, only wanting to stick around when I was in the spotlight. But all through rehab, my brother was there, and he helped me keep going when I wanted to throw in the towel. It had cemented our bond, and I couldn't imagine doing life without him now.

This competition was a nice break from my regular training, and a chance to see if I wanted to keep doing it or if I needed to find something else. The problem was, I didn't know what else I was good at. I had only one goal growing up and I didn't know who I was without the world records at this point. I'd done the one thing teachers told you not to do, put all my eggs in one basket. Of course, you never thought it would happen to you, so full of life and hope at that age. Coming back from the injury had been hard work, mentally, and physically, and I wasn't sure if I could do it again.

In part because my body was starting to wear down and needed more time to recoup. But also because I didn't know if my heart was in it anymore. I was almost twenty-eight, and my life had been made up of training and traveling. I'd recently stepped in for a friend on a gig as a stunt double, and I'd enjoyed it more than I'd expected. It might be something I needed to learn more about.

Opening the door, I heard the voices of my two oldest friends arguing over a girl, which I found interesting.

"You're the dumb one. You didn't see which direction they went. Now, we don't even know what hut they're in," Jett said.

"At least we know they're in the competition. Hopefully, we'll see them tomorrow or later tonight at the welcome dinner," my brother retorted.

Walking around the corner, I spotted him standing with his back to me. Running, I wrapped my arms around him, lifting him up. Perhaps it was odd, but at 6'4", I found it fun to pick up people and typically greeted others this way when I could get away with it. Aspen was shorter than me at 5'11" so I found it humorous to do every chance I got. I always joked I'd carry him around on my shoulder if I could get away with it.

Squeezing him tight, I jerked him a few times as he laughed before setting him down. He turned, giving me a big smile before punching me in the bicep.

"Coop, you big brute. How've you been? Come here and give me a real hug, asshole."

Giving him a hug from the front, I smiled, patting him on the back before letting go. I turned and gave Jett one as well.

"Hey, man. How are you?" I asked.

"Good, good. This place is pretty sweet. I didn't think it was going to be this nice."

"Yeah, yeah, we know. You dragged your feet so damn much about coming," Aspen groaned, giving him a look. "Then, of course, you meet a hot redhead in the airport, and now all of a sudden, you're all positive vibes. Yeah, no, I'm not buying it. You're just happy you're gonna get some."

"If it helps me write songs." Jett shrugged, not denying he wanted to sleep with her. It was funny to me *he* wasn't considered a player when he wouldn't touch commitment with a 10-ft pole, but me, who wanted to be serious, *was* one.

"And this is why you're called every name under the sun when you inevitably break their heart. Though, I think you might have your work cut out for you on this one. She seemed like a barracuda."

"Wait," I interrupted, part of their conversation sinking in, "did you say redhead? I just met the most beautiful redhead before I came back here." They both turned and looked at me with mixed expressions of dread and hope, waiting for me to explain more. "Hair about this long with the most amazing blue eyes and went by the name of Penny." Jett exhaled in relief when I finished, but I saw Aspen tense.

"You met Penny?"

"Yeah. Do you know her?"

"Sort of. I met her at the airport. She's friends with Poppy, who he's already been sucking face with."

I turned to Jett, taking in his smug expression. "Dang! I guess Aspen wasn't joking," I said, chuckling. "Poppy must be the friend she was with. She didn't introduce her, just said that she liked to be called Red."

"Good to know," Jett said with a smirk.

"Did you happen to see where their hut was?"

"No, but they were going in the opposite direction of the volleyball pool. So, I don't know if they have women and men, separate, or if that's just the location of their hut, but that's where they were headed."

"Cool. Maybe I can casually be walking in that area and bump into them later."

His plan had me realizing something. "Do you like her?"

"Yeah, I kinda do. Do you?"

"I mean, she's easily the most beautiful girl I've ever seen, and she groped my abs! I do think we kind of had a connection." I shrugged, not wanting to admit how much I liked her. This was uncharted territory. We'd never liked the same girl before.

"I kind of had a connection with her too."

"How could you both have a connection with the same girl?" Jett asked, wanting to stir the pot.

"Well, I guess we'll just have to wait and see who she likes best." I puffed out my chest before I realized what I was doing, and then deflated. "You know what? No, you're my brother. Surely, we can settle this like men."

"You're right. So what's it gonna be? Thumb wrestling, rock-paper-scissors, or chicken in the pool?"

"Thumb wrestling." I decided, nodding sagely.

"You guys are weird and dumb if you think that's how you're going to be able to decide."

"Hey, it's better than fighting over her," Aspen argued.

"Okay," I interjected, "what if we have a gentlemen's agreement, and we let her pick. We'll be happy for the other person."

"What about the brother that she doesn't pick?" Jett asked, again being an ass.

I shrugged, not understanding. "We both just met her today. It's not like we're in love with her. And this way, we're not fighting. I think I can agree with that." Smiling, I couldn't help but tack on a jib. "I'll try not to be too loud when she's moaning my name."

"Oh, you're so confident, are you?" Aspen laughed. "I happened to hold her hand the whole way here." He crossed his arms, a smug expression on his face.

"Well, like I mentioned, she's already very acquainted with my abs. So, abs over tattoos, I think I win. Your musical prowess isn't gonna win this time, Aspen.

"Okay, Coop, you're on."

"You guys are dorks." Jett rolled his eyes, turning to head to a room, but stopped. "Aspen, read the packet and let me know the important things. I'm crashing. Wake me later for dinner." He waved over his head as he started to shut his door.

Aspen, being the studious one, had, of course, already read the packet, and despite Jett bossing him to do it, we both knew he was the one to ask. "Basically, do what they say, be entertaining to get votes, and win. Don't be a jerk. Which undoubtedly will be hard for you, your highness." He bowed extravagantly, rising back up with a big grin.

"Haha." Jett flipped us off before shutting his door completely this time. I shook my head. Jett was still Jett. The fame only made him more arrogant at times. Glancing at Aspen, I noticed how tired he looked too. "What about you? Are you gonna crash?"

"Originally, yes. Nap, food, and shower were all I could think about. But now I'm thinking, shower, food, and then sleep."

"Want to go grab something with me after a shower, then?"

"Yeah, I'll change and meet you out here in a little bit."

"Don't go changing too much," I sang, one of our parent's corny jokes automatically popping up in my head. Aspen smiled and hugged me briefly again.

"Sounds good, bro. It's good to see you. I've missed you."

"You too, Aspen. Mom sends her love."

We both walked off to our rooms, and I hoped everything I said was true and that this girl wouldn't come between us. Our bond was tight, but I wouldn't deny Penny was someone I found intriguing enough to want to explore. I just hoped she felt the same. I guess I needed to see how she felt before I started planning our wedding.

CHAPTER
SIX

PENNY

Poppy and I found ourselves standing in a very misleading hut. When we'd walked into the "hut," I spun around in a circle ten times before I almost fell over, taking it all in. The word hut to me had implied a small dwelling. This place didn't even know that word existed.

It opened into a large area where a sunken spot included several couches facing a TV on a wall. A kitchenette area with a fridge, small burner, and sink ended with a breakfast bar and two stools. Behind the sitting space, it opened out onto a deck with a small infinity pool to the side and stairs that went down into the ocean. My favorite part had to be the areas that had glass floors showing the water below. The vaulted ceilings and airy drapes gave the whole place that Caribbean vibe that made you want to curl up in the hammock.

Because there was a hammock—two, in fact.

We were both finishing unpacking when we heard

someone else enter. A girl's laugh rang out, and I quickly shoved the last of my clothes into a drawer and walked out to investigate. A tall girl with dark hair, the ends tinted purple and a nose ring smiled when she saw us.

"Oh, hey! You guys must be my roomies." She bounced over, and I wondered if she was always this full of energy.

"Um, hey!" I waved. "I'm Penny. This is Poppy."

"Double P! Cool, I'm Jemma. So, what's your deal?" she asked, flopping down onto the couch like she owned it. She kicked her feet up over the armrest, her combat boots swinging as she waited for us to answer.

"Um, deal?"

"You 'um' a lot, Penny," she said, sitting up on her elbows with an assessing look. I tensed, thinking she was criticizing me, but she had a smile on her face as she spoke. "Own your womanhood. You're awesome."

"Oh, well, thank you."

"No problem. And, deal… like what are you known for?"

"Hm, well, I guess my cupcakes?" I shrugged one shoulder, looking over at Poppy.

She broke out into laughter, walking over to sit in the space next to Jemma. "She means on the app, dork." She turned to Jemma, completely relaxed. "Don't mind her. She didn't know until about an hour ago she was here for LiveIt. I wasn't completely honest about my intentions for bringing her down here. She does make awesome cupcakes, though. You might know her as DIYer girl?"

"No shit!" Jemma exclaimed, swinging her legs back around to the floor. "I thought you looked familiar, but I'm crap with faces and names. You're hilarious. I love your stuff." She turned, knocking her shoulder with Poppy while I stood confused, not knowing what she meant. "What about you?"

"Oh, me?" Poppy asked, sliding back smugly and moving the hair off her shoulder all diva-like. "I'm PopRocks, and you're JemmaDare, aren't you?"

"Yep!" She nodded, a broad smile on her face. "That's me. And you're awesome too! I loved the one you did back to that Heston song. You got some pipes, girl!"

"JemmaDare?" I asked, feeling out of the loop and not liking it. Sitting down in a chair, I crossed my arms and watched the two.

"People post the dares they want me to do and vote. The one with the most votes wins, and then I do it. If it's something I don't want to do, then there's a fun consequence. Like I refused to eat crickets, so I had to sing a Jiminy Cricket song in a busy intersection dressed like him."

"Okay, that sounds pretty fun. You're brave to let people pick things for you, though."

"That's the rush, though. I never know what it will be, and it gets me out of my comfort zone to try new things. I actually had horrible social anxiety before I started my account. It started as a way to save me, and now, I get to help others. My life has taken a drastic turn, and I owe it all to LiveIt."

"Wow, that's an awesome story. All I do is make paper mache crafts or repurpose cabinet doors," I mumbled, dropping my eyes to the floor. Why did I belong here? Surely there were other viral accounts that would fit this show better.

"Don't worry about her. She's just having a mid-twenty-something crisis this week," Poppy joked, sticking her tongue out at me. "So, have you ever done anything like this before?"

"Nope. First time."

"Score! We can all be newbs together."

"I'm just glad you're both so nice. I was afraid when I walked in and saw two hot redheads you'd be snobby bitches."

"We could say the same about you!" Poppy exclaimed.

As they continued to go back and forth about who was cooler, I got up to get some water. Poppy never had issues with new people, and well, I apparently said 'um' too much and was too sensitive. I was much better by the fifth time people met me... typically. When I stepped into the kitchen, I jumped back, a small gasp leaving me.

"Um, I'm sorry, who are you?" A tall, ripped man with dark hair pulled back at his nape stood in the kitchen eating a piece of fruit. I didn't know what was more disturbing. The fact he was casually standing in my hut's kitchen or that he was eating an apple while standing in my hut's kitchen. He lifted his intense dark eyes to me at my question but kept eating, not responding. Opening my mouth to shout for the others, Jemma and Poppy beat me to it by sauntering into the area.

"Quit being rude, Keelan. Double P are cool." She jumped on the counter, stealing the fruit from his hand, and taking her own bite. The man grumbled but let her do it, and I watched, suddenly fascinated by their dynamic now that I wasn't freaking out a stranger had broken in to steal from our fruit basket.

"The silent one belongs to me. He's *mostly* housebroken," Jemma teased. The man stared at her, but there was nothing but hearts in his eyes despite his scowl. It hit me a little in the heart, the slap of reality that Walter hadn't ever looked at me with even an ounce of that passionate possession. Hell, no guy I'd ever dated had.

"Well, damn, that's hot," Poppy said, fanning her face. Giggling, I leaned into her, knowing she'd understand what I needed. Her arm wrapped around my shoulders, pulling me to her. The best thing about having a friend for as long as Poppy and I had been friends, we didn't always need words.

"Yeah, he is," Jemma agreed, smiling a toothy grin at the man. He didn't disagree but took his apple back, biting into the last part before tossing the core into the trash can in a flawless move. I cleared my throat, bringing the attention back to me.

"I saw on the agenda that there's a pool party and barbecue tonight to welcome everyone. I guess it's the last time before the cameras start rolling too. Do we want to all go together?"

"You're not escaping me," Poppy said, bumping her hip.

I shrugged, some uncertainty filling me. "I figured you'd go make out with Mr. Rockstar some more."

"Maybe, but he can wait. This is our vacation, remember?"

I nodded and looked at Jemma. "What about you two?"

"We're game." She'd moved Keelan in front of her, draping over his back as she sat on the counter. It was odd watching their exchange but fascinating at the same time. I both enjoyed it and felt envious of the easy interactions between them. Was that how couples were meant to be? It looked nice. She wrapped her legs around his waist and then made a "giddy up" noise, and he pulled away, not even hesitating.

"Seriously, where can I get one?" Poppy asked, teasing.

We followed behind as we made our way out of the hut. We walked down the dock, leading back to the main area. There were several little offshoots for other bungalow sections, all trailing back to the pools and gathering places on the beach.

As we got closer, it was easier to hear the crowds of people. We walked out onto the beach, following the trail, and found our way to the food. My stomach growled, and I laughed.

"Your bottomless pit is speaking to us. Quick shove some food into her before she goes nuclear!"

"I'm not *that* bad," I argued.

"Uh, yeah, you are. But it's fine because you're practically perfect in every other way."

"Ah, you do love me." I smiled at Poppy as she scrunched up her nose.

"You guys are too cute. How long have you been friends?"

"Forever, and we've been saving each other since." Poppy wrapped her arm around my shoulders, pulling my head into the crook of her elbow to kiss my forehead.

We continued walking toward the tent that had the food, getting in line. I looked around, trying to see if I recognized anyone, but my lack of social media seemed to be hindering me. People smiled at me, but nobody approached us as we moved forward. It felt a little like a high school lunchroom, some small groups already forming. Once again, I was grateful for Poppy and not having to face the dreaded choice of where to sit. She pulled me along, making it easy for me.

Sitting at a picnic table, I started to eat my burger, or inhale it really. I'd tried to joke off the comment earlier, but I really did go hangry if I didn't get food in me. I was definitely one of those people you didn't mess around with when it came to food. I would stab a bitch if they tried to touch it.

Once my burger was finished, I started on the sides. It looked different than anything I'd had before, but I was curious to try it. It was around the third bite, I started to hear the sounds around me again. I tended to zone out when I ate at times, especially when hangry and in a new place.

"Don't worry, she's not ignoring you. Penny's just very serious about eating. She once zoned out for an hour when we went to a Brazilian steak house. I think food is her OTP."

"OTP?" I heard a familiar male voice ask.

"One true pairing."

Looking up, I found two gorgeous guys watching me with interest. One set of hazel, the other golden. When they noticed I'd stopped the love affair with my food, I watched as their mouths tilted up, smiles showcasing their gorgeous lips. Licking my own, I took another bite, finishing my food.

"Um, hi."

"Hey, Freckles," Cooper said, a smile on his face. I wanted to hate the nickname, but the way he said it had me reconsidering. He said it with a hint of suggestiveness in his voice, and I decided I'd wait and see how it played out.

"Hey, Dimples." The nickname left my lips without thinking, and I wanted to shove them back in once they registered. Not because I was embarrassed, but because I didn't want him to get any ideas that it meant more than it did. True to the nickname, the dimples popped out as he looked at me. "It doesn't mean anything. Don't go and get any ideas, sir."

"Oh, I like when you call me that, too."

"Really?" I rolled my eyes, but inside I was smiling. I enjoyed the playful banter with him more than I wanted to admit.

"I leave you alone for an hour, and you go and replace me. With my brother, nonetheless," Aspen joked, causing me to choke on the bite I'd just taken.

"Brother?" I gasped, gulping down the food as I looked between the two. Aspen smiled, the corners turning up a little lopsided. His hazel eyes seared me with sincerity, and I wanted to swim in them. While his apparent brother brought out the fun playfulness in me, Aspen made me feel grounded. He was probably the sweetest person I'd ever met, and the thought of him thinking I didn't like him hurt, sending panic through me.

"I-I-I didn't replace you, Aspen." His smile brightened, and I relaxed.

Poppy leaned in closer, whispering, "Oh girl, you're in *trouble*."

Ignoring her, I finished the last of my food before I attempted talking again. Taking a long drink of my water, I faced the two guys who had intrigued me.

"You don't look like brothers. Do you mean in the real sense or like a fraternity thing? If you made me choke on my food for frat brothers, I will seek my revenge."

"Told you she was serious about her food," Poppy whispered loudly behind her hand.

"Stepbrothers, actually. My dad married his mom when we were in high school, and we've been besties ever since," Aspen provided, smiling over at Cooper.

"He didn't give me a choice, is what he means. Aspen is a bit of a clingy puppy when he likes someone, so I gave in." Cooper shrugged his shoulders as Aspen punched him in the shoulder.

"Wow, can you make me sound any cooler?" They both laughed, and I liked their bond. It reminded me a lot of Poppy and me.

"Why would I want to do that? I gotta make Freckles like me better."

"Oh, is that how it is? I'm a prize to be won between you two?"

They both turned quickly, looks of panic on their faces as they tried to backpedal and save themselves. "No, no, that's not what I mean, promise."

"This is good. I feel like I should get popcorn," Jemma said. Keelan grunted next to her, eating his food and ignoring everyone else.

"Yes! Good call. The best snacks always make the mood," Poppy agreed.

Opening my mouth, I started to reprimand my best friend when the lady with the clipboard from earlier took center stage on a platform I hadn't noticed until then.

"Welcome everyone to the first-ever LiveIt games. We're all excited to have you here and not only get great coverage for LiveIt but get to know all of you on a real level. With each new endeavor, not only will you learn new things about yourself, but hopefully, open your eyes to the world around you. At LiveIt, we're all about getting out and living life to the fullest. Whether that's doing something fun with others, spending time in nature, or making the most perfect brownie, you're living life, and that's what we're all about. *If you're not on LiveIt… "*

"*…then you're dead!*" the crowd finished.

Crazy clipboard lady smiled wide, eating up the crowd's enthusiasm. I sat stunned, a little worried at what I'd gotten myself into, or my best friend had gotten me into. As if she could feel my panic, Poppy reached over and squeezed my hand, and I relaxed. I needed to stay out of my head and enjoy the time with her. Once the hoots and hollers had settled down, the clipboard lady grinned so wide, I was positive I could see her crown in the back.

"I don't have a good feeling about what she's gearing up to say," I mumbled, tightening my grip on Poppy's hand.

"So for the first surprise of the games, we're going to separate you into teams now and give you your first task. Please come forward when your name is called."

Glancing over to Poppy, fear surged forward at thinking about doing this without her. "We're on the same team, right?"

"Yeah, promise. It will be fine."

"Okay. I'm not doing this without you."

"You and me, Pen. PB&J forever." She wrapped her arm around my shoulders, pulling me into her.

The lady started calling out names, but I couldn't focus on them, too hyperaware of my own. When Jemma stood up, I realized her name had been called. Keelan got up, following her, not even waiting to hear if his was. The lady upfront rolled her eyes but called his next. I relaxed more, hoping it meant people who came together were on the same team.

Movement across from me had me looking up, and I realized Aspen was getting up. He winked, sauntering to the front, his tight jeans hugging his butt just perfectly. Jett already stood to the side, holding a sign with the #2 on it. They fist-bumped, and I looked over at Poppy. I hadn't realized he wasn't at the table until then. I hope he wasn't blowing her off already. She bit her lip, but when I nudged her, she shook her head, her confidence returning as she lifted her chin.

Cooper got up next, and part of me was jealous of whoever got to be with them. It was probably for the best, though. They'd be far too distracting, only confusing me and making me feel things I wasn't ready for.

"Poppy Jackson."

When her name was called, I tensed. Poppy only straightened, turning to me. "It will be fine, Pen, and if not, we'll fix it after. Don't freak out, okay?"

I nodded, but she still had to detangle herself from the grip I had on her hand. Finding myself alone at the table, I looked around at who was left. About ten people remained scattered throughout the area. I was focusing so much on not freaking out that I missed it when she called my name. Jumping up, my knees hit under the table, but I didn't stop as I power walked to the group, relief rushing through me.

Once I was near them, my exuberance took over, and I ran the rest of the way. They all cheered, laughing at me, but I didn't even care. Jemma waved from across the way, and I took a second to look at her team. There were three guys in total and two girls including Jemma. The other two guys looked just as cute, and the other girl was telling a story, the guys laughing as she recalled it. Keelan stood back, but Jemma seemed to be happy.

A few minutes later, all the teams were set, and we were given our first mission. Jett opened the folder shaped like a safe, pulling out a piece of paper, and the five of us gathered around it as we read.

Your first mission—name your team, make a home base, and come up with a mascot. You have until tomorrow at breakfast where everyone will reveal their new team. Good luck.

CHAPTER
SEVEN

PENNY

Poppy whooped, and I jumped, stumbling back into Aspen. He steadied me, his hands landing on my hips. My tank had ridden up a little, allowing his fingers to brush the skin visible there, sending shivers down my spine. His touch was light but firm as he held onto me. I could feel some of the calluses on his fingers from playing the guitar. When I realized I'd been standing there, staring up at him for a while, I stepped forward, out of his hold.

"Thanks," I whispered.

"It was my pleasure."

I didn't miss the sexual innuendo laced through his words, a blush rising to my cheeks. Whipping my head around, I attempted to focus on Poppy and Jett as they argued back and forth over the best place to make our home base so we could begin to brainstorm ideas.

"Have they fucked already?" Cooper asked, bending down to whisper in my ear.

Covering a snort with my hand, I shook my head. "They just met at the airport."

"Wow, that's some flaming sexual tension if I ever saw it."

"That's Poppy for you." Turning to the two who weren't arguing, I proposed a question. "Are you three all in the same hut thing?"

"Hut thing? Uh, yeah, we're in the same bungalow. Why?" Aspen answered, smiling at me. Having my answer, I walked forward and stepped in between the two stubborn prima donna's.

"Pop, we'll go to their place. It makes the most sense. All three of them are together, and this way, Jemma can use ours. Don't argue over the small details."

"Ugh, fine." She rolled her eyes and tossed her hair over her shoulder as she walked off. Squaring myself with Jett, I creased my brows at him.

"Whatever game you're playing with my best friend's heart, it stops now. Poppy doesn't need you swinging in with your bad boy swagger and then stomping on her heart. She won't admit it, but she's scared, and if you try to break her, I'll break your face. And hey, since the motto's 'LiveIt or die,' I'll even film it for all of the world to see. Understand?"

He scoffed, clearly not taking me seriously. Stepping forward more, I pulled my shoulders back even more as I attempted to intimidate him with my 5'5" stature.

"Don't believe me? I teach 8-year-olds. You should be terrified of the level of destruction I can cause without it even seeming like I'm doing anything. *Try me.*"

Jett finally had the good sense to stop, swallowing whatever smart-aleck remark he was about to say, and nodded. He stomped off in the opposite direction of our place, and I assumed it meant he was going to the base.

"That was kind of hot, Freckles." Cooper looked at me like he might want to lick me, and a blush rose to my cheeks. I shook it off, not wanting to explore if it was because of the nickname or that he thought something I did was hot. Or both.

"Is he always that intense?" I asked, avoiding eye contact.

"Yeah, he can be. He's pretty broody at times and has that need to be the center of attention thing. Which works well for the band, not so much for everyday life," Aspen verified.

"Not so well when you're trying to do a group project with him either," I muttered.

Looking back at the two guys I seemed to have formed a connection with, I shifted on my feet, unsure what to do now. Most of the other groups were mingling or heading off into directions assumingly to find a base. "Well, I hope he and Poppy can get along okay, or this might be a very stressful two weeks. I'm starting to think I preferred it when their lips were sealed together."

The two guys laughed, but I wasn't joking. If Jett kept blowing her off after sucking face with her earlier, Poppy wouldn't respond well. She was used to being the one to break hearts, not the one who was left.

"Don't worry about it, Freckles. We'll take care of you."

"Yeah, I'm not sure if I trust you two either." The giggle that escaped belied my words, and the two guys smiled at me. Cooper put his arm around Aspen in a move similar to Poppy's with me, and it softened me.

"Well, Aspen, it looks like we have a job to do then. Operation Prove to Penny we can be reliable."

"That's kind of a long title for an operation," I retorted.

"Nah, Operation PTP for short." Aspen winked, going along with Cooper's ridiculous suggestion. Feeling put on the spot by their attention, something I wasn't used to by guys, I spun and headed in the direction Jett had gone.

I followed along the path and stopped when I came to a fork, the piers branching off in different directions. The area looked pretty much the same on this side like ours, the docks leading into the ocean and the huts, or bungalows, stretching out on dock platforms in little groups.

Aspen grabbed my hand when he neared, pulling me along. It felt too nice to drop it, so I gave myself a moment to enjoy holding his hand. Cooper opened the door, and I followed them in. I could hear cabinets slamming off to the side where I assumed their kitchen area was. Shame heated my face when I realized Poppy wasn't with us. I glanced back down the path to see if she was coming, but she was nowhere in sight.

Pulling out my phone, I texted her the hut number, 520. Hopefully, she wouldn't hate me for leaving without her. I'd been a little dickupied. Taking a seat on the couch, I looked around to see if it was any different from ours, but it looked pretty much the same from what I could tell. Theirs just had a different color scheme, and the layout was flipped. So whereas our kitchen was on the right side, theirs was on the left.

Aspen sat down on the couch next to me, grabbing my hand in a playful gesture sending tingles through me. I was getting comfortable with his touchy nature and found myself missing it when it was gone.

"So, we need to come up with a team name, mascot, and home base. I guess we got a base covered. Now, we just need a team name and mascot," I rambled, turning sideways on the couch to look into the kitchen. Cooper was bent over to get something out of the fridge, and my words died on my tongue as I drooled over the man's backside. Seriously, I expected his shorts to split any second with how tight they were. *Damn.*

Aspen leaned over, wiping some imaginary drool off my chin. He didn't say anything but gave me a wink. I'd worried at first that their bid to win my affection would interfere with their bond, and I didn't want anything to do with that. But as I watched them, I realized it didn't seem to be the case. They weren't acting jealous, just trying to earn my attention. Cooper turned, spotting me, and gave me his gorgeous smile. He held up a water bottle, and I nodded.

It had nothing to do with the fact I was thirsty and everything to do with him needing to bend back over to grab some more. Hey, I could admit when I was shamelessly checking him out to myself.

Jett scowled while he poured a drink into a glass with ice, splashing some coke on it before he threw it back. Cooper came back into my line of sight, a smile on his face as he handed me the water.

"Thanks."

He leaned down close, whispering in my ear. "Anytime you want to check out my ass, all you gotta do is ask, Freckles."

My face heated, and I turned away. Being called out like that was starting to get to me. I hardly got embarrassed anymore after years of building up a thick skin, but at this rate, I'd be blushing nonstop around these two.

"Does anybody have any poster board or a whiteboard or something?"

"Why do you need those things, Pen?" Aspen asked, using a shortened version of my name only Poppy tended to do. His fingers continued to trail up and down my arm.

"I dunno. I feel like I need to teach a class or get us organized."

"Oh, I bet you're cute when you teach class," Cooper flirted, sitting down on the other side of me. I suddenly found myself the filling in a CooperAspen sandwich and I quite liked it.

"Oh yeah, teaching third graders, so sexy," I deadpanned, deflecting. "Let me tell you, the glue and paint I come home with on me. Oh, yeah, *sexy*." The giggle slipped again as I tried to hide my smile.

"Okay, okay, bad reference. I bet you're cute, at least."

Shrugging, I tried to hide my smile. "Yeah, maybe."

I knew he was being complimentary, but it felt weird with my current job situation, and I realized I was still feeling a little sensitive about the whole debacle. I'd already checked my email a million times despite it only being two days since the entire ordeal. There was still no word from the school board, which made sense, but my anxiety wanted to know now. I needed the answer so I could plan.

Which meant, I'd keep checking my email until I finally had one. Only then could I decide if my life was doomed to be over or not.

Overdramatic was my middle name.

There had been a couple of messages from my mom

and one from Walter, but I ignored him, and I would deal with my mother later. My parents weren't bad people. They just didn't get me and wanted me to be a carbon copy of them and my sister. And well, I didn't really like who they were most of the time. Or perhaps I just didn't like the same things as them. Yeah, let's go with that.

My parents had supported me growing up in whatever endeavors I wanted to do in school. Though, now that I'd thought about it, I hadn't been able to make my own choices. It was more of, "Penny do this," and "Penny do that," and then I did it. When I really thought about it, I'd hated most of the things I'd been forced into.

Shit. Had I always been such a pushover?

I'd never really examined myself before in that way. It was kind of mind-blowing.

"You look deep in thought, Freckles. What's going on in your mind?" His gentle touch on my chin pulled my face toward him.

"Hmm?" I lifted my eyes and found Cooper staring at me. His golden features were so attractive, they muddled my brain a bit when I looked directly at him.

"Oh, nothing. Just, nothing," I finished, shaking my head.

"Hmm, sounds like there might be something. If you find yourself needing someone to talk to, I'm available. I won't push, so you can come to me when you're ready."

I sagged in relief, not realizing how much it had weighed on me. His simple offer had me feeling as if maybe I didn't have to do it on my own, even if I had just met him. "Sure, sounds like a plan."

A few minutes later, Poppy walked in carrying a bag

overflowing with things. "Thanks so much, assholes. You left me to carry everything," she joked.

I jumped up, immediately feeling bad, as I rushed over to help. "Oh my god, I'm so sorry. I didn't realize, I just thought—"

"It's fine, Pen. I'm just giving you a hard time. Here. This is so up your alley, DIYgirl."

She handed me the bag, and I opened it, finding it full of so many treasures. To my delight, I found exactly what I had just asked for: poster board, markers, pipe cleaners, and different colors of construction paper filled the bag. It was craft heaven, or at least elementary school craft heaven.

"Yes! This will be perfect."

I started pulling everything out and sorting it up on the dining room table as I placed everything into sections to categorize so I could see everything we had. When I was done, I found all three guys staring at me with varying looks on their faces. Aspen looked excited, Cooper was in awe, and Jett seemed speechless.

"What?"

"I've just never seen somebody be so intense and organized about their craft supplies," Jett stated.

Aspen shrugged. "I think it's cute. Coop?"

"Yeah. It's making me wonder what else you can color code," he said with a wink.

"Ooh, speaking of! Perhaps this could be our first organizing class?" Aspen asked, sheepishly.

"Uh, sure, though, I thought you were joking about that or at least wanted a date."

"Oh, I definitely want a date," Aspen said, walking

closer. "But I'm also interested in learning more about you in general."

Poppy walked over, a drink in her hand, and sat at the table, ignoring Jett. "Just wait until she gets a hold of the label maker, then you're really in trouble. I took it out of her suitcase, but I bet she found a way for it to make its way back in."

"Hey! You told me I could go crazy in your apartment. I can't help that I like to label things."

"Yeah, well, I didn't expect you to actually label everything, including which tampons to use for different flow days or what lube was oil-based or water-based. But hey," she said, softening her tone. "I never have to worry about it anymore, now do I?"

"Exactly. You're welcome."

"I can't decide if this is the weirdest thing to ever make me hard or most wholesome," Cooper mumbled.

"I'm still stuck on the fact there are different types of tampons," Aspen added.

"It was the lube that got me," Jett admitted.

Tuning out the three men at the end of our table, I focused on the task at hand as an idea struck me for our team name. Grinning wide to myself, I took out a marker and started to draw the letters on the poster board. Poppy leaned over, snorting, and then went back to drinking her beer while avoiding looking at Jett. After I'd been quiet for a while, the men finally noticed and watched as I worked.

"Should we be scared?"

"Nah, she's in the zone," Poppy answered them.

Smiling, I kept writing. I was already done with the title and added some little characters for balance. I wasn't the greatest at it, but small things were easy enough.

Writing a tagline, I stood back, pleased with the poster. Picking it up, I turned it for them to see.

"Ginger Nuts. Hard to crack, but we go hard," Aspen read.

I waited, some apprehension setting in now as I waited to see what they thought. The guys looked at me, blinking, before breaking out in laughter, falling into each other. Even Jett seemed happy, and I relaxed.

"You're alright, crazy, but alright, Penny," he said, smiling at me.

The guys kept joking about what our mascot could be along with many more nut puns and jokes. Satisfied for now that we'd accomplished something, I sat back down and leaned into Poppy.

"You okay?"

"Mmhmm," she said, running her fingers through my hair. We stayed like that for a while until a shadow darkened our little corner.

"Red, a moment?"

I was about to spout off how I didn't like to be called that when I realized he was speaking to Poppy. She sighed but hugged me before getting up. I watched as she followed him into a room, the door shutting. Biting my lip, I stayed, making sure she was okay. When I didn't hear any shouting, I got up and joined the guys on the couch.

"Wanna go night swimming, Penny?"

"Um, sure."

"We can leave a note for them if that's what you're worried about."

"Oh, no, it's fine. I mean, but yeah, that would be nice."

A loud bang sounded, causing me to jump. Standing, I started toward the door to bust into the room and kick Jett in his nuts when a loud moan sounded out, followed by more thumping.

"Well, I guess they got over whatever had crawled up Jett's butt. So, swimming?" I asked, moving toward the door in record speed to get out of there. I loved Poppy, but I didn't need to hear her getting it on. The two brothers followed, laughing at my red face, but I didn't care. Some things should be kept private; even PB&J had limits.

"I just need to grab my suit. Meet you at the pools?" I asked once we were clear of the sex hut.

"Sounds good, Freckles. Don't take too long though, I'll miss you." Coop winked, and I smiled, heading toward my hut.

CHAPTER
EIGHT

RAFÉ

PACING, I RUBBED THE BACK OF MY NECK, THE ACHE GROWING
the more my mother lamented about how foolish I was,
and how if I was a better son, I'd be home helping manage
the household. She conveniently forgot she could only
afford my father's medical bills because *I* sent her money.

But it wasn't enough.

For my proud, Catholic, first-generation immigrant
mother, it really wasn't. I was meant to be the answer to all
of their struggles; all their hopes and dreams pinned onto
my coattails. It was a lot for one person, and I struggled
each day with doing right by my family while also doing
what I needed to be happy.

But I wasn't happy. Not really.

"Yes, Mamá. I'll call Lucinda and make sure she
doesn't buy the car without having it checked, and I'll
remind Será to check on Mrs. Baldwin. Uh-huh. Yeah.
Okay, well, I gotta go. I'll call again tomorrow. Love you."

Sighing, I dropped my head, taking in a few deep breaths. Every day I called my mother, and every day I wished I didn't have to. The guilt of feeling that way was what kept me calling her despite my desire to throw my phone into the ocean when I was done.

Guilt had become my constant companion these days.

Guilt for not doing enough for my family. Guilt for wanting my own life. Guilt for pursuing a job that took me away from them on purpose. Guilt for hating the job I so desperately held onto and had fought for.

I carried so much guilt that I had constant heartburn which would no doubt cause an ulcer to develop in the long run. I knew something had to give soon. I just wasn't ready to face the inevitable decision. Everything was balanced precariously and it would only take one thing to tip it over.

My job was joy-destroying at best, soul-sucking at worst.

And yet, I couldn't quit.

I made a good living, had great benefits, and got to travel. So, why did I hate it? Because in order for me to be successful, I had to make other people miserable. When your income and job performance were based on catching others in vulnerable, humiliating, or even scandalous moments, it didn't make you feel good about yourself. At least I didn't.

Lifting my head, I watched the last of the sun dip below the horizon, and I couldn't decide if it was relief or despair I felt at making it through another day. Each day felt more unbearable than the one before, the inevitable crossroads looming closer. But with my father's illness and treatment weighing over me, it didn't feel like I had any other choice but to continue down this path of destruction.

The phone started to ring, and I glanced down to see who it was. It was a habit despite knowing it was one of two people at this time of night. Seeing it was my boss, I exhaled and straightened my spine, hopeful it would give me the confidence I needed.

"Rafé!" she barked, starting in immediately. "How is the footage? Have you been able to talk with any of the contestants yet?"

"Good evening, Georgina."

"For fuck sake, Rafé. You and your manners. I swear, how you're able to get me the best content always blows my mind." Her smoky voice chuckled down the line, and I took another breath. I might want to avoid my mother at times, but she'd taught me to be polite. And even if I thought my job was despicable, I was still courteous about it.

"Everyone just arrived and has been given their first mission. I'll be ready to go in the morning when they announce the team names. I have a few interviews scheduled after that. I've gone over all the files of each contestant, and I know which ones have the juiciest backstories. There's no need to worry. Like you said, I always deliver. I'll get your footage, but I have a system."

"Yes, yes, you and your system. Fine. Just send over the dailies, so I can see how things are going. Anyone surprising you yet?"

"There might be a few wild cards, but I'm waiting to see how it plays out before I say anything."

"Fucking hell, Rafé. I swear, your lips are tighter than a

virgin on prom night. *Fine.* Keep your secrets. Don't forget we have a meeting to discuss your future with us when you return from this, assuming you hand over gold content. *Don't* let me down."

She hung up, her farewell as abrupt as her greeting. "Good evening, Georgina," I whispered into the wind. Shoving the phone in my pocket, I mimed strangling something as I screamed internally.

"Argh!" Okay, so one scream slipped out. Spinning, I took off and immediately slammed into someone.

"Ack!"

Her scream had me reaching out to grab her, not wanting any harm to come to the person who had the misfortune to stumble into my path. Turning mid-air, I managed to roll us enough that I landed on my back, with her lying across me in the sand.

"Shit, I'm so sorry! Are you okay?" I asked, my hands tracing her face. She laid on my chest, braced on her elbows as she stared at me, her big blue eyes blinking at me.

"Did you just do one of those movie things?"

"What?" I asked, a crease forming between my brows. Did she know who I was?

"You know, where the guy manages to turn, so the girl falls on him? That thing!"

"Oh, I, well, yeah, I guess I did." I looked to the right and left to check my whereabouts despite knowing full well I was on the ground, the hard feeling of the sand underneath me. We were at the fork for the huts, so I'd managed to at least fall on the side that wasn't water. It would have to be my positive thing for the day.

"Wow, I'm impressed then."

"Um, thanks?"

"Sure, no problem." She giggled.

We stared at one another, and I lifted my brow. "You going to camp out here, or will I have the use of my upper half back anytime soon?" The slightly flirty tease slipped out of my mouth before I could think about it.

"Well, I didn't know camping was an option, but now that you mentioned it?" she teased, smiling at me.

I smiled back, and despite having just fallen, the tension had seeped out of my body, and I felt relaxed for the first time in forever.

"That so?"

"Yeah, I could make it work. You're pretty comfortable." She bent her elbows and laid on her hands, smiling at me. She looked so cute. I didn't have it in me to ask her to move.

"Do I get a name since you're moving in? I like to be on a first name basis with my tenants?"

"Penny, and yours?"

"Rafé."

"Well, it's nice to meet you, Rafé. And I'd like to thank you for your generosity to let me move in and live on your chest, but I think I'm going to have to decline, despite it being my idea. You see, I'm kind of partial to food and water and bathing, and while you make a comfortable pillow, it doesn't make up for not having those things."

"I respect your decision, Penny, and applaud you for knowing what you need in life. Don't ever settle." The words had been genuine, but an ironic voice asked me if I was doing the same.

"That's great advice, one I should probably follow more in my own life."

"Yeah, as soon as I said it, I wondered if I even did it," I admitted.

"It's funny how that happens, right? You say something, and then it hits you. I had a moment like that earlier today."

"Oh yeah?"

"Yeah, I realized that I've pretty much done everything everyone else has wanted me to do my whole life. Excluding recently. And now, everyone is losing their shit over it, which then makes me wonder if I'm in the wrong, but I don't think I am."

She scrunched up her nose, the gesture both adorable and familiar. The freckles across the bridge drew my attention, and I wanted to trace them with my thumb. I shifted unintentionally, drawing her attention.

"Oh! Here, let me get up."

Her legs slid off to the side of mine, and she sat up. The pressure on my chest was gone, but the lower half of me became more aware of where her body touched me. She froze for a second, and I prayed she couldn't feel anything. Penny stared down at me, licking her lips. Sitting up quickly, our faces came even closer to one another. She cleared her throat, hiking one leg over the side, and kneeling in the sand next to me.

Every part of me missed where she'd touched, and the strongest urge to reach out and grab her fired through my body.

Clearing my throat, I turned in the opposite direction, shifting my erection, and standing. Dusting off the sand, I held out a hand for her to take. Penny peered at it briefly before reaching out and accepting it. Her hand was small, delicate, and it fit nicely in mine. Her creamy skin contrasted against the dark bronze of mine, and I had a brief flash of what her naked body would feel and look like against me.

Pulling her up, I considered making the small space between us disappear, but I didn't. That wasn't who I was. Stepping back, I cleared my throat, suddenly shy now that we weren't on top of one another.

"I feel like I owe you a drink or something for saving me from falling into the water or a worse fall."

"No, that's not necessary. I'm sure you have plans, people waiting on you."

"You know what? They'll be okay without me. Come on, I insist. Plus, I haven't explored much of the resort. It would be nice to do it with someone. Please?"

It was the please that sealed it, appreciating her use of manners. I couldn't deny her, and any attempt was feeble at best.

"Well, if you insist." I smiled, my body relaxing again. If I kept feeling this way around Penny, I'd quickly become addicted to her. We took off in the direction of the main resort area, the bright lights calling to us.

"Wow, it's stunning here at night too. I can't wait to look around more."

"Did you just get here today?"

"Uh, yeah. My friend and I came together."

"Sounds like there's a story there," I joked but then swallowed as I realized how easily I'd slipped into the producer role, digging for information.

"Yeah, well, there's a lot of stories, I'm afraid." She laughed, her hip hitting me slightly as she walked. "My life kind of took a tailspin over the past few days. I broke up with my boyfriend after realizing my vibrator made me happier, to only then sing karaoke into said vibrator while recording it, and then sent it out to the entire school. Now, not only am I single, I might be jobless when I return home. So yeah, *tailspin*." She huffed, throwing her hands down in a cute fashion. Everything about Penny was cute.

"Okay, that does all suck. But…" I turned, grimacing at her, "I might have you beat."

"Highly doubtful, but go ahead, let me hear it."

"Well, a year ago, I was left at the altar, found out my dad had cancer a week later, and apparently, I'm the only one in my family to keep a job since my four sisters all keep getting pregnant. I hate my job and the person it makes me, but it's the only thing that pays enough to help my family. So, I'm stuck, and yet, it still feels like it's never enough. My mother called tonight telling me how I'm a bad son because I'm off gallivanting instead of home taking care of Papi. I often wonder if it's all worth it. Okay, wow, that got dark." I stopped, turning to her with wide eyes, and she watched me. I was relieved to see she didn't have any pity in her eyes, but understanding.

"I promise. I'm not normally this forthcoming or someone who spills their baggage onto a stranger."

"To be fair, I spilled mine first, and hey, that's kind of what strangers are good for, you know? Spilling secrets."

"Yeah." I gulped, the implication was innocent, but it hit too close to home and how often I played that card too.

"Though, if you think about it, we're not really strangers either. I did practically lay on top of you for a solid ten minutes. I'd say we're only a few steps away from besties at this point." She smiled, making it all okay.

"I like how you think, Penny." My shoulders dropped in relief, and I felt relaxed again. Even the heartburn seemed to ease the more I was in her presence.

"Ha! It scares most people." She beamed at me, and I didn't believe her. There was no way she wasn't popular, she was too nice.

"But hey, all that you're dealing with, that's a lot of heavy shit. It's okay to not have it together. Most people would be hitting the bottle for just one of those things." She leaned in close to me to whisper, "It's me. I'm most people."

I found myself laughing, the sound foreign "Thank you for saying that, but I still feel guilty."

"You can be a good son and a good person, and still feel resentful about not getting to feel what you want. They're not mutually exclusive. It doesn't make you selfish to want to have your own feelings."

"That's profound. I guess I've just never known how to separate myself from my family or my job. I'm the oldest of five with four younger sisters, and it's always been expected of me to do these things. I've never even questioned it. It wasn't until my ex-fiancee said I was more concerned about my family than her that I started to notice it, sad as that might be. I'm 30, and I still fear my mother."

"Do we ever outgrow that, though?" she asked, chuckling. "You know what, new friend, this calls for the hard stuff. Come on. Let's see if we can find the perfect place to wallow in our feelings."

"This feels like a bad idea."

"Nah, it'll be great."

Smirking, Penny grabbed my hand and pulled me into the resort. Despite not knowing where to go, she led the way, dragging me along, and I was happy to just let her. Penny had this thing about her that made you feel comfortable. She didn't claim to be perfect and admittedly called out her faults. It was refreshing to be around after being surrounded by faultless socialites. Though, it made my own guilt increase. I didn't want to tell her what I did; the look on her face would surely change with the information.

So maybe I'd live in denial a little longer, enjoying this one night until she looked at me like everyone else.

When she pulled up to a door, I was shocked when it wasn't the bar. "*This* is where you want to go?"

She turned her head, a toothy grin on her face. "Yep. The best place to drown your sorrows is with ice cream. The only thing you regret in the morning is the calories. Come on. I read about this in the brochure. They have a sundae bar and 50 different types of toppings. It's my goal to try them all in as many combinations as I can before I leave. I even have a spreadsheet to use to track which ones are the best."

"Whoa, that's some intense ice cream game you got there."

"Some people are good at sports. I'm good at trying out different combinations of things. I happen to love food and trying new things, so this is a paradise for me."

"Well, lead the way, Penny. I'm curious to see what combination you start with."

"Watch and learn, young grasshopper."

Penny pulled me into the ice cream shop, and I found myself matching her grin with ease.

Earlier, I'd been close to pulling out my hair and drowning myself in whiskey. Instead, I found myself at an ice cream bar with a beautiful girl not hating my life at the moment.

As I took a bite of the crazy concoction she'd made, I tried to memorialize each moment to have when it all blew up.

I wasn't naive to think it wouldn't.

Because it would. It always blew up.

CHAPTER
NINE

PENNY

W̲HEN MY ALARM WENT OFF, I WAS ALREADY FINISHING UP the poster board I'd started last night. I'd snuck into the guys' bungalow at 6 am—I'd decided it wasn't a hut, no matter what the clipboard lady said. It had been way too easy to get a key, making my sneaking adventure a success. Though, it did make me doubt the security of the place and I would be sleeping with three locks from here on out if they just gave keys to anyone.

I'd felt guilty for ditching the guys last night for Rafé, so I'd gone and procured coffee and donuts. There was a full breakfast at the announcements this morning, but I hoped it'd be a peace offering and tide them over until then. Plus, I wanted a donut.

I knew Poppy hadn't come home last night, her bed was still made this morning, and I doubted anyone else would've finished our first mission, so I made it my priority this morning to complete it. It might be a stupid contest, but the thought of not doing well was giving me anxiety. I liked to succeed.

I guess I needed to own that about myself. My parents might've pushed me into things I didn't have a lot of interest in, but my need to win at them had caused me to stay involved long past when they were fun. Though, perhaps it was their fault for making everything a competition between my sister and me. Prue was a natural at most things and succeeded in school. It came so easy to her; I didn't think she ever stressed about anything.

I'd both admired and envied her as I grew up, always in her constant shadow and never able to keep up with her accolades.

The dourness of that thought made me realize it was time to add more to my list.

4) It's okay to lose—it builds character. Try something you suck at, and just have fun.
5) Say no every once in a while. You don't have to do things for people to like you.

New items added, I fell back into the quiet zone I found myself in when crafting. A door opened a moment later as I finished gluing the last pipe cleaner to the board. Glancing up, I froze, my hand hovering over the poster board as I stared at the magnificent display that was Cooper. His hair stuck up in a few places as he scrubbed his eyes. He was shirtless, only a pair of *very* tight boxer briefs that left nothing to the imagination. Fucking hell, I suddenly found myself shifting my legs.

Remembering I was staring, *again*, I closed my mouth and returned back to packing up the supplies as I tried to keep my eyes lowered. The noise had Cooper stumbling, and I looked up to find him blinking at me.

"I must be asleep still," he mumbled. "No, wait. If I was dreaming, you'd be in something sexy like my favorite t-shirt. So, if I'm not sleeping, then how did I get so lucky to wake up to you first thing this morning?" He smiled with no irritation in sight about standing him up last night or finding me randomly in his dwelling.

"I, um, came to finish our assignment and brought coffee and donuts." I pointed to the items, tucking my hair behind my ear self-consciously.

"Okay, now, I'm convinced this has to be a dream again. Coffee *and* donuts?"

He ran forward to where they perched on the table, not minding at all that his massive thigh muscles and abs were out on display for me to drool over. Cooper grabbed a donut, and I stared at the part of him I wanted to lick that was very happy this morning. He moaned as he inhaled the yeasty concoction, and I was done for.

Cooper opened his eyes, finding me practically panting at his naked body as he licked his fingers clean.

"I think you're my dream girl in real life, Freckles. If you keep looking at me like *that*, though, I might have to take this box of donuts and leave crumbs for you to follow me to my room with the trail ending with a donut on my long john."

I leaned forward in my chair, licking my lips as I debated doing what he said and licking that donut clean. Cooper's eyes heated, his "long john" growing bigger by the minute as the tension between us thickened. The door to the master suite swung open, breaking our focus and Jett walked out with Poppy under his arm. They were in a sex-crazed bliss state, not paying attention to anyone else as they made their way into the kitchenette all loved up.

"Coffee over here," I hollered, gaining their attention. Poppy saw me, untangled herself, and skipped over to me with a huge smile on her face.

"Pen! You're here! I've missed you."

She wrapped her arm around me, rocking us side to side. She just stayed there for a second, and I patted her back, not used to this level of lovey-dovey from Poppy.

"Missed you too, P. You okay?"

She pulled back, a bright smile on her face and her cheeks rosy. "The best! And now, I'm even better because you're here. Oh, donuts!" She moved over, and grabbed one, licking the sprinkles off as she stood over me.

That was when I realized what was going on. Sitting her down in a chair, I walked over to the man who was sipping coffee with a smug grin on his face. Clearly, he didn't understand the damage I was about to bestow on him. Grabbing Jett by the ear, I yanked him down hard so I could whisper-shout at him. He yelped, followed by a slew of cussing as he attempted to break my hold.

"Fuck, woman. Ow! That shit hurts!"

"I warned *you*."

"I didn't hurt her! I swear."

"No? You got her fucking high! Poppy doesn't react like the average person who gets high and then can go on with their day. Poppy—" I stopped, catching my breath as I tried to reign my emotions in. It wasn't my place to spill her secrets, but it didn't mean I wouldn't protect her with every breath I had in the process.

"Don't *ever* give her drugs again, or I'll twist more than

your ear next time. Do we have an understanding, asshole?"

"Yes, fuck, just let go, okay. I didn't know."

I did as he asked and let go. Jett scooted back, his hands held out in front of him as he regarded me.

"I'm sorry, truly. I thought she was acting differently, but she's unlike anyone I've ever met, so I didn't think anything of it. She hasn't reacted to anything like most girls. What can I do?" He dropped his hands, his question sounding sincere, but I was too pissed to hear it.

"Right now? Nothing. But in a few hours… " I shook my head, a hard laugh leaving me. "We'll see if your dick is good for more than screwing over women."

I turned on my heels, not waiting for a response. Poppy was oblivious at the table, nibbling on the donut in a daze. Cooper watched me seriously, no longer looking at me like he wanted to fuck me and I didn't have it in me to feel bad for how I'd treated his friend. Guys could come and go, but Poppy was forever.

Grabbing her face, I peered into her eyes, checking them to assess the level of worry I needed to have. Her pupils weren't too dilated, so maybe she hadn't had much. Even just a smidge made her giddy until the crash, it was the crash that worried me though.

"What did you give her and how much?"

"It was just a pot sucker. I had a few left from the flight. They help me calm down before having to fly. She said she was hungry and started to rummage through my stuff I had out. She found one laying out. I don't think she realized what it was, honestly. When I told her, she was already dancing around the room, acting funny, so I took it from her." Jett had come over to the table, a sincere look on his face as he spoke to me, no traces of the smug asshole from earlier.

"She always thinks she can do it, forgetting how messed up it makes her no matter how little she has. Poppy has a slight allergy to THC, among other things. At first it makes her all flirty and high, but then she crashes, and if she has a large enough dose, it can be bad. If it was a small dose, she should be okay. Once when she ate a pot brownie, she was in the hospital for a week. It took them a few years to figure it out, just thinking it was other things causing her illness."

"Shit. I'm so sorry. Seriously, what can I do to help?"

"Mostly, just wait it out. We can try to flush it from her system, but it's probably already in her bloodstream at this point. Grab some water, and I need to go grab some allergy meds."

"Let me," Aspen said, touching my arm softly. His touch surprised me since I hadn't heard him enter the room. I looked up into his hazel eyes, a refusal on my lips, but something in his gaze had me stopping and considering. Swallowing down some panic, I nodded.

"Okay. We're in 240. My room is the first one. In the bathroom, there's a small bag about this big," I gestured with my hands, "it has peanuts on it. Just grab that. It has everything I need in it."

"I'm on it. Can you let your roommate know I'm on my way?"

"Yeah, good call." I started looking around for one of the room phones. When I found it, Cooper was already holding it to his ear.

"Hey, this is Cooper, I'm with Penny and Poppy. My brother Aspen is headed to you to get something for

Poppy. Can you let him in when he gets there?" Cooper paused as he waited, a smile on his face as he turned to me. I was still in shock he'd jumped in to help so effortlessly. I wasn't used to this. I was the fixer, the planner.

"Jemma wants to verify that it's you and not some 'polite psycho' calling before he comes to kill her, so could you please tell her something only she and you'd know since you hadn't gotten to the secret handshake or password portion of your friendship yet." He finished, taking a breath, and I laughed, relaxing some. Cooper standing in his briefs on the phone had nothing to do with it. Nope.

"Um, tell her Double P dares her to let Aspen in."

"Okay, Freckles said, "Double P dares you to let Aspen in. Uh-huh, yeah, okay. Thanks, Jemma."

He hung up, winking at me and I could've kissed him for taking care of that. Poppy was starting to get sleepy, her head resting on Jett's shoulder as he encouraged her to drink some water. I hadn't noticed him bring it over, and I softened a little more to him. Another wave of relief washed through me, and I sagged back in the chair. Poppy was still holding my hand and I squeezed it, feeling like everything would be okay for once.

"She gonna be okay?" Jett asked, looking at me earnestly, and I nodded.

"Yeah, I think so. Thankfully, she doesn't seem to have ingested too much. Some antihistamine and sleep, and she'll be good as new."

"I didn't know. I wasn't trying to get her high, so I could sleep with her," he pleaded.

I met his eyes, sincerity shining through again, the bad boy nowhere in sight. "I believe you, and you couldn't have known. You did just meet her. Plus, she's usually much better about checking things, but I think she's just been so stressed, worried about me," I cringed, some guilt filling me, "and it slipped her mind."

I could feel their eyes on me and I swallowed down the lump building in my throat. It was time I got my shit together. I couldn't have Poppy bailing me out of every-thing. She had enough of her own shit to deal with as it was.

I felt Cooper squeeze my leg, and I looked up to find concern on his face. I gave him a wobbly grin. This was too heavy for people we'd met only twenty-four hours ago. Though, I had dumped all my baggage on Rafé last night within ten minutes of meeting him. So, perhaps that was something else I needed to work on. This list would be long by the end of the summer at the rate I was adding things to it.

Aspen ran through the door a moment later, the peanut bag in his hand. He held it out like a baton, ready for the next person to take it in the relay as he bent over, trying to catch his breath, making me chuckle. Cooper jumped up, taking the proffered item from him and handing it to me with a bow. I still found my eyes drawn to his thighs each time he moved.

"Did you run there and back?" I asked, concerned when he was still panting.

He nodded his head, still bent over. "I should have sent Coop. He's at least fit. Water?" he croaked.

Cooper laughed, but jogged over to the fridge and grabbed some water, and I had to forcibly turn away from the delicious sight while I opened the bag, discreetly taking out the pink antihistamine and a white and blue capsule. Tapping her cheek, she sat up, touching my hair in a dreamy state.

"I love you, Pen-Pen."

"I know. I got something to make you feel better. Open up."

"No, I don't want it." She shook her head, her lip quivering a little, killing me inside.

"It'll be okay. I'm here, and I'll take care of you," I whispered, smoothing her hair back.

She nodded, tears springing to her eyes, but opened her mouth. I covered my palm as I placed them on her tongue and handed her the water. She swallowed them, thankfully, and handed me back the bottle. I could already tell she wasn't as affected as some of the other incidents, but I knew she never liked feeling weak.

For some reason, the allergic reaction always offset her moods, and if she wasn't careful, she'd spiral into a deep depression. I'd given her one of the emergency pills she took at times when it got too much for her. Poppy hated them because they made her feel like a zombie, but she also knew the alternative was worse, so she took them, despite knowing the day would be rough for her.

I kissed her forehead, smoothing her hair down. "I love you too, Poppy. You're gonna be okay. I'll see if we can get an extension or something."

"Um, about that," Aspen interrupted, reminding me we weren't alone. "I read the rules, and, um, it says if one member of the team isn't able to make it, then it's up to the others to take their place or all forfeit. No exceptions."

"Well shit."

"I'm good. I can rally," Poppy said, yawning a little, the antihistamine already kicking in.

"I think it would be better for you to sit this one out. I'll join you and keep you company. You guys okay to do it without us?" I asked, looking at them.

"No," Jett said vehemently, startling me. "I'll stay. I can do that much."

"I don't think—" I said, shaking my head before Poppy cut me off.

"Let him," Poppy whispered. I peered down at her, trying to gauge everything. She opened her eyes, looking at me. Her pupils weren't as dilated anymore, and she'd be out for the count in ten minutes as it was, sleeping most of the day. I didn't think she'd have any further reactions either.

"Are you sure? I don't want to leave you."

"We both know I'll be sleeping. Go have fun. Don't let my stupid mistake spoil it."

"Poppy, like I could have fun without you."

"I think you can." She yawned bigger, but not before she lifted her eyes to the two guys standing beside me. Sighing, I knew I wouldn't win this argument.

"Fine. But only under duress."

"Dressed is the best way to go unless it's a nudist camp." She laughed at her lame joke, and I smiled. At least she still had her humor.

"She'll just need to be monitored closely," I ordered Jett and he grabbed some of my paper and started to write it down, reassuring me he'd take it seriously. "Water and food in a few hours, but mostly rest. You'll call me if anything changes? *Anything*, even if it's minuscule?"

"Sure, I can do that." He nodded, finishing the list.

"My threat still stands, but if you do this, I might be willing to forgive you."

"Well, then count me in, little gangsta. You've officially scared me." He lifted his lips a little, but I didn't think he was joking. Feeling appeased for the moment, I turned to the two who'd been watching me through it all.

"I guess it's just us three."

"Works for me." Cooper winked. "How much time do we have before we need to leave?"

"Um." I bit my lip, looking down at my watch. "Like negative 10 mins."

"Which means 10 mins, 5 if you really like her," Poppy said in a sleepy voice. "She's always early to everything, so if she says something is 'negative time', you're still good. But, go, quick!"

The guys blinked at Poppy. When she sat up, staring at them, they finally jumped into action. She rose out of the chair, kissing me on the forehead this time before pulling me into a hug.

"Thank you. Go, have fun, and then later, I can tell you about the most amazing sex I've ever had, and you can tell me where you were last night."

She pulled back, raising her eyebrows at me. Blushing, I nodded, pushing her toward the bedroom. Jett walked with her, and for once, I felt confident leaving her with him. Gathering up the last of the stuff we needed to take with us, I was impressed when both guys rushed out dressed, hair wet as it laid against their foreheads.

"Wow, okay. Maybe we can do this. Can you grab that bag for me?"

Cooper nodded, stuffing another donut in his mouth as he picked up the bag I'd pointed to. Aspen came over and took one of the ones I held in my hand, ignoring my protests.

"Let's go and show them what Ginger Nuts is all about, Freckles."

"Ha! Time to go *hard*, guys."

Laughing, we hurried out of their bungalow, heading toward the central area, and I mentally added the two items I needed to my list.

6) Quit apologizing for things you have no control over
7) It's okay to ask for help every now and then

Walking into the main area, we took our seats, just as the clipboard lady took the microphone. She started to welcome everyone when Aspen nudged me. Looking over, I found him holding a plate full of food out to me, and now I wanted to kiss him.

Grabbing it, I dug in, no longer caring what she had to say as I inhaled pancakes, bacon, and fruit. "Oh, man. I think I love you."

"Is she saying that to you, or the food?"

"Not sure, but I'll take it."

"Man, no fair. I was this close to getting my donut licked. I get to bring her food tomorrow then."

"I don't even want to know what that means. Besides, you gotta be quicker. I'm not giving up *that* just so you can have a turn. This isn't little league, bro. All is fair play in winning Penny's heart."

Snorting, I took a drink of juice, feeling better now that I had food in me. I ignored their bickering, finding the banter cute, and not wanting them to know how much I liked the fact they were fighting over who got to bring me food. The real answer, both.

Cute guys, bacon, and swim trunks. I guess this day was still salvageable.

CHAPTER
TEN

ASPEN

Coop nudged me as we walked, motioning with his eyes to look at Penny. It was unnecessary since I hadn't stopped looking at her since the moment I met her. She was fiddling with her hair as we walked, twisting it around her index finger, and I could tell she was miles away in her thoughts.

"So, Penelope, what do you think should be on our flag, our mascot, or just our name?"

"Hmm?" she asked, peering over. When her eyes met mine, she startled, focusing on what I said. "Oh, right. Why not both in a way?" She shrugged one shoulder, and it was almost back to the carefree one she had when we first met.

"Are you able to draw it?"

"A squirrel, yeah, or well, I can print one off and trace it."

"Huh, never thought of that." I smiled at her, our arms rubbing against one another as we walked.

"It's a little cheat I learned when doing crafts. I can do lettering well, but outside of a few small things, I'm horrible at drawing. Tracing something is the way to go."

"Sounds like a plan. Just one thing, where are you going to print it?"

"Right." She stopped and then turned back around. "Come on." Then stopped and spun back in our direction. "Actually, first, we need to come up with it, then print it. For that, I need my iPad."

"How long do we have to do it?" Coop asked, watching her closely.

"Um, I'm not sure. I was kind of zoned out."

She definitely had been. I had to nudge her to stand when they called us to announce our team name. Penny had said it and then sat down, so I lifted the poster board and said our motto with our mascot that she'd made out of pipe cleaners. It was awe-inspiring. Penny didn't appear to have heard the comments or how everyone laughed, thinking it was brilliant. Despite Poppy assuring her that she was fine, I could tell Penny was still worried about her friend. At least today's activities weren't too intensive, more focused on getting to know one another, and we could do it back at home base, allowing her to check on her friend.

We all walked silently to her place, and Coop and I waited outside while she ran in to grab some items.

"I'm worried about her. She seems withdrawn. The food was the only thing that made her smile," Cooper mumbled, his brows dipped down as he tried to work out how to make her smile.

"Yeah, hopefully, once we get back to our place, she'll see Poppy is fine, and it'll help."

"Hope so. Man, I can't believe I'm this torn up about a girl already." He rubbed the back of his head, fidgeting as he waited.

I lifted my eyebrow at him, an incredulous look on my face. "*Really*? You can't?"

Coop chuckled at my comment, shaking his head. "Okay, you're right. I tend to fall in love after ten minutes, but you're one to talk. You're just as bad."

I shrugged. "Maybe, but I wasn't claiming *not* to be." Coop pushed my shoulder, laughing at me. Some of his nerves had dissipated though.

"Fine. Though," he started, peeking over at me before he finished, "I was surprised when I wasn't jealous. I thought with us both liking the same girl, I'd be fighting you for her. And I think at first, that was some of the fun, but this morning, it was nice working together to help her."

I mulled over what he said. "You know, you're right. I was glad you were there when I left. It was easy to divide and conquer. Still doesn't mean I'm not going to give you a hard time about trying to earn her time the most."

"I wouldn't want it any other way, bro." Cooper wrapped his arm around my head, giving me a noogie as I attempted to punch him in the stomach.

"You know, I always thought I wanted a brother, but maybe I don't."

We both straightened, sheepish smiles on our faces at her voice. "Nah, it's in good fun. Come on, Freckles, let's go and make a flag." Cooper directed her down the dock, placing his arm around her shoulder. He peeked over her head, sticking his tongue out at me as he kept walking with his arm there.

I was satisfied to follow along behind, hands in my pockets as I watched them. Coop had his head bent down, whispering in her ear as they walked. An odd feeling of happiness stole over me at seeing him so content. He acted unaffected by things, but I knew Coop struggled to let people see the real version of himself. He was comfortable being the flirty guy, but his heart was big and he loved deeply.

If I was a better man, I'd step back and let my brother have his chance.

But for some reason, it didn't feel like that type of situation. I didn't know what it was yet, but it felt necessary for both of us to be in her life.

The fact I didn't want to back away had nothing to do with it.

Probably.

Maybe.

Or it could just be purely coincidental.

Yeah, that.

They'd just made it to the turn to head down the dock toward our bungalows when Penny stepped out from under Coop's arm and waved down someone headed down the other path.

"Rafé, hey!" she yelled, and the man in question stopped, turning. He smiled brightly at her, and they started to have a conversation a few feet ahead of where Cooper had stopped. Coming flush with him, I leaned on his shoulder as we both silently watched.

"Who do you think that is? And when could she have

met him? She's been with one of us the majority of the time," I asked.

"Hmm, if I had to guess, maybe last night when she was supposed to be meeting up with us. This fucker swooped in and stole her. You know what this means, right?"

"We no longer compete against one another, but him."

"Damn straight. Bros before… wait, that doesn't work out the way I want it." Coop's brows creased as he tried to figure it out. Chuckling, I stepped away while he thought it out and I decided the best defense was a good offense. Walking forward, I causally interrupted.

"Hey man, I'm Aspen."

"Oh, sorry. Rafé, this is Aspen, and that's Cooper," Penny said, motioning behind her toward my brother.

"Yeah, I know," he fawned, "Aspen Cooper from Shadows of Mayhem. I love you guys."

It still blew me away when people recognized me and even more when they liked our music. I'd walked over here with the intention of asserting some dominance, but I couldn't hate the guy when he was a fan. "Ah, well, that's cool. It's nice to meet a SOM fan, Rafé. How do you know *our* girl, Penny?" I wasn't ashamed that I emphasized the our.

"Oh, well, we um, met last night when I tackled her to the ground in an attempt to run away from a bad phone call."

"More like he saved me from falling into the water. I was on my way to change when the collision happened. The only cure from that point was ice cream," Penny admitted, a little remorse seeping through her words at standing us up.

Well, at least her flaking out on us hadn't been intentional. That had to count for something. I started to ask another question when Coop swooped in, no longer able to stand back, and stuck his foot in his mouth like he did when he was nervous.

"And here I thought I was special, Freckles. I guess I'm not the only handsome guy you're vibing with, huh?"

Penny bristled at the slight insinuation, and I turned, giving him a look. Widening my eyes, I shook my head slightly, warning him off from whatever path he was taking.

"Cooper Aspen! Oh, man! You're amazing to watch when you do your tricks. I've been following your career for a few years," Rafé exclaimed, fanning over Coop more than he had me. I wasn't jealous. Nope.

Cooper jolted, almost having the same reaction as I did to him. It was hard to be mean to someone who was spewing nice things about you. He stopped, his mouth parted as he assessed Rafé.

"Wait, your name is Cooper Aspen, and you're Aspen Cooper? What the fuck?" She looked between us, a slight hysterical look on her face as her eyes scrunched up and her cheeks heated. "And don't get me started on the idiocy of your comment. Wow, just wow!" Penny's nose screwed up like she smelled something bad, and she looked back and forth between the three of us, none of us answering.

"Okay, well, awesome. Glad we had this talk. I'm gonna go and check on Poppy and do our task. You both can *vibe* yourselves since I'm too busy to entertain dicks."

Penny walked off, but stopped, looking over her shoulder. "In case it wasn't clear, you're the dicks, and I don't mean the ones in your pants." She turned back, mumbling and we only caught some of it before she was too far away. "Seriously, of all the things to say! He has the gall to call me out!"

I stood stunned, not sure what had just occurred.

"What just happened?" Coop asked, the same look of confusion on his face.

"You made an ass out of yourself," Rafé supplied. I turned and looked at him, realizing he was being serious. The last five minutes had given me whiplash, so I laughed, not sure how to make sense of anything. My laughter set off Cooper, and Rafé even joined in with us.

"Shit. I did, didn't I? Okay, time for some damage control. Any ideas?" Coop asked, looking at me.

"First, you need to apologize for being a dumbass. Second, you need to do something to make it up. What, I'm not sure."

"Hmm, I might have an idea," Rafé said, drawing our attention back to him.

Raising my eyebrows, I observed him. He seemed sincere, confusing me yet again. "You're kind of a strange dude, aren't you? You have this vibe about you that makes me want to trust you, but I can't work out why you'd want to help us? It's obvious you like her."

He shrugged, something passing over his features before shutting them down. "I'm not the type of guy to get the girl in the end. I'm just biding my time until she discovers who I am and hates me."

"Whoa, cryptic enough there, dude? What, did you kill someone? Do you secretly hate kittens and rainbows? Take all of her glue guns?" Cooper teased.

"No, why would you think that?" Rafé asked, looking between us, genuinely curious.

"You just seem like a nice guy, and yet, you sound like a tortured hero. The one I usually root for in the story, if I'm honest. Ah shit, now I can't wish for you to fail. Is this some type of Jedi mind shit where you make me like you and want to see you happy instead of my initial intention to come over here and insert my dominance?"

"You were trying to pee on Penny? She won't like that," Coop said, snickering.

Pushing his shoulder, I rolled my eyes, focusing back on the solemn man. "Seriously, what's your play?"

"No play. I just won't be the one standing at the end. I know my fate in life."

"Sounds depressing, mate," Coop replied, a serious look on his face. He sighed, dropping his head. "Fucking hell, I'm with Aspen." He lifted his head, staring at Rafé. "I want to hate you too, but the romantic in me can't help but wish for a happily ever after for your tormented soul. Shit, you're right Asp, those are totally my jam too."

"Are you two for real? I feel like *I'm* being played now." Rafé looked between the two of us, and I shrugged.

"We're both complicated in the easiest of ways. We both enjoy a good love story but can't ever seem to get our own. Girls don't always want the nice guy. They like us for the crying shoulder, but when it comes time for the one who stays, it's the guy who hurts them a little. Which, obviously, we both get, but just can't seem to cultivate for ourselves. Something about the tension and pinning, well, it makes for a great story. We're champions of love at the end of the day," I sighed, "even if it's not ours."

"I think I just had my first guy crush," Rafé admitted, laughing. He shook his head, though, looking at us with regret. "I wish my story could play out like you both think it will, but I know how it ends for me, and it's not with someone as good as Penny."

Placing my arm around his shoulders, I steered him in the direction of the resort. "Well, Rafé, welcome to the Heartbreak Club. Our first official meeting will be Apologies 101. Let's hear this idea you have, and we'll see what we can do to make it work. Teamwork just might get one of us the girl at the end."

"This is the weirdest club initiation I've ever been part of, but Hell, what do I have to lose?"

"Exactly," I agreed, nodding. Peering over my shoulder, I hollered for my brother, "Coop!"

He jogged around us, spinning to run backward as he looked at me with a smirk. "Yes, Captain?"

"I think it's time for a reprise."

"No!" he shouted, grinning eye to eye, and almost jumping on the spot. "Don't joke about that if you don't mean it."

"Oh, I mean it."

"Um, do I want to know what you're talking about?"

"Just the greatest matchmaking duo in history, formally known as Casper."

"Casper?"

"Cooper and Aspen merged together," Coop said, beaming.

"Our greatest achievement was reuniting our parents when they called off the wedding, both too stressed to deal with the planning and ultimately scared. We rose to the occasion, and Casper was born. We got several of our friends together, and even two teachers."

"So if you're so good at matchmaking, why don't you just do yourselves?"

"Because you can't use your powers on yourself. Everyone knows that!" Cooper laughed, spinning around, so he no longer walked backward. It was in the nick of time as he dodged a few people and a pole. It was like he'd known, his weird spatial thing coming into play to tell him where things were like Daredevil.

"Listen, I appreciate it, but I know there's no future for her and me. You'd be better off doing it for yourselves."

"Okay, how about a compromise. We'll resurrect Casper and help all three of us, giving us an equal chance, and let fate and Penny decide? You only regret the chances you don't take, Rafé."

He observed me for a few seconds before he sighed. "I feel like I'm going to regret this a whole heck of a lot. But what the Hell, it's not like I have anything else going for me."

"Such the downer, Rafé," I tsked, directing him toward the resort. "Okay it's time to share your knowledge and start phase one. What's this secret apology gift idea you have?"

"Ice cream."

"Ice cream? Really?"

"Yeah, she loves the stuff and plans to try all these different kinds of combinations. I figured you get a few different pints to go and some toppings, and you'll be back in good favor."

"Penny does love her food," Cooper said, shrugging.

"Well, it's worth a shot. Alright, it's time to upgrade our original operation from P.T.P to operation W.O.P. It's Casper time! Let's do what we're good at."

"Be cute, friendly, but most of all, *invisible*," Coop whispered, making us laugh.

"Yeah, well, he might need to be visible for this mission."

"You guys are weird, but I kind of like you."

"Same, Rafé. Same."

"What's the PTP and WOP, though?"

"Ah," I answered, smiling, "first we were proving to Penny we could be trusted, but now… "

"Winning over Penny?"

"You got it!"

Rafé laughed but nodded and we walked into the ice cream shop, a mission in front of us, and I felt confident we'd be successful.

I'd gone over to knock Rafé out of the way, and now I was eagerly helping him. Either I was crazy or Penny just had that effect on people.

Now, I needed to prove to her that one of us was the right man for her.

Though in the back of my mind, I knew something wasn't right about that, but I was too scared to look too closely.

CHAPTER
ELEVEN

PENNY

I was losing it. The tightly wound facade of having it all together was starting to crumble at my feet. One minute, I felt on top of the world and like I had it all together. The next, I couldn't even formulate a sentence or go two seconds without wishing I could rewind time and make a better choice.

It didn't help that I was worried about Poppy but then I would get distracted by hot guys, only making me feel guiltier.

I was sick of feeling this way. I needed to get it together. Wasn't that the whole purpose of this trip? To quit all this wallowing and insecurity?

Stopping in my tracks, I took a few deep breaths. The Penny that rushed to do everyone else's bidding needed to take a backseat.

"Do you need to pee or something?"

"Huh?" I opened my eyes and found Jett staring at me.

He was leaning against the porch railing of their hut. I blinked, not realizing I'd speed-walked this far in my angry, confused lust haze. His words seeped in after a moment, and I scrunched up my nose at him.

"Do you really go around asking girls if they need to pee? That's weird, and that's coming from me."

"What? No! I didn't mean it like that." Jett sighed and his hand went to his temple as he rubbed the area, taking a lungful of air himself. "You stopped and then took a few breaths. I thought maybe you had to go or something. Sorry, I wasn't trying to be weird. I haven't slept a lot in the past 48 hrs, and I'm a bit jet-lagged."

"I'd feel sorry for you except for the fact you chose to stay up all night boinking with my friend."

"I'm not asking you to! Geez. Is everything a battle with you, little gangsta? I apologized for the weed thing. I didn't know. But it's like you hated me from moment one, and that's not fair to make a snap judgment about me."

I clenched my jaw, not liking that he was right. "Fine. You're right, I did, and it's not fair. I just know guys like you, and you're all the same. You're gonna make promises to Poppy and then break them. Sorry if I don't want to see my friend hurt."

"Wow, and here I thought you were better than that. Glad to see I'm only a stereotype." He turned to go, a hurt expression on his face.

Blowing out a breath, I counted to ten. "Stop." He did but didn't turn around. "Ugh," I groaned, tapping my foot. "Listen, I'm not going to apologize for caring about my friend, but I will give you the chance to be you. I owe Poppy that as well. My threat still stands, though."

He glanced over his shoulder, giving a nod. "I can

accept that. And for what it's worth, I like her. I don't have any plans to hurt her." Jett walked in, and I followed close behind, but the thought, *"they never do,"* flooded through my mind anyway, and I hoped he would be the exception to the rule. Poppy deserved someone who worshipped her.

"Did you really say boinking?"

Ignoring him, I asked what I really wanted to know. "How is she?"

"Asleep."

"For how long?"

He spun, his eyes filled with a challenge as they seared into me. "Listen, little gangsta, I get that you and Poppy are like two peas in a pod, or whatever—"

"We're actually PB&J because we stick together," I muttered, crossing my arms. For some reason, I had no qualms about standing up to him. He rolled his eyes, ignoring my comment this time.

"But I'm not a fucking asshole. I can watch over a person."

"I'm not saying you're incompetent. I'm simply asking a question because I need to know. You don't know the full scope of things, and it's important that I stay aware. I'm not sure what happened between us leaving and now, but I prefer the Jett I left my friend with, not this one. This one, he's an ass." I waved my hand in his direction, not biting back my words for once. Perhaps I just needed Jett to follow me around and then I could tell people how I felt.

He stewed in his spot for a minute, his jaw clenching with each breath. Growing tired of waiting, I walked around him toward the bedroom. I'd figure out the information for myself.

"Sorry. I… I got a call before you showed up. It's why I was outside, so I didn't wake her. She just fell asleep, so I wouldn't go in there just yet," he said calmly. I guess the breathing worked.

"Thank you. I'll just go work on this then." I walked toward the table, placing the supplies down and grabbing the stuff I'd left out. Jett went into the kitchen, grabbed a drink, and walked over, leaning against the wall as he watched me.

"Where are the other two?"

"No clue." I shrugged, sorting the markers. "I left them back at the front where they were measuring their dicks."

Sputtering, Jett smiled, softening to me a little. "Good for you. I don't mind your attitude when it's not directed at me."

"Well, don't be a jackass, and I won't have to aim it toward you." I glanced up, grinning mischievously at him. He shook his head, giving me a smile.

"See, that's hard because it's kind of my go-to nature."

"I'm going to pretend you're joking because I saw glimpses of a nice guy this morning. So be more of that." Looking back down, I pulled out my iPad and searched for an image I could trace for our flag. I wanted to know the size before I started with the letters. As I browsed photos, Jett kept watching me.

"When did you become the bad guy police?"

"When I was twelve and the first guy broke Poppy's heart."

"Pftt, what did you do? Punch him?"

"No, that's more Poppy's domain. I made him laxative brownies, and he pooped himself in front of the whole class."

Jett spat his water out, laughing so hard he almost choked. "Shit, okay, you're hardcore, Penny."

"I've gotten more creative since then too." I looked back up, smiling this time. Jett shook his head, still chuckling. Grabbing some paper, I placed it over the iPad, figuring I'd try it this way before I had to seek out a printer.

"Yes, something about eight-year-olds?" Jett asked as I traced the squirrel.

"Yep, I'm a teacher. Or well, I think I am." I kept tracing, not wanting to look at him now.

"Ah, now that sounds like a story."

"Not a good one."

"In my experience, the 'not good ones' are usually the best ones. I find we're at our best when we're at our worst."

Stopping, I looked up through my eyelashes at him. "That doesn't make sense."

"Sure it does. When we mess up, that's when we have a choice to either embrace the pain or ignore it. When we embrace it, we drop the pretenses. I think that makes us better versions of ourselves."

"Pretty deep for a bad boy rockstar."

"I'm not really a bad boy, you know. I'm more of a broody asshole."

"Well, at least you admit you're an asshole." I smiled but kept drawing. Once I had it done, it was good enough to use to trace on the fabric we'd been given. At least one step was done. I started to mark off the measurements on the flag, so it would be proportionate.

"You put a lot of effort into something that doesn't even matter."

"It matters to me."

"Why?"

"I don't know." I shrugged, focusing. "It just does."

His question rattled me, but I didn't want him to know. Starting on the letters, I was surprised when the door opened. I kept my focus on what I was doing, not wanting to be persuaded by two cute guys distracting me. I wasn't furious at them per se; the guilt I'd let someone down had risen, making me strike out at the closest recipient.

Which were both things I needed to work on. Not apologizing and not having to be perfect for people to like me. I didn't know if I agreed with Jett, but maybe there was some truth there. He did seem to be okay with himself. Poppy was like that too. Was I the only one who struggled to accept myself? I didn't like to think I was. But maybe.

"Freckles, I came off judgy back there and it wasn't my intention. I was attempting a lame joke, and it didn't work out. I'm sorry if you thought I was implying something. To make it up, we've brought loads of ice cream and Rafé."

I snapped my head up, looking at the three guys standing at the end of the table. True to his word, they all stood holding pints of ice cream. I licked my lips, my eyes shifting to Rafé. He had a lopsided smile on his face. It was interesting to me he'd willingly shared this info, knowing it would help them.

Sitting back, I crossed my arms, not wanting to show how much what they'd done excited me. Honestly, I didn't know how to take it. Most of my relationships had been me apologizing for things they'd done when it wasn't even my fault. Perhaps I attracted manipulators? Was this a ploy? Shutting my eyes, I counted in my head, not wanting to go down that spiral. It didn't matter. I was single now. I was here with these guys. Everything else was background noise.

Opening my eyes, I found the three of them watching me closely. Cooper walked forward, holding out a pint with a spoon toward me. "I heard about your combo goal, so I made you my favorite. It's the Coop Special. Godiva Dark Chocolate, caramel sauce, sea salt, and marshmallows."

Carefully, I took the spoon, scooping out a bite. It wasn't something I'd had before. Tentatively, I placed it in my mouth, rolling it over my tongue. It was a good balance of sweet with a little salty kick, the bitter richness of the chocolate rounding it out.

"Yum, I'd say a solid 8 on the perfect combo."

"Yes!" Cooper fist-pumped the air, a massive smile on his face. I held out my hand for the next one, needing to test them all like some Goldilocks of ice cream. Aspen walked over but refused to give me the spoon.

"Close your eyes, Penny. The Aspen delight is best tasted in the dark."

"I feel like this might be a bad idea, but fine." Shutting my eyes, I opened my mouth, assuming he wanted to feed it to me. A cold spoon met my tongue, followed by the sweetness of cheesecake ice cream, a fruit, and a creamy tart sensation. Swirling it around, I rolled it over my tongue.

"Raspberry and… custard?" I asked, opening my eyes.

Aspen blinked at me. "How did you do that?"

"It's her superpower," Poppy said from the doorway, causing me to look over. She perked up when our eyes met, giving me a small smile. I watched as Jett walked over, handing her a cup of coffee. If he kept this up, he'd definitely leave the shit list.

"Superpower, huh?" Coop asked, winking at me.

"I worked at an ice cream shop for several summers. I picked up a skill. It also started my obsession with trying the best combinations and finding the perfect scoop of ice cream. If it exists."

A throat clearing had me turning back to the end of the table where Rafé still stood with his creation. Cooper was sitting in a chair eating his now. He grinned wide when he saw me, and I knew I couldn't be mad at him any longer. He was like an adorable puppy that kept getting into your stuff but then would lick your face and you'd melt for them.

"I still have one flavor for you to try," Rafé said, walking forward.

I'd been happy to see him out on the docks; our time had been fun last night. I wasn't sure how long he was here, and I hadn't thought to exchange any info with him. Mostly because I'd felt guilty for liking three guys and figured if I never saw one again, it made it easier. It hadn't stopped my mind from thinking about him this morning or my heart racing when I saw him though.

"I'm curious about what you have after last night." He smirked, handing me a spoon as he lifted the lid from the container. It was hard to tell from just the top, so I put my spoon in, scooping some out. Placing it in my mouth, I was greeted by coffee ice cream followed by a crunch of almonds and chocolate with a caramel swirl. I couldn't work out the chocolate, the coffee flavor masking it.

"Okay, I'm stumped on one thing. Coffee ice cream, almonds, and caramel I get, but it's the chocolate I can't place. What kind of candy is it? I'm racking my brain trying to remember what kind they had, but I'm coming up blank."

He smiled wide, and I heard Aspen and Cooper groan behind me. "Heath bar."

"Heath bar. I don't think I've had one of those in years. Well done. It's a good combination. I'd say a 7 on the flavor scale, and Aspen, yours was 7 as well. Does yours have a name?"

Before he could answer, Cooper cheered, jumping up and running around the table. "Yes! I win overall flavor!"

Ignoring him, I looked to the others. "I'll have to add those to my spreadsheet later. What did you call yours, Rafé?"

"Oh," he blushed, shuffling his feet. "Rafé's café extremo."

"Yum, I like it. Well, we um, need to finish this." I pointed at the piece of fabric on the table. "But what are you up to, Rafé?"

"Um, not much." It didn't sound accurate, but I wasn't going to be the responsibility police here, so I let it go.

"If it's okay with the others, would you want to hang out?"

"Yeah, I'd like to."

"Cool." I turned to the guys, but they were already smiling.

"We're cool with it, Freckles."

"Thanks, Coop." I smiled softly back, standing up so I could check on Poppy. She watched me approach as she sipped her coffee. She was wearing a t-shirt I assumed was Jett's and some joggers. I'd need to go and get her some clothes soon.

"How are you feeling?"

"Groggy, but otherwise fine. I think I bypassed any rash or hives this time."

"I'm more concerned with the way it attacks your insides, but I guess if it didn't have any outside reaction, you're good. You've gotta be more careful, Pop."

"I know. I'm fine, though."

I gave her a look, not budging on this. "We both know it's more than just a careless oversight. You can't forget to take your meds. I know you hate the ones that make you a zombie, but if you keep pushing yourself like this, you won't have an option anymore if you can take them or not."

"I know, Pen, okay! Geez, you're not my mother." She turned, walking back into the bedroom, shutting the door hard. I stood there, the tears fighting to leak out of my eyes. This was the only thing we ever fought over. But I cared too much about her to let her self-destruct. She could be mad at me all she wanted, but I'd never stop caring for her, no matter how many doors she slammed in my face or how bad it hurt.

My sinuses burned, and I took a few breaths to swallow the emotion clogging my throat. Placing my hand on the door, very quietly, I stated, "PB&J forever. You're stuck with me P."

Wiping the one tear that fell, I turned and walked back to the table to finish the flag. I didn't even care about it right now, but it helped distract me from breaking down into tears. The guys gave me space, which I appreciated. A few minutes later, I had everything outlined.

"Does anyone want to help me paint? You just have to stay in the lines."

"Sure," Aspen answered, grinning. I scooted over, and we sat silently side by side, painting the flag with a squirrel holding nuts, the words Ginger Nuts in big, bold letters.

I felt him squeeze my leg under the table when we were done, and we sat there looking at it.

"I like it."

"Yeah?"

He squeezed again, and I found myself leaning into him. "I was thinking we should do something?"

"Hmm, what are you thinking? I don't want to do anything outside for too long so I don't get burned."

"Ah, well, maybe we could play a game or something?"

"Yeah, that sounds fun."

"What you guys talking about?" Cooper asked, coming to lean over my head. I peered up, but he was looking at the flag. "Oh, nice, I like the squirrel dude."

"Yeah?" I asked, still upside down. "I traced it."

He peered down, the corners of his eyes twinkling back at me. "Still better than I could do, Freckles. How are you still so cute even upside down?"

I blushed, not used to being this adored. "I guess it's just my natural ability." I cheesed a smile, and he bent down, kissing my nose. It was sweet and endearing, taking me by surprise. When he pulled back, his eyes glimmered, and I wanted to bottle that shimmery sunshine up and keep it in my pocket so I could always have a part of Cooper with me.

"Looks like we have our next task," Aspen stated. Righting myself, I found him reading his phone. "We're to do a charades game that's based on current events with a focus on media, entertainment, and sports."

"Oh! That sounds fun. Rafé, do you want to help? I know you're not part of our team, but maybe you could be the scorekeeper or something?"

"Um, yeah, I could do that." He swallowed, looking nervous and I worried I'd pushed too far.

"Do we want to see if Poppy or Jett want to join us?" Coop asked, looking at me.

"Um, let Poppy sleep," I suggested, moving over to the couch area. "In fact, maybe the deck, on the shaded part would be a good place so we're not too loud out here."

"Good idea! Though, I'll grab you some sunscreen just in case," Aspen offered, getting up to grab some.

It was one of the most romantic things a boy had ever said to me.

Making myself comfortable under the umbrella, I watched as the guys gathered around. Aspen handed out paper and pencils for us to write ideas on and a bowl to place them in. I struggled to think of anything so decided to be cheeky and wrote Aspen's band, the only movie I could remember seeing the past year, and some slang words my students taught me. I hoped they were current and not recycled ones. You never could trust an eight-year-old.

We placed our answers into the bowl, and Jett walked out, eyeing us. "You guys playing something?"

"Yeah, want to join?" Aspen asked.

Jett looked between us all, a notebook in his hand and shrugged. "Sure."

He filled out some answers quickly once Aspen told him the topics, and then decided to go first. He pulled out a piece of paper, rolled his eyes, and stood, sighing heavily.

"Why did I stop writing for this?" he muttered, glaring at all of us.

"I just asked if you wanted to, no one forced you. Do two and then leave. You're no fun to be around when you're in one of your moods," Aspen said, not taking his friend's crap.

"Fine." He started to mime some things, but I had no clue, so I sat back watching in amusement. Rafé came over, sitting next to me and I smiled at him.

"Hey."

"Hey," he replied, smiling.

"I'm glad we ran into you. Any massive ice cream hangovers this morning?"

"No," he chuckled, "though it was hit or miss there for a while last night."

"Yeah, the peanut butter crunch isn't for amateurs," I joked.

Over the next thirty minutes, we took turns acting out the words we'd put into the bowl, laughing at some of the guesses. Despite his glower, Jett stayed the whole time. Rafé sat back, keeping the time and score, smiling at the guys' antics with one another. I'd gotten stuck on "And I, Oop" and "WAP" neither of which I knew. Of course, when I tried to act out "WAP" I had no clue it was a song, or what the song was about, so the guys laughed for a solid ten minutes when I read my card out loud.

"I can't believe you've never heard that song," Cooper said, laughing through his tears.

"Yes, well, now you know why I kept falling to the

ground and smacking my butt thinking it was just a sound."

"Penny, don't ever change, please," Aspen said, sincerely.

"You're alright, little gangsta, even if you have no clue what anything current is and thought AF meant always and forever," Jett added.

Smiling, I sat back down, leaning closer to Rafé. He smiled over at me, and I couldn't deny the spark I felt with him, the memory of how his body felt beneath me rising to the surface.

"Well, I think that's all of them. I got enough footage to loop together to submit. Come on, let's watch a movie or something and relax before dinner," Cooper suggested, standing.

"Yeah, okay," we all agreed.

Getting up, I walked over to the couch, not sure where to sit. Rafé was sitting on a small two-seater couch, and Cooper was spread out on the longer one. They had put on some sports competition that barely even registered to me. Folding my arms over myself, I debated just going back to my hut and curling up in my bed. Aspen walked over just then, directing me to the long couch.

He sat down, pulling me with him. Cooper sat up when he saw us, moving closer to my side. Aspen placed his arm around me, pulling me into him allowing Coop to put my feet into his lap as he softly caressed my ankle. I fell asleep a few minutes later, the comfort of them both giving me the peace I needed to shut my eyes, hoping things would be better when I opened them again.

CHAPTER
TWELVE

PENNY

Soft music woke me later, and I opened my eyes, surprised to find Cooper and Aspen had shifted, and I'd somehow been wedged between them horizontally on the couch. Aspen was higher up, my head on his abs, and Cooper was lower, cuddling my legs. And well, using a particular body part of mine to place his head.

My butt. It was my butt.

Cooper's head was perched on a butt cheek, and I never wanted to have the ability to fart on demand than I did right then. A giggle escaped at the thought causing my whole body to shake.

"What are you laughing at, Freckles?" a sleepy murmur asked.

"Nothing," I squeaked, followed by another giggle.

"Yeah, I don't buy it."

"You're awfully brave there, chap," I heard Poppy utter as she moved closer. Her head appeared over the couch, as she leaned on the back, peering down at me with remorse in her eyes.

"What do you mean?" Cooper mumbled, snuggling in closer to my ass.

"You're about to become a Cooper wedgie or potentially get hit with a one cheek squeak," Poppy informed him.

Cooper stilled, and I wished I could see his face. Peeking over my shoulder, I watched as he lifted his head, realizing where he was, and shrugged. Cooper started to dive forward, aiming his nose right between my butt crack.

"Nope!" I shrieked, rolling off Aspen and falling to the floor in surprise. "Well, that worked out surprisingly well. And Cooper, I'm not a dog; you don't need to smell my butt."

"Who said I was going to smell it," he mumbled, falling back to the couch. I eyed him but dropped it, not really wanting to know. He curled his arms around Aspen's legs, snuggling back down and I laughed. Aspen yawned, and stretched before he looked down at his brother. When he saw him holding his legs, he smiled and patted his head, making me giggle more.

"Penny, I was wondering if we could go grab some clothes and talk," Poppy asked, biting her lip.

Nodding, I grabbed her hand, pulling her along with me. Once we were clear of the guy's place, she tugged on my hand, halting us midway down the dock bridge.

"I'm an ass. I'm so sorry." She pulled me into a hug, her tears hitting my shoulders as I wrapped her up.

"Ssh, I know you are."

I smoothed her hair down, giving her time to let her

emotions out. That was the thing with Poppy. She worked so hard to not let her diagnosis control her; she often stuffed her feelings down too much. Poppy felt that if she pretended she was okay, she would be, and it worked 90% of the time. That was until it didn't, and her volcano of feelings erupted.

"I just hate it. I hate it so much," she cried. "Sorry, I took my stupid mistake out on you. I love you for making sure nothing worse happened."

"You know I never hold grudges. We fight, we yell, and we always make up. That's us. Though you did miss an epic showdown between Jett and me."

Poppy laughed, pulling back to wipe her tears. "That explains the new nickname. I wondered what went down for him to start referring to you as little gangsta."

Locking our elbows together, I pulled her along toward our bungalow. "Just a reminder that you don't mess with an elementary school teacher. Or well, *former*, I suppose."

"Hey, none of that. You don't know yet. It's still too early."

"Yeah, I guess. It just feels final. Like that one incident shut the door to that life, and now I gotta figure out which door to open."

"I know you're probably freaking out about it, Ms. Spreadsheet-for-everything, but I think that idea sounds amazing. You have a whole world of opportunities in front of you now, and only your voice to choose which one to go with. Not your mother's, not your sister's, and not your father's. *Yours*. This could be great for you, Pen."

"It seems terrifying." She squeezed my hand, encouraging me to not give up.

"I realized through all this that I don't know who I am,

Pop. I'm just the girl who did what everyone told her to do. Go to this school, date this guy, study these subjects. Before the whole vibrator incident, when have I ever made a decision for myself?"

"Um, being friends with me, and look how well that turned out." Poppy grinned wide, bumping her hip with mine as we walked.

"You know what? You're right. So basically, I need to find that five-year-old mentality where I thought I could do anything and just do it."

"Yasss, queen!" Poppy giggled, and it was good to hear it. I'd missed her, even if we'd primarily been together most of the day.

"Soooo," she drawled, "now that my drama is over, and your future is decided, tell me how you found yourself in a situation with three hunky guys drooling over you?"

"Pfft, you're insane. They're just being nice. Aspen, I'll admit, when he held my hand, I did get butterflies. Then I promptly screwed it up when I freaked out. And, well, Cooper, he's just naturally flirty. Rafé, we bonded over break-ups, so I doubt he's ready to be in a relationship."

"Girl, you can deny it all you want, but what I saw was three guys who, by the way, weren't even jealous of each other but appeared to be working together to win your affection. How cute was that whole ice cream stunt? I practically swooned and my heart's black," she teased. "I'd say you're well on your way to a nice threesome, foursome?" She scrunched her nose up in thought.

Gasping, I turned to her in shock, pushing her shoulder a little. "What? I could never!"

"Oh, you so could. Don't knock it until you try it, Pen." She winked, grinning mischievously.

"No way! You're saying you've had a threesome?"

She rolled her eyes, raising one as she looked at me. "Like you hadn't assumed I'd had one."

"Contrary to what you may believe, P, I don't sit around thinking of your sex life. But besides that, with who? When? Why am I just now hearing of this?"

Her face changed then, and her cocky attitude slipped a little as she tried to avoid directly answering. Deflecting, she laughed it off. "Um, hello, it's called college?" She looked at me like I'd grown three heads.

"If I hadn't thought it before, I can safely say we had very different college experiences. Come on, out with it. I'm your bestie, and you've been holding out on me all these years. Spill!"

She shrugged, peering off into the distance as we walked. "I was kind of, I don't know, embarrassed, I guess."

"Poppy Jackson embarrassed? No way! I don't believe it for a second." She groaned, rolling her head around to look at me.

"Fine, maybe it was more that I was embarrassed because I thought it meant something."

"Oh, are you saying it was with '*he that should not be named*?'" I whispered.

She nodded, not able to say anything for a few seconds. "Yeah, well, I don't feel like dragging all that back up, so let's focus back on *your* potential harem." She peered at me, the pleading in her eyes clear. Two things Poppy didn't like to talk about—her illness and him.

"Well, first, they're brothers. I don't want to come between them."

"I think that's exactly what you should do between them, *cum*. Sometimes, I wonder if you're still a virgin with your level of prudeness," she tiffed.

"Sure, that makes sense." This time it was my turn to roll my eyes.

"Speaking of coming, hot damn! Jett might be an ass a majority of the time, but the man knows how to use it." She fanned herself at the memory.

"You know, I was about to bust down that door when I heard the thump."

"Ha! You would've gotten a show. Jett isn't afraid to toss a girl around and make it a little rough, and you know that's how mama likes it." She shimmied a little, pulling her arm from me.

"Ew! Don't call yourself mama!" I swatted her arm as we neared our bungalow and pulled out the key. Poppy laughed at my discomfort, following me in.

"Regardless, I think you should take the blinders off and embrace this new Penny with no limits. Have some fun outside of vibing, especially if they aren't going to get all up in arms about you liking all three of them. I say, give in while you're here and explore. You're all adults, and they know about each other. You're not cheating, and they can deal with it if they have a problem. You're not committing to anyone. It's vacation booty! The best way to get boring Walter out of your system is with a healthy diet of cock. Four out of five women recommend, and that one holdout, well she's a nun, so, do with that what you may."

"I feel like you made that up?" I asked, peering at her suspiciously.

"Who cares! I'll poll five women tonight, and I guarantee it will stay the same. Hell! It will probably be five out of five because I was being generous with the nun. It's vacation. Why can't it be a sexy one? Hmm?" She stopped in the hallway, assessing me as she waited for me to respond.

"Why does it sound so simple when you put it that way?" I asked.

"Because it is simple. You like them; they like you. Duh."

"And that's all it takes, huh?" I laughed, rolling my eyes. Poppy stepped forward, grabbing my hands.

"Seriously though, there's no nosey parents, no judgmental classmates, and no boring ex-boyfriend here to ruin things. Do it, Pen, or at least be open to it."

"Okay, but if they're only being nice and I get rejected, then I'm cutting holes into all your favorite shirts and shaving your eyebrows."

"You wouldn't!" She gasped, but then laughed. "But also, fair." We both giggled as we made our way into the main area and were greeted by Jemma. A barely dressed Jemma holding a hairbrush out like a weapon.

"Phew, okay, it's just you guys." She exhaled, crossing her legs as she tried to keep her shirt down.

"Who'd you think it was? We kind of stood there awhile."

"Oh, just somebody breaking in." She shrugged like it made complete sense to her.

"You have a phobia of people breaking into places?" I asked, getting it.

"Not typically, but they just give keys out to whoever! I wouldn't put it past another team to try to sabotage."

"Oh yeah, they gave me one this morning! But people do that, sabotage others?" I asked, my nose scrunching up in surprise.

"Uh, yeah. It's cutthroat. You guys have missed a lot."

"Huh." For some reason, I didn't mind it.

"So, where's the quiet one?" I asked, leaning against the doorway.

A head poked up from behind the couch, and I jumped back in alarm, making Poppy laugh at me. "What the…"

Keelan gave Jemma a look, and she rolled her eyes. "He's just mad I pushed him back there to jump out and surprise the attacker." I nodded, but I was suddenly transfixed by the man's naked, bronzed, and tattooed skin. Each inch he revealed, I found myself tracking his ink until I realized he was naked, *completely* naked. Keelan stood, not ashamed at all about being in the nude, his massive cock out and hard for us all to see. Covering my eyes, I turned quickly, bumping into the doorway as I made my way to my room. Poppy laughed more but stayed. Turning back, I grabbed her arm, pulling her with me into my room. Jemma's laughter carried into the room, followed by the sound of her door shutting.

"Hot diggity, that man!" Poppy teased, fanning herself.

"Yeah, well, she probably doesn't want you leering at her boyfriend."

"I don't think she noticed, considering the other half-naked dude that climbed out from underneath her legs."

"*What*?" But then I stopped, smiling. "You know what, good for her!"

"That's the spirit! See, even Jemma is having a vacasome. It's practically required."

"Vacasome? Nevermind. Anywho," I deflected, "we

need to change. What's going on this evening? I haven't looked at the agenda yet."

"Hold the phone! Someone call the Pentagon! The press! This is breaking news if you haven't looked at the agenda! Are you sick?" Poppy grasped her chest, falling onto the bed dramatically.

"I know, I know," I huffed, rolling my eyes, "but I was kinda busy making sure you didn't die. Then I had to deal with the wonder twins and go off on your bed-partner. It's been a busy morning."

She burst out laughing, and I relaxed, joining in.

"Okay, fair. But I think it's good for you to let loose. There's some type of competition tonight, so wear something sexy."

"Have you met me? I don't own anything sexy."

"I'm sure I can make something work."

"Fine. Are we grabbing stuff or getting ready here?" I asked, trying to decide if I needed to take more than one night if we did.

"I don't think we're at the level yet to introduce them to how long it takes me to get ready or the number of products I use."

"Oh, yeah, good call." I nodded sagely.

"Hey! Be nice or I won't do your makeup, Miss it only takes me five minutes to get ready." She narrowed her eyes at me, and I sheepishly shrugged.

"Sorry?"

"Whatever. I'm taking a shower first. You get whatever is left. Humph." She turned and went into our communal bathroom to head into her room. While she was gone, I looked through my clothes, pulling out a pink dress with large flowers on it.

Once Poppy had finished her hair and makeup, she obliged and did my eye makeup for me. I slathered on some more sunscreen and then stepped into my dress. Poppy walked over, shaking her head at me.

"What? I like it." I placed my hands on my hips, ready to fight for this dress.

"No tank top. If you're gonna wear a dress that covers your ankles, then you gotta show the cleave."

"Cleave? Did you just make that up?"

"Does it matter? Do it before I make you lose your bra too."

I rolled my eyes but hurriedly took off the tank top. The dress dipped down low, my bra almost peeking above the deep-v. Poppy walked back over in a tight, white, body-hugging dress that accentuated every curve the woman had. With her red hair down, she looked amazing.

"Damn! You're hot, woman!"

"Why, thank you! I have another one if you wanna change out of that flowy dress."

"No, I'm good." I didn't want to admit I was already getting hives from the amount of cleavage, or "cleave" as Poppy would say, showing. But it also made me feel a little powerful, like I was taking back my sexuality and letting all the modesty comments I'd been drowned in since I could remember float away.

We headed out the door and had timed it perfectly with Jemma. She was walking ahead of us with two guys. Poppy lifted her eyebrows at me, reiterating her vacasome rule. Maybe it was a real thing, like a buy one, get one free promotion?

My cheeks heated as I thought about being with two or three guys at once in a vacasome. Could I do that? I guess the better question was, why wouldn't I? Poppy was right —it was time for my vibrator to warm the bench.

CHAPTER
THIRTEEN

COOPER

THE ENERGY BUZZED INSIDE OF ME AS I WAITED AT THE entrance of the outdoor eating area. Penny would be here soon, and I couldn't wait to see her again. She'd been gone over an hour, and I'd missed her terribly. She made me feel like I could be myself, and after years of doing the opposite of that, it felt freeing, and a sense of excitement had taken root in me.

"You spot her yet?" Aspen asked. I shook my head, not turning to look at him. I knew he'd look as hopeless as me. He liked to pretend he wasn't pining as much, but Aspen was just as clingy, if not more, when it came to girls he liked.

"Oh, there's the roommate!" he shouted. I peered out but only spotted a brunette with Keelan and Alistair.

"I don't— " but stopped when my girl appeared. Her red hair sparkled under the setting sun, the rays of the day gravitating toward her hair to grab some last bits of light.

She was wearing a flowy dress, and I swallowed as I watched her grow closer.

"Hey," I said, internally berating myself for the less than stellar greeting.

"Hey, back," she said, smiling warmly at me.

That simple phrase was the air I needed, and I inflated, puffing out my chest as I held out my arm for her to take. Aspen rolled his eyes but led us toward the spot Jett had spread out in.

"So, Freckles, did you miss me?" I gave a cheeky wink as I asked, wanting to hear her laugh.

"You know, I did, Dimples." Her smile was radiant as she looked up at me.

"Well, good, I missed you too."

"Just no more smelling my butt. A girl has limits!"

"Ha! Okay, not my finest decision, but in all fairness, your butt is just so cute." Her face blushed, and I recorded it as a win. "You look gorgeous tonight, Penny; I just wanted you to know that."

We made it to the table, Aspen had beat us there and was already pulling out a chair for her. Poppy was on the other side, meaning I could be a dick and take the chair next to her while he won gentlemen points, or I could be a nice brother and let him have this one. When Penny stopped, pulling my arm to lower me, I was confused at first. The soft kiss on my cheek and the whispered message was worth more in the end.

"Thanks, Cooper. It's nice to hear that."

"Anytime, Freckles."

She squeezed my arm, walking forward to take the chair he offered, and I walked around to the empty one. All through dinner, I couldn't keep my focus off her. Every little move, sound, or laugh she made stole my focus. I found myself captivated by her more than anything had ever been able to capture me before. It appeared Aspen was just as enthralled, his gaze fixed on her as well. I hoped we could figure this out together. Because I didn't think, at this point, either one of us was willing to let her go. Hopefully, that dedication and bond we had as brothers would be enough. So far it seemed to be.

"So, where's Rafé? Is he here?" I heard her ask, looking around.

Aspen shook his head. "He's not part of the competition. He left when you fell asleep and said he would try to catch up with us later, but that he had some things to do."

"Oh." Her shoulders dropped, but she quickly dismissed it, turning to Aspen. "So, what's this competition that we have tonight? Something to do with dancing?"

"Yeah, it's basically like a dance-a-thon. But with doing all the different dances that have gone viral on LiveIt."

"Ha! I'll suck at this. I doubt I'll know any of them."

I scrunched my nose, not sure how that could be accurate, even I knew a few. "Have you been living under a rock?" I joked.

"Well, you see—" Penny started, but Poppy interrupted her before she could finish with a mischievous laugh.

"She's *on* the app, but she's not *on* the app."

"That doesn't make sense," Aspen said, looking between the two of them.

Penny cleared her throat, fidgeting with her silverware. "I like making stuff." She shrugged like it explained everything. "Poppy suggested I record them. She'd just started out on the app and liked it, finding a new audience for her music. But, you see, I'm horrible with techy stuff, and I couldn't figure it out. Nor did I have enough of an interest in it to learn."

"So, wait a minute, do you have an account?"

"She does, but I manage it for her," Poppy said, grinning. The mischievous glint I noticed earlier reappeared, and I had a feeling the videos weren't what Penny thought they were.

"Yeah, that," Penny answered, pointing at her friend.

"So… you've never actually seen your videos?"

"No." She shook her head forcibly. "The thought of seeing myself is cringeworthy."

"I gotta see these then." I pulled out my phone and went into the app. "What's your user name?"

"DIYgirl," Poppy offered, grinning more.

Smiling, I typed it in and waited for it to pull up her videos. Aspen leaned over to see as well. Penny huffed, crossing her arms, which only distracted me as her breasts pushed together more. Blinking, I remembered what I was doing and looked back at my phone as I clicked on a video. Aspen and I leaned closer to the screen as Penny came onto it.

She was showing how to make bath bombs. The first few seconds were a fast version of the steps, but the last part had to be bloopers Penny had wanted cut-out. Water sprayed everywhere, soaking her, as well as another outtake where glitter erupted everywhere, coating her. It was only a minute video, with half of the actual project sped up and the other half of funny moments. Grinning as I watched, I found Penny just as enchanting, especially for someone who didn't know anything about trends or filming.

"Is it awful? I've never watched them."

"No, you're adorable."

She blew out a breath, not completely buying it. "Okay, well if you're going to watch my videos, then I want to see yours."

Penny grabbed her phone out of the bag she'd carried and looked at us, waiting for something. Aspen laughed as well, and she seared him with a look, causing him to place his hands up in a placating measure.

"I'm staying out of this, even if I agree with Cooper."

"Ugh," she groaned, turning back to me.

"Yes, Freckles?"

"Well, I need your name."

"You probably need to know how to sign in first," Poppy teased.

Penny stuck out her tongue and went to log in. We all waited a few minutes as we watched her grow increasingly more frustrated when she couldn't.

"Ugh! I can't get into this stupid app. What did you make the password, Poppy?"

Her friend laughed, unable to contain her giggles. "Capital M, lowercase a-g-i-c-s-p-3-r-m." Poppy could barely get out the last letter before she burst out into a fit of giggles. When what she'd spelled penetrated, I laughed as well. Penny had been typing it in and looked up, confused.

"What?"

"Your password," I said, watching as she said it to herself.

"Really, Pop! You're so fired!"

"Hey, I never forget it!"

"Fair," Penny said, letting it go.

We all laughed, and Penny shrugged, not feeling all too put out about it, and I liked that she didn't get upset about things.

"Okay, I'm assuming I can use this little magnifying glass to search, so what's your username?" She pinned us with a stare like she dared me not to give it to her. I smiled, wanting her to watch my jumps. I knew they were entertaining, and most I had my shirt off, my abs already proving to be an attraction to her, so I figured it could only help my chances.

"CoopJumps," I replied, setting my phone down and propping my chin on my hands as I waited, wanting to catch her expression.

She blinked but typed it in. I watched as she clicked on a few videos, her eyes going wide as she moved the phone closer. Even Poppy moved, mouthing 'whoa' at one point, and I smirked, knowing she'd fallen down my thirst trap. I worked hard to stay in shape and willingly flaunted it.

"See anything you like there, Freckles?"

"Um, yeah, they're not terrible."

"Hmm. What about the boyfriend application one? You thinking of applying?"

"Oh, I don't think I saw that one," she lied, her face revealing more.

"You can play it off all you want, Pen, but I'll show you *where* to apply later."

She sat up, no longer embarrassed as she stared at me, biting her lip, and suddenly, I was the one blushing. "So you think I want to apply?"

"Well, I hope so," I replied honestly, causing her to soften.

"Then, I guess, um, I need to watch more."

Nodding, I let her off the hook as she started on some of my jump rope videos. As she kept scrolling, I picked up my phone and continued to watch hers. Clicking on the next one with the most views, I tumbled willingly into the Penny trap. In each one, the same trend followed where she showed how to do a project and then the funny bloopers. Whether Poppy had stitched it together or if Penny had naturally said it, a motto of "Pen Can" emerged in each video. I started to read the comments and found how much people loved her. It was obvious why the show had picked her, whether she knew it or not.

"Wow, you're quite good, Cooper. I could never do the crazy things you do. I'm impressed."

"Yeah?" I looked up, smiling broadly at her as she nodded. "Thanks, Penny, so are you. I definitely want to make some of that manly soap, and the man cave liquor bar was amazing. You're very charming for someone who doesn't like to be on camera." She blushed, and Poppy nodded, pointing to me in agreement as she chewed her food.

"See! I told you!" she exclaimed once she'd swallowed. "It's how she hypnotizes the little rascals she calls students, too."

Penny's smile dipped a little at the mention of her job, and Poppy cringed. I wondered what that was about, but Aspen took the opportunity to lean in to distract her as he spoke low in her ear. Whatever he said, she smiled, nodding.

"Of course, what's your name?" she asked, turning to

him, forgetting he was so close. Their noses brushed, and I watched as they became mesmerized by one another. I thought I'd be raging mad, or even sad, their undeniable attraction clear for all to see, but I wasn't. I didn't know if it was because I was used to not being chosen, or if perhaps, this was meant to be; no matter how it looked.

Jett cleared his throat, clearly over their cute flirting. "It's Aspen," he answered in a deadpan.

Aspen moved back and acknowledged Jett's reply with a sly grin. "I'm not as entertaining as Coop, but look up AspenMayhem."

"I'll be the judge of that!" Penny smiled, and I plunged into her orbit, no longer wanting to watch the video when I could watch the real one in front of me. I took the opportunity to memorize everything about her. She swayed to the music as she listened to Aspen, his videos consisting of his shows and mashups he did. There were even some behind the scenes from his performances. After a few minutes, Penny glanced up, addressing my brother.

"Wow, okay, you were right. The first time you told me you were in a band, I wasn't that impressed. But… listening to you, you're not bad."

Aspen chuckled. "Not bad. You hear that Jett? Penny said we're not bad!"

Jett scoffed, acting as if he wasn't paying attention to the girls. Except, each time Poppy wasn't paying attention, he watched her. Jett didn't want to admit he was a smitten kitten and was falling for Poppy. He tended to have two speeds—all in or all out. Right now, it seemed like he didn't know which one to be, meaning he over-exaggerated his disinterest.

Poppy turned to him, bumping him with her leg. Jett

raised his eyes up slowly, not able to turn off the heart-breaker he pretended to be. Poppy wasn't deterred and gave him a knowing look as she licked her lips. "How did you like *my* videos?" she purred.

He sat up from his spread-out state, searing her with one of his trademark looks, lifting his eyebrow. "Hmm, you think I've seen them?"

"Oh, I know you have."

We all watched as they eye fucked one another, the compulsion to keep watching was there like with a train wreck. Except when they just kept staring at each other I grew bored and turned back to the other two, an idea coming to mind.

"So… following this dancing thing, do we have to do anything afterward?"

"No, I think we're free to go when we get out," Aspen replied, looking between us.

"Perfect." I smiled wide. "I say we go swimming."

Aspen sat up, catching on to my idea. "Yes, that's a brilliant idea. It's nighttime, so no worries about the sun," he said, looking at Penny.

Penny beamed, and I internally sighed in relief. "I'd like that, especially since I kind of missed out last time in my pursuit of ice cream."

"Awesome!" I fist-pumped, and they both laughed, but I was excited so I ate it up. "Let's go then. I'm ready to get to the after part."

We all gathered our things, leaving Poppy and Jett to figure out their own way when they came up from the kiss they'd fallen into. Penny fell into step between Asp and me, and I smiled over her head at him. This felt right, and I hoped it meant because it would work this time.

CHAPTER
FOURTEEN

ASPEN

WALKING OVER TO THE DANCE FLOOR NEAR THE FRONT OF THE stage, I found myself smiling, happy for no reason other than just enjoying my time. Things had been interesting since Penny had crashed into my world, and I was loving every minute of it. Her hand grazed mine again, and this time, I took it, linking our fingers together. I caught her smiling wide out of the corner of my eye, and I couldn't help but match it.

The event organizer walked up to the microphone, tapping it like she thought it worked that way. When she seemed satisfied, she cleared her throat, the noise echoing out around the speakers. *Amateurs.*

"Hello, and good evening. The leader boards have been updated with the points you've received so far and the current standings..."

As she prattled on, I glanced around at the other groups, greeting a few people I knew. It was an odd sensation meeting people in person who I've grown to know through their online profiles. I wonder if people felt that way with me sometimes? Imposter Syndrome was a heavy thing at times. I still didn't understand why girls became so squealy when they caught sight of me. It was an odd, out-of-body experience I hadn't gotten used to yet.

The LiveIt community was friendly, though, and everyone here appeared genuine. I hadn't paid much attention earlier, but I could tell the teams were evenly dispersed, with two females and three males competing per group. Creators from book enthusiasts, make-up tutorials, life hackers, and comedians filled the space. It made me wonder what the rest of the tasks would be with the diversity of contestants.

When I'd completed a full sweep of the area, I turned back to the woman at the front. She was one of those people who assumed you knew her, so she never introduced herself, the inflated sense of self-importance too big for anyone else. She started to explain the rules, and I perked up, wanting to know them.

"This will be based on two things. Your teams' knowledge of the viral dances from the app, and your ability to perform the moves to some reasonable degree. At least one person on your team has to perform the steps. When you get to a point where no one knows it, then your team is out. You will get points based on the degree of accuracy for the dance you perform and the number of rounds you last. Since there are five teams, you will rotate around who you battle."

"Battle? Oh man, I'm so going to suck at this," Penny whispered.

Cooper pulled her close, comforting her. "We got this,

Freckles. I happen to be a great dancer." He circled his hips as evidence, thrusting forward, making Penny giggle.

"Let's hope Jett and Poppy join us soon. I think we're going to need them."

"We're here. Don't get yourself all worked up there, Aspen," Jett teased, knowing I hated to be unprepared.

Ignoring him, I focused back to make sure we were ready when it was our turn. We would be up against a team of six, and I wondered how that worked but then saw one of them sit out. It was the married couple who took classic songs and made them into parodies about marriage, so I guess they were considered as one contestant. I wondered if that was the case for the twins too.

"Are you ready? The LiveIt dance-a-thon battle begins now!"

Music started, and the first group instantly went into one of the viral dances together, tapping their shoulders in synchronization as a country song about beer played.

"Whoa, that's impressive," Penny said, watching them.

"Yeah, they must've practiced," Cooper acknowledged, his brow creased in worry.

After thirty seconds, they tossed it to the next group, and the song changed. That group wasn't as coordinated as the first, but there were at least two who knew the music and dance, pulling it off. We were up next, so I readied everyone as best I could.

"Alright, Ginger Nuts, we got this!"

They all looked at me with only slight panic in their eyes, as the group tossed it to us. The song changed, and thankfully it was one I knew. Going into the hip roll, I laughed when Penny tried to fake it, not knowing what she was doing, only confirming her claim to not being active on LiveIt. I decided right then, it didn't matter, that enjoying the moment was the true reward. The sappy romantic in me swooned, while the battered heart portion drew up, wanting to take cover and batten down the hatches.

We finished, successfully making it through the first round, and moved down, facing off with Jemma's group next. The girls did some funny 'you're going down' motions, and we all relaxed as we waited for our turn again. We ended up making it to the top three but got knocked out when a song started, and none of us knew it, so Penny improvised and did the macarena, at least getting everyone to laugh as we joined in. It was the classiest losing dance there ever was.

"Oh man, that was terrible," Poppy said, laughing through her tears. "And yet, the best thing ever. Have I told you how amazing I think you are, Pen?"

"Hmm, nope, not today!"

Chuckling, the two girls embraced as they walked away from the dance floor, not wanting to stay and watch the other two.

"We're going to swim. Do you want to join us?" I heard Penny ask as we started down the docks.

"Nah, I think I'm going to hang with Jett."

Poppy looked back over her shoulder at the man in question. He didn't say anything, but he didn't deny it either, lifting an eyebrow at her as he walked with his hands in his pockets. When she turned back, putting her head together with Penny, Jett's eyes went right back to her ass as it swayed. Snickering, I elbowed him, but he shrugged, not caring. The girls whispered something, and

I saw Poppy nod, agreeing with whatever Penny had told her.

"Yes, I promise," Poppy finished, stopping. "You guys take care of my girl." She narrowed her eyes at Cooper and me.

"Absolutely," Cooper said, grinning. "She'll be in *good* hands."

I didn't miss the innuendo, but apparently, no one else did either, as everyone laughed, and Penny elbowed him in the stomach. Poppy rolled her eyes and bent down to kiss Penny on the cheek. "Don't forget what we talked about earlier. Your voice, remember? Vacasome over vibing for the win!" She fist-pumped the air in exuberance.

Penny nodded in response, biting her lip, with anxiety more than excitement. "Yep," she answered, breathing in.

The three of us watched Poppy and Jett walk off in the direction back toward the resort, not sure what they were up to, but I'd take the opportunity to have some time with my girl. I turned to Pen in excitement. "So, do you want to go to your place or ours? Do you need a suit or something?"

"Um, yes, I do need a suit. I'm not brave enough to go without." Her cheeks blushed adorably, and I wanted to kiss them all over.

"Wait," Coop interjected, looking between us, "that's an option?"

Penny laughed, some of the tension leaving her, ignoring Coop as she continued speaking with me. "So, yes, I need to go get mine from my place."

"How about this," I proposed, "I go with you back to yours, and since we know Cooper is the fittest of us, he runs back to ours. If your hut is empty, then we can chill there this time, so it's not always on our turf, and he'll bring back our suits. But, if your place isn't free, then you and I can head back to ours?"

"Yeah, that sounds like an excellent plan. You're very strategic for being so disorganized."

"That was just my suitcase after a two-month stint on the road!" I protested. "I'd like to see you try to have it organized after that!"

"Hmm, I probably still could." She winked, and I knew I was gone. I'd just fallen over the cliff and was head over heels for her.

Laughing, I nodded to Coop as he set off toward our place to grab our stuff. I was oddly hoping we could stay at hers, wanting to see more of her world. We walked in silence for a bit, the sounds of the night and the soft crash of the water the only noise. Deciding to show Penny how much I liked her, I chose to put myself out there.

"You know, I'm glad things have worked out how they have. I've really liked getting to know you." I stopped, looking at her. "I really like *you*, actually."

"You do?" she asked, some doubt in her eyes as she peered up at me.

"I do. You're so different from other girls," I started but was interrupted by her.

"Different. Yeah, I get that a lot."

"You didn't let me finish, sassy pants! Different in a completely magical and enchanting way, and from the moment I met you, I've been pulled toward you. I can't seem to stop smiling when you're near, and I feel excited to see you. You surprise me with what you say, and my status as a musician didn't make you go goo-goo, letting me know it's me you like, or at least I hope you like me."

"I do. And wow, I've never had anyone describe me like that before."

"And to think you almost brushed it off."

"Sorry." She cringed. "I guess I'm still a little gun shy after my break-up."

"Was it recent?"

"Yeah, like three days ago."

"Oh, wow. So am I barking up the wrong tree?"

"No! I like you too. I like you and Cooper. I just don't want to come between you as brothers."

"What about the other guy, Rafé?"

"I mean, I felt a spark with him, but he's not here at the moment, so I'm just focusing on who is."

"What if I told you that Cooper and I seem to be on the same page about how we feel about you and aren't jealous of one another?"

"I'd wonder if you really liked me if I'm honest." She started walking again, some of her insecurity coming to the surface. Jogging, I caught up to her, linking our hands. When she didn't resist, I smiled.

"I think you've dated the wrong type of guys, Penny."

"You're probably right, but why do you say that?"

"Jealousy doesn't necessarily equal how much a person likes someone. Possession shouldn't be the goal. Cooper and I can both like you and be happy for one another for finding someone they mesh with, even if it's the same person. We trust one another to not sabotage or try to ruin the other person's chances. I guess I've been in enough relationships that weren't right that when one feels like it is, I don't want to throw it away just because I'm not the only person."

"It sounds simple when you say it." Her acceptance of

my response felt like the best gift, spurring me on to keep opening up.

"Why can't it be? If we're adults and promise to manage our own feelings of jealousy if we have them, I don't see how we couldn't at least have some fun while we're here."

"Only fun?"

"Well, I'd like more, but I tend to scare girls when I start spouting all poetically." I shrugged, my cheeks blushing at the admittance.

"Ah, I've found the flaw in your argument."

"What's that?"

"You said I was different but then expected me to react the same as other girls."

I stopped, realizing what she'd just said. Staring, I pulled her close, wanting to hold her. I squeezed her forearms, looking at her.

"You're absolutely right. So, I'm going to give you the full Aspen package, no holds barred, and trust that you'll be okay with it."

"Well, I guess if you're going to give me the non-watered down version of you, it's only fair I do the same."

"Great. We're going to see where things go then and take it one step at a time, and maybe someday, those steps lead us to forever."

"I'm on board with this plan." She smiled up at me, her eyes twinkling in the moonlight, and I really wanted to kiss her. Bending down slowly, I waited to see if she'd move out of the way, but when her eyes closed, I met her lips. It was a simple kiss, only lasting a few seconds, but it felt magical. Pulling back, I found her grinning as wide as me.

When we got to her door, it opened with Jemma and Keelan exiting. He nodded, moving out of the way as he stepped down the dock a few paces.

"Oh hey, I was just going to see if you would be here tonight. We were thinking of going swimming."

"All yours! We're headed over to Alastair's." She wiggled her eyes at Penny. "Great moves earlier. I can't believe you guys beat us!"

"Me either," Penny said, laughing. "Okay, well, I guess we'll see you tomorrow then. Have fun!"

"Oh, I will. You do as well, and be as loud as you want!" Jemma winked and then ran up and launched herself onto the back of Keelan. He let her, carrying her off as they went. Penny tried to hide her blush as she walked in.

"Um, alright, how about I go change, and you can call Cooper. The phone's over there."

"Sure." I walked over, taking in the place more this time since I wasn't in a rush. Picking up the phone, I punched in the digits for our hut and waited for it to connect.

"So, what's the scoop?"

"Game time, Coop." I chuckled at the unintentional rhyme.

"I'm on my way!"

"Hey, wait!"

"Yes?"

"I kind of talked to her about both of us, and she's cool with, you know, seeing where it goes if we're okay with it."

"Really? Well, then I'm doubly on my way!"

"See you soon, bro."

Hanging up, I peered out at the water, the serene scene calling to me. When I heard her footsteps a few seconds later, I turned, not prepared for what awaited me.

Penny walked toward me in a modest swimsuit, but it still made me swallow as I tried to convince my lower half to behave. The bottom piece came up to her belly button, and the top covered her chest, tying around her neck. There was only a sliver of skin showing, but I still found it sexy as Hell.

"Wow, you look… *wow.*"

"Thanks. I know I'm not as out there as Poppy, but I do feel good in this suit." She twisted a little, popping a pose.

"You do that a lot, you know, compare yourself to Poppy. I think you're perfect as you are, Penny, and you should embrace it. I know that I'm happy to have found you."

Her face sobered, and she nodded seriously. "You're right, it's just hard, but I'm trying to do better." I pulled her into my arms, rubbing my hands up her biceps as I peered into her eyes.

"Coop's on his way. Let's see if he makes it here out of breath or not and puts me to shame."

She giggled, and I realized it had become my favorite sound. "I love when you do that."

"Do what?" she asked, giggling again.

"Giggle."

"Well, I like when you make me giggle, so I guess we're a good combination."

"That we are." I found myself leaning forward, her eyes flickering closed again right as a door crashed open loudly, and Cooper barreled through, skidding to a stop. "I'm here!"

"Of course, he's not out of breath," I mumbled, acting put out, but the sound of Penny's glee at the comment was worth it.

Laughing as well, I walked forward and grabbed the shorts he had dangling from his hand, and headed to the room Penny pointed out. Changing quickly, both Coop and I headed out in anticipation of what awaited us, pushing us to return quickly to the beautiful redhead.

CHAPTER
FIFTEEN

PENNY

When Cooper and Aspen returned, they stared at me with hunger in their eyes, a look I'd never experienced before. There had been guys who desired to sleep with me and the ones who wanted to win me or even use me. But there had never been the ones who looked at me like *that*.

Swallowing, my heart raced as I tried to gather my bearings. "Well, okay, you guys need towels?"

"Oh, yeah, I suppose we do." Cooper cringed, a slight blush to his cheeks, the dimple winking at me. For some reason, it made me feel better. If he was so gung-ho to get back here that he forgot to grab a towel, it had to mean he was just as excited about the conclusion of this night. Right? It felt inevitable now.

The desire had been building over the past few days, and dinner had been a massive flirt fest. The looks, the casual touches, the innuendoes… it had all been leading us here and I knew Poppy was right. This was the time to ignore all the noise and do what I felt like. It was time.

Smiling, I walked over to the cabinet I knew had towels and grabbed three. When I turned back, Cooper was there, ready to take them from me. Handing them off, I felt the buzzing sensation under my skin as his hand grazed mine. Locking eyes, I remained frozen for a second, held captive by his champagne orbs. They were light and fun, and I wanted to drink them.

"You know the water is this way," Aspen teased, pulling us from our stare-off. Laughing, I blinked and headed over to the door. Anxiety that I was making a colossal mistake rose up for a split second, tightening my chest. Ignoring it, I knew it was only fear.

Fear had held me captive for far too long. It no longer had a place here.

Opening the doors, the sound of the waves filtered in, the smell of the saltwater a calming reassurance. Flicking the lights on, I couldn't help but calm just by the sight of the deck's ambiance. It truly was paradise, built for comfort, fantasy, and relaxing. The hammock swayed with the breeze, and I placed my phone down onto the large circle bed, kicking off my flip-flops as I turned to look at the guys.

I found them both gazing at me, and I blushed. Never in my life had I blushed as much as I had since being here. They made me feel giddy, filling me with a confident reassurance.

"Um, so, do we want the jets on or just to swim in the little pool?" I asked, turning my toe in a little as I fidgeted.

Each deck had a small, private Infinity pool that looked out over the ocean with steps that led down into the water.

I wasn't the best swimmer, though, and being that deep at night was a little scary, so I hoped the pool would be good enough.

"Let's just chill for a bit, and then we can see if we want the jets," Aspen suggested.

Nodding, I walked over, stepping down into the pool. The water was a perfect temperature, and I sunk into it, walking over to the side where a bench was. Sitting down, I watched as Cooper stripped off his shirt, the abs I'd fondled day one on display. Fucking hell, the man's body was perfection. Watching his videos, I'd gotten to see him move it in amazing ways as he flipped and jumped through routines. It was incredible the way he could move his body all while jumping rope! Hell, I couldn't even do half of them standing.

"So, Coop, how did you get into jump rope? I didn't even know competitive jump rope was a thing."

He smirked, settling back into the water. His arms braced against the back, his legs spread out, practically touching mine as he did.

"How I started jumping is kind of a sad story, but one I love telling. My dad was in the army, and physical fitness was important to him. One summer, he got tired of coming home to me sitting on the couch playing video games. So he told me if I could out jump rope him, then he'd take me to any theme park I wanted to go to. My dad was a bit of an adrenaline junkie and passed it on to me. Even at the age of 10, we'd been to quite a few already. So, I started training. Every day he'd come home, and I'd challenge him."

"And every day he'd lose," Aspen piped in, smiling fondly over at him.

"Wait, did you know each other then?"

"No," Aspen answered, shaking his head. "I've just heard this story enough; it's become part of me too. Get to the next part," he urged, settling down into the water next to me. I blinked as his tattoos came into view, but Cooper began again, pulling me back.

"Yes, like Aspen said, every afternoon, I'd think I'd finally beat him, improving on my time and number of jumps I could do, but somehow, my dad still bested me. When it was the end of the summer, I only had a few days left, and I wanted to give up, figuring I wouldn't be able to at that rate. But my mom told me to keep trying, and that was the lesson my father had been teaching me. So, I did, I dragged my jump rope out there, and I jumped for so long, my legs were jelly, but I knew I had him. So that day when he came home, I challenged him, but this time, I asked to go second."

He paused, some emotion coming over him, and I remembered him saying now that it wasn't a happy one, and I regretted asking.

"So, did you win?" I asked when he seemed to have gotten lost.

Cooper looked up, a sad smile on his face. "I did. My dad went, and I counted, and when he stopped, I knew I could beat him. Smiling, I tried to hide my victory as I started, going into the place I'd found to focus as I counted the rhythm. When I got to his number, I kept going, so focused, and before I knew it, I was 50 jumps past him. When I stopped, my dad had the biggest smile on his face, and he gave me a hug, telling me he was proud of me."

"That's beautiful, Cooper. I don't get how it's sad, though."

"Yeah, well, that's the after bit, how I got into competing. We made our trip plans, and I was excited to go the last weekend before school started, but life had other plans, and he died at work during a training accident, a day before we were meant to go. He saved three cadets' lives but wasn't able to make it out in time."

Gasping, I sat up, the water dispersing around me, and I reached out to touch his arm. "Oh, I'm so sorry, Coop. You should've told me it was too private."

He smiled at me, patting my hand but I didn't understand why he didn't seem to care. "It's okay, Freckles. It's nice to talk about him. It was a long time ago, and while it's sad, it no longer defines who I am. My love for jumping rope had been activated, and mom pushed me to continue, finding new ways for me to keep the memory alive. I started to jump rope for my father, and I found a passion and way to make him proud. I never imagined it would lead to the life I get to have now. And as much as I miss him, I'm glad my mom got to meet Aspen's dad and find love again. I gained a brother and a best friend."

"Wow, that's beautiful."

"Nah, it's just life. You can choose to see it how you want. At first, I wanted to avoid the world and the inevitable pain I would feel, hiding away from everything and everyone. But avoiding things wasn't a way to live either. It might hurt at times, hell, there have been some things that have hurt a lot, but it doesn't diminish the good. In fact, it makes it better because I know what it's like to be on the other side of that pain."

"I think you just got even hotter to me," I whispered, not caring I'd said it out loud.

Cooper chuckled, moving forward toward me. "Oh yeah? So, you thought I was hot before?"

Splashing him, I smiled. "Don't you do that too! I already yelled at this one for acting like his backward cap ensemble at the airport wasn't hot guy catnip."

Aspen chuckled. "She did, and it made me instantly like her. A woman who can put me in my place and not get all swoony just because I'm in a band, winner."

He grinned at me, his thumb casually grazing the shoulder he'd dropped it around as Cooper spoke. The golden cheeseball didn't deter from his path, and I soon found them on both sides.

"Bro, move your arm. You're touching my girl."

"Um, *our* girl, Coop. You're gonna have to learn to share."

He sighed dramatically, scooting closer, practically pulling me into his lap. He smirked, and I could tell he had something naughty planned, and I hoped it was for Aspen, not sure if I could resist a naughty Cooper. He leaned in close to whisper in my ear.

"Don't think I didn't notice you calling me Coop. I think it means we're official now, right? Cutesy nickname level means we're serious," he teased. His warm breath skated across my skin, and I sucked in a breath.

"Oh?" I choked, not sure I could say much else. Both of their bodies pressed into mine, and every part of me tingled. He trailed his nose down the crook of my neck, breathing me, and my eyes rolled to the back of my head. "But Aspen calls you that too, so does that mean you guys are in a relationship together?" I asked in a husky voice.

The thought left my lips, and I wanted to slap myself for my mastery of ruining moments. His head snapped up, his eyes wide as he looked over at Aspen. I was too scared to turn my head, nervous they'd both think I was a weirdo.

"We've been busted, Aspen. Our torrid love affair is no longer hidden."

"Wait, what?" My brain short-circuited, and I couldn't tell if I was excited about the prospect or relieved he wasn't taking my comment the wrong way when they both started laughing next to me.

"Fine, Freckles, you make a valid point. I hereby request a Penny-made couple name. I'll wait."

"But," I stuttered, words leaving me. "I can't just make something up on the fly!"

"Then I guess you have homework. Did you hear how she didn't deny we're a couple, though, Aspen? It's a sealed deal, brother!"

"I agree, no take-backs now."

"I'm way in over my head with you two, aren't I?" I asked.

Their laughter didn't make me feel any better, but it did seem to dispel the tense moment, giving me more time to prepare for being between them both.

"Wait! I called you Dimples, doesn't that count?" Cooper only winked, making his pop out, ignoring my answer.

"I have an idea," Aspen said, butting in.

"Go on…"

"To get to know each other better, but to maybe avoid the whole emotional minefield of topics we don't know, we do it in a safe way."

"Safer? I feel dumb that I'm not getting this," I admitted.

Cooper chuckled, his whole body moving next to me. "You're not dumb, Penny. Aspen's being obtuse on purpose. For a songwriter, he sometimes has a hard time expressing what he really wants to say without the riddles or metaphors."

Aspen flicked Cooper's ear, his arm still around me and close to the appendage. Cooper chortled, moving away but not letting it stop him from teasing Aspen. "As your Aspen translator, he's saying we should do something like 20 questions, or the ever-popular Never Have I Ever."

"I don't think I've played that one."

"See, you're already playing," Cooper teased.

Sticking my tongue out at him, I caught the way his eyes dilated and drooped as he watched my mouth. Clearing my throat, I turned to Aspen. "What are the rules?"

"We take turns saying things we've never done. If you have done it, well, there are different versions. Some, you start with 5 fingers up and put one down for each thing you've done, and others, there's alcohol involved, but the same concept. A drink or shot for everything you've done."

"Shit, Poppy would be drunk with this game. Um, well, I'm cool with the hand thing. I don't know what the alcohol situation is inside, and after my last drunk debacle, I'd rather steer clear for a bit."

"Good for me," Aspen agreed, smiling. "Plus, it means we keep our inhibitions about us."

"Oh, what do we need those for?" I teased. Cooper didn't like being ignored and started to trail his nose up my neck again, his hands rubbing on my leg he had draped across his.

"I'll go first while you two have your little witty banter battle," he breathed into my neck, causing me to close my eyes as my breath hitched. Cooper pulled away, and when I opened them, I saw Aspen's flick up over my head. I'd give almost anything to know what he found behind me, but I was too nervous to turn around and find out.

"I think instead of holding fingers up though, we up the stakes a little," Cooper suggested, and my assumption had been correct. He was plotting, and I was about to fall into his trap.

Swallowing, I turned, bracing myself for the sexual swagger he oozed. "Like what?"

His eyes heated, and my leg moved under the water, rocking against him. His hand gripped my thigh, and I focused on keeping my breathing even.

"A kiss."

"A *kiss*?" I blinked, not getting it.

"Yeah, for each thing someone has done, they have to kiss someone."

"You mean me because I don't see you guys kissing each other."

"Well, I guess it's your lucky night then, and you can choose between us for yours."

Nodding slowly, I gave into his game. I knew what he was hoping for, but I was kind of glad for it. It would provide us with the chance to cross that line without having to be awkward, or at least *I* wouldn't be awkward. I never knew how to broach the subject in relationships. 'So, wanna bang?' or 'Time to get it on?' Yeah, smooth was not in my DNA.

"You go first, Coop," Aspen suggested, somehow moving closer to me. At this point, I was sitting in both of their laps with one leg draped over each of them.

"Never have I ever kissed a guy." Coop looked at me with his bedroom eyes, his hair falling slightly across his eyebrows as it curled up at the ends. Narrowing mine at him, I figured out his play there. So, I turned my head, grabbed Aspen's cheeks, and pulled his lips to mine.

I'd caught him by surprise, his lips slightly open as our lips pressed together and I waited to see if he'd respond. Our kiss earlier had been sweet, but this one felt so much more. Within seconds, Aspen eagerly met my efforts, the pressure perfect as his soft lips touched mine, his tongue slipping in this time. When it started to go deeper, Cooper pulled us apart, pouting.

"Okay, okay, point made, Penny. I won't lowball next time. Your turn."

I blinked, licking my lips, still tasting Aspen there. I'd forgotten about the game the second our lips had touched.

"Um," I said, trying to find something. "I've never—"

"No, it's 'Never have I ever,'" Coop interrupted, winking at me.

Rolling my eyes, it at least helped me return back to my body and what I wanted to know. "Never have I ever… tried sushi." I wanted to facepalm, the question tame compared to Coop's, but it was what came across my tongue at the moment. I looked between the two, waiting to see if they had.

"Me either," Aspen admitted when I looked at him.

Looking back at Cooper, he winked before grasping my chin in his hands. He waited, holding my eyes, not using the moment to surprise me like I had with Aspen. Cooper wanted me to know he was kissing me and needed me to want it. I could see it in his eyes that it was important to him.

Nodding, I licked my lips as I waited. He leaned forward, his grip staying on my chin as he met me. His kiss was so different from Aspen's. It was soft at first, almost like Cooper was still testing it out. Once he was confident I was going along with it, he parted my lips, his hand sliding down my chin to wrap around the back of my neck.

Cooper kissed with his whole being, consuming me as he showed me what it felt like to be kissed by him. He pulled back, and I panted, wanting to follow his lips. He smirked, but I caught the relief in his eyes that I'd responded that way toward him, and it made me want to make sure he never felt anything other than wanted. It made me realize I wasn't the only one with insecurities, opening my eyes that maybe I did get too in my head at times over things.

Clearing my throat, I turned to Aspen. "Um, so is it your turn now?"

He smiled, and I relaxed when I didn't see any anger in his expression. "Sure, hmm, never have I ever been arrested."

Laughing, I raised my hand to the shock of both of them. "What? Wow! I thought that was a safe one," Aspen admitted.

"Well… *Poppy*." It was all I said, and they both laughed, understanding.

"I want to hear this story sometime," Cooper said, "but right now, you've got a kiss to deal out."

I looked between the two of them, gulping. I didn't

know how to pick. Closing my eyes, I started to sing the classic picking song when in doubt. "Eeny, meeny, miny, moe, catch a tiger by his toe. If he hollers, let him go. Eeny, meeny, miny, moe. My mother told me to pick the very best one, and you are not it."

"Did she just 'eeny, meeny, miny, moe' us?" Aspen whispered.

"Looks like it," Coop agreed.

Opening my eyes, I turned to Cooper, smiling. Shrugging, I cupped his cheek, leaning up to meet his lips. The kiss turned heated quickly, and I was panting as I pulled away. Turning to Aspen, I ran my fingers through his hair and waited to see if he would be okay if I kissed him too.

"I couldn't choose," I admitted, and he smiled, closing his eyes as I leaned forward.

As I started to kiss him, our tongues twirling this time, I felt hands running up my legs, and I knew the game portion of the evening was over, our lust ramping things up. Cooper began to trail kisses down my neck, down my collarbone and shoulder. I never knew that area could be so sensitive, but I felt myself growing more aroused with each lick.

Moaning into the kiss, I went willingly when Aspen grabbed my hips under the water, pulling me entirely onto his lap. Rocking into him, I found the friction I'd been needing. Feeling two sets of hands-on my body was erotic, and the thought of it sent my desire sky high. Gasping, I pulled back from Aspen and tilted my head back to capture Cooper's waiting lips.

Aspen took the opportunity to kiss down my front, and Coop somehow managed to untie my strings while he kissed me. Aspen slowly pulled it down, giving me time to stop him if I wanted, and it made me like them both even more. It wasn't that I didn't have a choice in the past, but when I thought about it, it also didn't feel like a genuine choice. It had been expected of me, so I did it.

But here, with them, I felt in control of my actions and desires, and the difference was staggering in how it made me feel. Taking the option myself filled me with a sexual power I'd never felt before, and I'd wager it increased my desire along with it. Each touch felt more sensual, each kiss a little more dangerous, and as we headed toward a new destination together, I knew what I needed.

Pulling back, I bit my lip as I looked between the two of them as we all breathed heavily. Their eyes zeroed in on me, waiting to see what I wanted to do next. I knew it was now, the time to make my voice loud and clear for both of them and me.

"I want you both. I want you both to take me to bed and fuck me... *together*."

CHAPTER
SIXTEEN

PENNY

For half a second, no one moved, and then the energy snapped. Cooper lifted me off Aspen's lap and into his arms as he surged out of the water. I was surprised when he didn't barge into the hut but stopped, setting my feet down, and wrapped a towel around me, taking the time to dry us off. It was sweet and endearing.

Cooper quickly picked up the other and tossed it to his brother before taking the last one and drying himself. I watched enamored as he rubbed it over his skin and then roughly over his hair. He tossed the towel on the bed, and then with a smirk, lowered his shorts, dropping the wet fabric to the ground.

I gulped, the urge to lower my eyes and take in his dick hard to avoid. Slowly, I started to rub the towel over my arms and dried my middle. My top was practically hanging off as it was, so I undid the bottom clasp and dropped it next to his shorts, holding their eyes the whole time as I glanced back and forth between them.

Next, I pushed down my bottoms, kicking them off with my foot. Gulping, I forced myself not to cross my arms over my body to hide it. They both made me feel as if the flaws I saw didn't exist, and I liked that feeling. Looking at Aspen, I waited to see what he would do. He stood frozen, his swim shorts tented as his eyes trailed over me, leaving a heated touch on my skin as he did.

"Sorry, I just need a minute to take you in," Aspen whispered.

"Fuck that," Coop bellowed, stepping forward as his dick slapped against his leg. The sound drew my gaze down, distracting me. I was so transfixed by the size of him, I didn't notice when he stepped forward, resuming his earlier trek. This time, he scooped me up, kissing me as he walked forward, and I wrapped my arms around his neck, enjoying how he seemed to want to carry me. Any girl that denied fantasizing about being carried by a strong man had to be lying. I'd just never found a man who could do it before now.

"When you look at me like that, Freckles, you make me feel like I could do anything."

"You don't already think you can?" I asked, curious, my brow creasing at the thought.

"Most days, I'm not even sure I can dress myself," he admitted. "It's why I opt for athletic shorts and tee shirts, they're easier to match."

"And here I thought you just liked to go without a shirt. The scandal!" I giggled, and he gently laid me down on my bed. I hadn't even realized we'd made it there, so focused on his face.

"You caught me, Penny. Ssh, don't tell my secret." Cooper smiled down at me, and my heart warmed at the look.

"I hope you know, I do believe you can do anything, and I'll believe in you double until you can as well." He jerked back in surprise, a wide serene smile coming over him.

"And you wonder why Asp and I are both smitten with you."

It was said with such reverie, I knew it wasn't a line. Brushing the back of my hand over his cheek, I melted when his eyes fluttered closed at the touch. Shit, Cooper Aspen was breaking all my barriers and making me fall for him bit by bit.

"You're the kind of guy girls dream of meeting, you know."

He smiled, shaking his head. "No, I'm not. I've never been *the one* at the end, just the friend or a convenient fuck buddy. Girls trust me, but they never give me their heart."

"Oh, Coop, I think it's my turn to say that you've dated the wrong type of girls."

"Your turn?" he asked, ignoring the other part.

"Aspen said it to me earlier; that I've dated the wrong guys, and well, I think it applies to you as well."

I kissed his cheek softly, holding his face still as I laid kisses all over his face. His eyelashes closed again as I kissed his whole face. He was bent over me on his elbows, our naked bodies touching almost everywhere, but he wasn't trying to be sexual at this moment, letting me care for him. It was a nice feeling.

When I pulled back, I smoothed his hair away from his face, and his eyes opened, swirling with an enormous amount of emotion—hope, fear, joy, lust, and perhaps even love. I just didn't want to look at that one too closely yet.

A knock at the door had me peering over his shoulder. Aspen stood, an odd look on his face, almost as if he was pained.

"I'm just gonna go." He pointed over his shoulder, and my face dropped. Cooper had been watching me and noticed, turning his head slightly to glare at his brother.

"Dude, get your ass in here and make our girl feel better. She legit got sad when you said you were leaving. We were having a moment; it doesn't mean you can't have one too. Quit being a dummy and join us."

Aspen swallowed, looking at me. "I'm sorry, I didn't mean to make you think I didn't want to. I just thought I'd be a third wheel."

"No," I answered, reaching my hand out for him. "I want you both here, remember?"

He nodded, walking forward, pulling his shirt over his head, and dropping his shorts in two steps. Cooper rolled to one side of me while I ogled his brother's cock. I knew they weren't real brothers, but yet it shocked me how different they were.

Cooper's was long and cylindrical with a fat tip. Aspens' was thicker, a couple of inches shorter, but looked to have a slight curve. I licked my lips as I watched him place his knee on the bed, settling down next to me.

"I'm impressed, Aspen, you've emerged into a man." Cooper chuckled, causing Aspen to reach over and slug him in the shoulder.

"I don't want you looking at my cock, weirdo. It's for Penny's eyes only."

Cooper leaned down, whispering into my ear, but

loudly enough for Aspen to hear. "That's because he has penis envy." Giggling, I shook my head and elbowed him in the gut, not wanting to make Aspen feel inferior.

"Ow! Okay, okay, I'll stop."

Aspen moved forward, wrapping his hand around the back of my head, threading his fingers through my hair. "Don't stop on my account, Coop. I'm not afraid of a little cock war. I know how to use *every* inch of mine."

He purred the last part, pulling my face to him to fuse our lips together. Aspen's other hand went to my hip, apparently no longer worried I didn't want him there, and pulled it up over his. The angle was almost perfect for him to hit my clit, and I rocked forward, seeking the friction I craved. Little moans left me as his hands started to explore.

Except he tugged my hair back a little and pulled my hip more, and I realized it wasn't his hands. Breaking the kiss, I leaned my head back, finding Cooper leaning over me. He winked, his dimple poking out as he lowered his mouth to mine. One hand traveled up top, caressing my breasts in soft touches, while the other made its way painstakingly slowly down my belly. A whimper fell from my lips, and he smirked, knowing what he was doing to me.

Aspen's mouth descended onto my nipple, swirling his tongue over the bud, and I trembled, the sensations overtaking me. I didn't know if it was them specifically or the fact there were two, but I'd never been brought to the brink of an orgasm so quickly.

When Cooper's hand finally made it to my clit, I practically wept when he began to circle it. Aspen's tip rubbed against my folds, and I wanted to push forward, taking him into me. Cooper's hand lifted off my breast and shoved Aspen, and I opened my eyes to see what they were fighting about now, disappointment filling me at the realization this wouldn't work.

Except when I opened my eyes, I found Cooper handing his brother something. "Don't be stupid."

It was interesting seeing this side of Cooper. When I'd initially met them, I figured Aspen was the older of the two, but the past few interactions had me wondering. Cooper acted so carefree at times; I'd wrongly assumed it meant he was also careless.

"I wasn't—" he started, then realized I was watching. "I would never, Penny. Sorry if it seemed that way."

"I don't even know what you're apologizing for," I admitted, tilting my head to look back at Cooper. He bent down, kissing my forehead.

"Freckles, in our haste to get naked, we didn't talk about the big things like contraceptives and all that jazz." He smiled, but I realized he was right, and some of my 'practical Penny' wanted to chastise myself for getting carried away.

"Okay, um, so I'm clean. Since my ex, I haven't been with anyone, and we hadn't had sex in at least a month. I have an IUD. I think that covers it?"

They both smiled at me. "You're so cute, and I love how easy you make everything," Aspen whispered, kissing me. He pulled back, only looking at me as he spoke the next part. "I haven't been with anyone in a few months, and my last test results were clean, but I respect you enough to wear a condom for now."

"I never knew talking about condoms could be so sexy."

"Well, Freckles, I think it's just who you have it with. It's not been as long for me." He cringed, embarrassed. "But I always wrap it before I tap it, and I had a test before I left to come here, and it was clean."

Laughing, I shook my head, kissing his nose from upside down. "Coop, you say the weirdest things, but I love it. Don't ever stop."

"Deal."

He kissed my nose back, his hands going back to my body, tweaking my nipples between his thumbs. Gasping, I arched my back into him, bringing my body closer. He started to kiss down my neck, sucking the skin as he traveled lower, licking the dip of my collarbone.

Aspen focused back on my clit, his fingers dipping in as I moaned out even more. "Fuck, yes. Don't stop, *please.*"

Writhing between them, I rode his hand as Cooper sucked my neck, massaging my breasts. Out of nowhere, my orgasm peaked, and I tumbled over the edge as I cried out. Aspen covered my mouth with his, swallowing my cries as he surged up into me. The sudden fullness took me by surprise, and I gasped, my moan of pleasure leaving me. His thickness filled me, stretching my walls as he moved. Our foreplay had crescendoed to this moment of pleasure, and he didn't last long as he pumped into me, pulling me tight to him as he hit a spot I thought was an urban legend.

Stars filled my eyes, and my head fell back onto Cooper, the spasms ringing out as I trembled between them. "Fuccck."

When I came down, he was kissing my cheeks and nose. When he saw I'd returned, he kissed me briefly, before helping Cooper turn me onto my back. When I opened my eyes, I found the golden God above me, his long dick in his hand as he rolled the condom down. Hooking my knees into his arms, he speared me onto him in one move, stopping as we both caught our breath.

I was boneless as I laid there, barely able to wrap my arms around his neck as he lowered himself down. Cooper fucked hard and fast, and I felt him deep, making me wonder just how big he was. His head fell to my neck, his breathing heavy as he thrust forward.

"I'm sorry, Freckles, I wanted this to be longer, but you're so fucking sexy, I can't hold back anymore."

He pulled back, kneeling, and wrapped his arms around my legs, holding them to his chest. Quickly, he pistoned into me in short thrusts before he pulled back and impaled me hard. After a few of those, he stuttered, moaning out as he came.

"Fuck, you feel too good. Shit. I'm coming."

I didn't know what the big deal was. They'd both lasted longer and been more impressive than any other man I'd been with.

"Ssh," I slurred, patting his cheek. "That was perfect."

He kissed me, smiling into it as he pulled out, curling around me once he'd removed the condom. Aspen was already back, his shorts on as he laid and watched us. He seemed calmer as he peered at me, a sense of acceptance in his eyes. Cooper let me go after a minute, getting off the bed, and I grabbed Aspen's hand, pulling him over to me.

"Do you need to do anything before you go to sleep, Pen?"

"Hmm?" I opened my eyes, his question hitting me. "Oh, um, yeah, probably."

Chuckling, he helped me up, handed me his shirt, and

followed me out to the main area. I made sure the door was secured with all three locks, the lights were turned off, and the sliding door was bolted. Grabbing some bottles of water, Aspen took them from me as we walked back to the room.

"I'll put these on the nightstand. The bathroom is free now." He kissed me, and I found I was becoming addicted to their small pecks, their lips needing to touch my skin as much as I wanted them to.

"Mmhm."

Floating, I walked to the bathroom and somehow managed to wash my face, brush my teeth, take my vitamins, and pee. Walking out, I realized I was mostly naked, only his shirt covering me, but I no longer felt self-conscious about it.

The lights were out, only a lamp lighting my way as I crawled over Cooper, who made no effort to help me other than touching all over my body. Giving him a narrow-eyed look, he laughed, not ashamed at all of his blatant groping.

Crawling under the covers, I found myself cocooned by them within seconds. It was everything I'd ever hoped sex could be, as well as blowing my mind on what a threesome could be like. Not once had I felt dirty, but a sense of empowerment. Cooper pulled me tight into his chest, his hands running through my hair as I held Aspen's hand. It felt perfect, well, almost. There was one thing, or person missing. But it was perfect for now.

As Coop kissed my neck, whispering, "I don't think I could ever walk away from you." I smiled, hoping he heard my reply before my eyes shut.

"Then don't."

CHAPTER
SEVENTEEN

RAFÉ

Knocking on the door, I held my breath as I waited for someone to answer. I hadn't been able to get away the past few days and seek out Penny. I didn't know what to think about the two brothers, yet. They'd seemed so genuine in helping me, but I also could see their desire for Penny just as clear and they'd been able to spend time I hadn't with her. And yet, they were my best chance at getting closer, so I'd take it for whatever it was, even if it meant I had to win her over them in the end.

The weird part was, it didn't feel like a competition.

Cooper had sent me texts the past few days, letting me know what they were doing, but I hadn't been able to join them yet. So, here I stood in front of 240 with a box of breakfast treats and a carafe of coffee I'd taken from the hotel, hoping I'd be greeted with welcoming arms after ghosting them. One of the assistant producers had looked at me oddly but let me go without asking the question clearly written on their face.

I knew my time was running out before I was discovered either by Georgina or Penny and the guys. The problem was, I didn't know which way I hoped it went anymore.

The door opened, and I found a beaming redhead peering up at me.

"Rafé! You're here!" She hugged my middle, and I awkwardly patted her head with my fingers, my hands both full. "Oh! Sorry, I'm just so happy to see you, I didn't think. Here, let me help."

Penny took the carafe and stepped out of the way so I could enter.

"Hey, hope it's okay that I stop by. I'm sorry it's taken me so long to get away from work. Coop had texted me you guys were here, so I hoped showing up with breakfast and coffee would buy me some goodwill."

"Most definitely! Especially because you have coffee and food. Though truth be told, you could've shown up empty-handed and I still would've been over the moon to see you. "

Her smile was everything as she walked in, placing the coffee down. Penny took the box from me, opening it up and deeply inhaling the smell of the food. "Oh my, that smells delightful." Her eyes had closed, a soft moan escaping as she fantasized about the food. I couldn't deny it affected me. Shifting myself, I looked around at her place.

The network had placed us in the hotel part, wanting to keep us separate from the contestants. Probably for the same reasons I found myself currently in, struggling to stay impartial in order to do my job. If I couldn't be objective, it was harder to separate myself from the task at hand. I'd been up most of the night going through the footage of the first five days, and I couldn't help but make sure the ones of team Ginger Nuts were fun and painted them in a good light.

Not that there was anything that would make people hate them, but there was always a way to splice and edit scenes to seem like something else. There had been one small piece with Poppy and Penny that I'd buried, not wanting it to be distorted into something it wasn't. Georgina would eat it up if she caught wind of it, and that was something I couldn't allow.

"You're officially my favorite person today! Coffee and food! You know the way to my heart," Penny sang as she poured some of the hot beverage into a cup and then picked out a massive cinnamon roll. I was so transfixed by watching her eat the thing, I hadn't noticed the other two. The clap on the back brought me back to the present.

"Hey, Rafé! How's it going, man?"

"Oh, good. How about you, Coop?"

"Can't complain. It's been a kickass morning so far. We've been out on the deck, just watching the waves and swinging in the hammock until it's time to do our task for the day." He wrapped his arms around Penny, resting his head on top of hers.

"Nice. Sounds like an enjoyable time." I cleared my throat, not sure why I felt awkward all of a sudden. His hands landed on her waist as he leaned over, taking a bite out of her roll. Penny tilted her head, narrowing her eyes at him.

"I know you didn't just steal my food. I've maimed

others for less." She glared at him for ten seconds before giggles erupted, and the feeling of jealousy slammed into me.

I wanted to feel that comfortable with her. I wanted to be the one stealing her food and then being yelled at. I wanted to be in her life.

"What do you have going on today, Rafé? I'm not even sure what day it is anymore. They kind of all blend together after a while," Coop said, bringing me back to the conversation. Penny took a seat next to me at the table, her leg rubbing against mine, and I lost all brain function. When I looked up, finding Cooper staring at me, I remembered he asked me a question.

"Oh, it's Wednesday if you're curious, and well, I guess I'm free at the moment. What about you?"

"There's some contest on the beach later," Aspen offered, rubbing his eyes as he walked in from the deck.

"Right, I knew that," I said it before I thought about it, and they looked at me, but thankfully dismissed it.

"Have you heard from Poppy or Jett?" Coop asked, shoving another pastry in his mouth.

"Hmm, let me check." She reached around me, her breast rubbing against my arm in the process. I stifled a moan, not wanting to alert anyone, but when I looked up, I found Aspen knowingly smirking at me. When Penny leaned back, she stayed close to me, though, and I pressed my side into hers more.

"Okay, there's a text that says to meet them on the beach when we're ready and to dress accordingly. What does that mean?" Penny asked, scrunching her nose as she looked up from her phone.

Aspen chuckled, leaning against the counter on the

other side and snatching a coffee cup. He waited until he had it filled, and everyone looked at him before he answered.

"The theme for today is 'Bringing Sexy Back.'"

"That sounds dirty," Coop stated, snorting.

"You think everything sounds dirty. I said something about taking out the trash yesterday, and you said 'I'd like to take out your trash.'" Penny gave him a look, though the edges of her lips fought not to curl up. Her tone had been exasperated, but it was clear she was poking at him. It seemed things had progressed between them all in the time I'd been away, and it was clear to see I was intruding. I hadn't realized a few days could change things so much, but that had been a desperate wish on my part to acquiesce my own guilt.

"Well, I guess I'll get out of your way then."

Sadness filled me at the thought, but I didn't want to be second fiddle… again. Turning to leave, I made it four steps down the hall before I felt her hand on my arm.

"Do you really have to leave?"

"You're busy. I don't want to be in the way." I didn't turn around, just spoke to the void in front of me.

"Stay… please? I'd like you to be here too."

Turning, I met her blue eyes. Her face was open, and I couldn't detect any deception. I knew it was stupid to think something from a vacation romance would be lasting but I wanted to try. "I don't think I can be here like you want me to, Penny."

"Why? Did I say something wrong to hurt you? Did the guys?"

"No, it's not that. I just can't be around you feeling this way and not want to kiss you," I admitted. "I want to be more than friends and you seem to have that covered. I'll just be in the way."

"Kiss me."

"What?"

"Kiss me."

"But—"

She shook her head. "No buts. Just kiss me. *Please*, Rafé?"

I quit thinking and bent my head, wanting nothing more than to fulfill her request. The please had been heavy, filled with desire, and I couldn't deny I aspired to fill it. Our lips touched, and sparks flew. I'd never had such an explosive kiss. I could still taste the icing on her lips as I pressed mine into hers.

Penny moved them slightly, a moaning sound escaped, lighting a fire in me. It was the kiss of death for me because it killed any hope I had of walking away or believing this was nothing and of thinking I wouldn't be changed from her kiss alone.

Lifting her up, I felt her wrap her legs around me, and I turned us toward the wall. Nothing else seemed to matter, everything falling away. Where we were, who was here, or the fact my job was to exploit the contestants. All I could breathe, taste, and feel was Penny. She'd become my entire world in a matter of seconds.

Her moans spurred me on as I rocked into her, our tongues now joining in the fun as they battled one another. Her fingers raked through my hair, pulling the strands and making me want to return the favor. I was rock hard, and my dick was in agreement that nothing else would suffice until we could feel her around us.

Letting go of one of her cheeks, I smoothed my palm

over the round globe, hooking my finger beneath her dress and panties, feeling her skin against my fingertip. Her moan encouraged me as she bucked her hips into me, rubbing against me. Dipping my fingers in from the back, I felt her wetness beginning to drench my fingers. Using some of it to lubricate my digits, I slowly made my trek forward, seeking her center. The closer I got, the more wetness I found, and soon I was sliding in between her folds, her hot wetness coating me.

Breaking the kiss, I sought out her neck as I laid a kiss there, her panting breaths loud in my ear as I plunged deeper into her. When I'd worked her over more, I was able to get two fingers in, pushing faster. Each thrust of her hips had her riding my fingers and bucking into my erection. She pulled my head back, locking eyes with me as she came around me, her eyes only shutting as she spasmed.

When she blinked back open a few seconds later, I slowly pulled my fingers out, licking them as I brought them to my lips. Penny's breath caught, and she dropped her legs from me as I swirled my tongue around, drinking in her desire. Closing my eyes as I cherished the taste, I stepped back until I hit the opposite wall. Shock filled me a few seconds later when I felt my shorts being unzipped and my cock freed. By the time I opened my eyes, Penny already had her hand wrapped around my dick, her tongue swirling out to lick the drop of cum that had beaded there.

I wanted to tell her that she didn't have to, that I was okay. But the words never left me as she started to pump her hand up and down, taking me deep into the back of her throat as she sucked. My head fell back against the wall, and I moaned, the sensation of her lips around me a dream come true. This was mind-blowing, and it was only a blow job. I guess it was cock-blowing then? Dick-blowing? The ridiculous thoughts floated to the top of my head, floating around merrily as all the blood stayed in my cock, every nerve ending firing as she devoured me. Sooner than I'd like to believe, my balls drew up tight, and a tingle ran down my spine.

"Pen," I gasped, "move."

"Mmhm," she hummed, not helping. The sensation of her voice was all it took, and I erupted, the cum squirting down her throat as she held me tight to her. I cried out, the moan funneling through my whole body as I shuddered, sagging against the wall.

I watched as she licked her lips, tucking me back in and fixing my pants before she stood.

"I don't think you're real," I mumbled, pulling her toward me.

"I could say the same about you." She kissed my lips, and it melted the last bit of reservation I had. I'd figure out a way to be with her, no matter what, because everything with Penny had felt better than anything else had in the past five years. I'd become so jaded, unsure of what I wanted, and going through the motions. Even my engagement hadn't been what I needed, only going through with it assuming it would make me feel happy. But it had been a lot of work and a mutual arrangement. It wasn't real love, and the fact she was able to identify that and save us both from a life of misery made me respect Rebecca.

"Do you have time to hang with us today?"

"Yeah. For you, I have all the time in the world."

And I did. I hoped she was my future, but I knew she was my present, and I didn't want to miss it.

CHAPTER
EIGHTEEN

POPPY

JETT KISSED MY NECK, AND MY TOES CURLED IN MY SANDALS. His arms were wrapped around my waist, and he had me pulled tight to him as we waited for the three musketeers to arrive. I'd had so much sex the past few days, my vagina was starting to yell at me. But when Jett looked at me like he might die if he didn't have me right then, my pussy started singing "Bow Bow Bow" and doing the "Apple Bottom Jeans" dance. Needless to say, I hadn't been able to say no once.

"How long is this going to last?" Jett asked, nipping my ear.

"Why, do you have plans?"

He pulled me tighter, his lower half brushing against my ass. I felt the hard length twitch, and I stifled a gasp. He hummed against my skin, but didn't say anything.

"Oh, so you want to bake cookies?" I teased, unable to let it go.

"I want something sweet and hot, but it's not a cookie, *Red*."

My whole life I've been waiting for a man to call me Red in that way. I knew Penny hated obvious nicknames, but I was a bit of a romantic in the sense that if a man growled it, I was putty. I'd read a book, okay, was *forced* to read a book once, and the male love interest had been this growly, tattooed hunk, and he called his girl, Red, and for some reason, it became the epitome of love to me.

We all had weird goals in life—this one was mine.

And Jett was fulfilling the fantasy perfectly.

Before I could respond, Penny arrived with her pack of love-sick puppies trailing behind her. I smirked wider when I saw she'd even picked up a stray.

"Hey! We're not late, are we?" she asked, looking around at the other contestants.

"Nope. We went walking on the beach after we ate, then came here instead of going all the way back."

"Wow, that sounds kind of nice, actually." Her eyes flicked up to the man behind me, his head still resting on top of mine, and I could imagine the cocky eye lift he was giving her. She opened her mouth right as the event coordinator began to speak into the microphone, giving an update on the rankings.

"In first place, we have The Quirks." She nodded to a group of people close to the stage. Grumbling, "They should've been named Overachievers." Jett snorted into my hair, and I realized I'd said it out loud unintentionally.

She droned on, letting us know we were in 4th place. Jemma's team, Aces, was now in 2nd. Jemma blew me a kiss at the announcement. I noticed how all three guys hovered around her, and I wondered if it had developed beyond just the two we saw at the hut. Her other team member, Meredith waved, but then returned to her phone. She was quiet in person, but her videos were fun. She did a thing where she blind reacted to thirst trap videos and made funny faces at them.

"Today's challenge will be a decades contest. Your team will be given ten songs that were popular during a certain decade. You're to pick two people for the challenge from your team. Each song you know, you get a point. Get them all right, and you get a bonus. Up first will be team Quirks."

We all watched as they grabbed hold of the microphone, a screen appearing behind them with ten spaces. Music started, and I wanted to sing along to it, the familiar tunes making me move my hips to the beat. After a few songs, it was clear that team Quirks had met a challenge they couldn't win, and when the tenth song played, and they dropped their heads, I couldn't help but smile.

"So, who's gonna represent our team?" Cooper asked, looking at Aspen and Jett.

"Penny and I got this," I interjected before they could make a suggestion. The boys stared at me, but Penny nodded, giving me a fist bump.

"PB&J are gonna rock this!" Giggling, I winked at the guys, noticing nerves on their faces. "Don't worry, guys. Penny, she's not the best singer, but what she lacks in tone, she makes up for in her insane knowledge of pop culture songs. Not to mention, we've basically been performing karaoke every week for twenty years."

Aspen lifted his hands in defeat, bowing to us. When Ginger Nuts was called, we walked up casually to the stage. I was surprised Penny hadn't argued with me on doing this, typically needing liquid courage to do karaoke. A smile radiated off her face, though, and I smiled, liking the effect the sun, waves, and multiple dicks seemed to be having on her.

"Peen does a body good, huh, Pen? Oh my god, Peen Pen. I'm gonna call you that now."

"Don't you dare," she hissed.

Smiling, I brought the microphone up and nodded for the tech assistant to start. The first song came on, and I immediately began to sing, "I'm a Barbie girl." Penny joined in, and we shimmied together as we laughed. The next song started, and Penny instantly went into her best boy band dance.

We belted out Adele next, Fall Out Boy, and The Killers. At this point, we were just having fun, singing and dancing together as the songs transitioned into one another. When we got to the last song, an emotional Eminem song, we both leaned against one another, singing the parts. When it ended, we both bowed, knowing we'd nailed that. Jemma was dancing all around for us when we walked by, and it made me like her even more. She was competitive, but she wasn't a bitch about it.

"Okay, that was impressive," Coop admitted when we got back to our spot. "I'm in awe, actually. There were only like four songs I knew."

"I could've done it," Jett mumbled, rolling his eyes.

"Sure you could, stud." I slapped his stomach, not buying the pout. He grabbed my hand, pulling me close and my heart took off. I knew I was in danger, but at this moment, I couldn't seem to find it in me to care. I'd seriously become dickupied.

When the contest ended, our team jumped up a position, putting us in third, just behind Jemma's.

"So, what are you all up to now?"

"I can tell you what's up?" Jett purred into my ear. I ignored him though, realizing I missed my friend.

"Oh, I don't know," Penny said, looking between the guys hanging off her every word.

"What if I commandeer one of the volleyball pools and we have a friendly match?" Cooper offered.

"Yes! That sounds perfect. You guys in?" Penny asked. I tilted my head up at Jett, giving him a look. He looked down at me before he rolled his eyes and then growled, pretending to bite my nose.

"Fine, little gangsta. Let's play some volleyball."

"Ah, look guys, I think Jett's heart just grew three times its size."

Laughing, we all headed over to the pool. Sunscreen and a few cocktails later, I'd never had so much fun with a group of people. I could tell the guys cared for Penny too, and it made me happy for her.

When Jett got me back to the hut later, he reminded me just how much he liked me or at least liked being between my legs. I wasn't fooled that it was anything more. It was a classic vacation hookup, no matter how gooey he made my insides.

CHAPTER
NINETEEN

PENNY

RAFÉ BUMPED MY HIP, AND I LOOKED OVER, SMILING AT HIM. We'd spent almost every day together since he showed up with coffee and donuts, and he'd become an integral part of our group. He wasn't able to always be here, his work calling him away at times, but every moment I got to spend with all three of the men who'd infiltrated my heart felt right.

"I can't believe this is the last week we'll be here," I said, a frown overcoming me.

"Hey, don't think that way, we still have this weekend and Ginger Nuts is now in second place. You guys have a chance of winning this thing."

Smiling, I nodded, wrapping my arms around his waist. "Yeah, you're right. I'm glad you get to hang out longer today. I've missed you." I snuggled into his chest, feeling his soft shirt against my cheek. Despite all the time we'd been spending together, we hadn't crossed the sex line yet. Rafé was a pro at oral, something he demonstrated to me this morning as he ate me out on the deck before everyone woke up—but I wanted more. Each time we started to go further, something held him back, and I hoped he'd tell me soon what it was. The reality of the situation was that I didn't want to ask either.

"You guys ready?" Cooper asked, bounding toward us with a big smile on his face. Grinning up at him, I found my heart racing as he neared, the butterflies coming to life each time I saw him.

"What are we doing today, anyway?" I asked.

"It seems the show is doing a scavenger hunt," Aspen answered as he joined us.

"Scavenger hunt?" Poppy asked, sipping a coffee as she walked up. Today she had on one of my favorite shirts that said "It's okay guacamole, I'm extra too."

"Yeah, there'll be various clues that lead to the next one and we have to record them as we go around town. Sounds fun." He shrugged, putting his phone away.

"Oh!" I clapped. "That sounds awesome! I've wanted to tour the town. We've mostly been stuck here, so I'm looking forward to getting off the resort. I hope they have one of those open-air markets."

Everyone laughed at my enthusiasm, but I really was excited. As the vans pulled around, and we all loaded up inside, I sat between the brothers, and practically bounced the whole way into town. When the van pulled up to a curb, and we all bustled out, I couldn't contain my glee.

The city sounds hummed around us, coursing under my skin, making me feel alive. I found myself dancing through the streets, happiness wanting to burst out of me at every chance. I felt on top of the world, a powerful feeling making me believe anything was possible.

"Let's get this over with. What's the first clue?" Jett asked, scowling as he shaded his eyes.

I'd learned over the past week or so that any time Jett had to do an activity, he acted affronted, but would join in and by the end, have a smile. It was like his bad boy, broody exterior had to make it seem like he didn't like to be around others before he could shed it.

"It says, 'To win, you can only move by jumping. Find the place where you can jump, and you will find your next clue.' So, what do we think that means?" Aspen asked.

"Hmm, that could mean a lot of things."

"Wait, did you say jump?" I asked.

"Yeah, why?" Aspen looked up from the map we'd been given curiously.

"There!" I pointed to a sign on a shop across the way. It said Knight in all caps with a chess symbol behind it. "A knight can only move by jumping."

Everyone looked at me, not sure what to think.

"Worth a shot." Coop shrugged, grabbing my hand as he pulled me across the street. I couldn't contain my smile at the gesture, and he caught it as he peeked out the corner of his eyes.

"Whatcha smiling at, Freckles?"

"Nothing."

"Hm, I don't buy it. I think you're feeling all giddy because you got some extra lovin' from Rafé this morning."

"What?" I gasped, slapping his arm. "How? You know what, I'm not even surprised that you know. And yeah, I had some fun with Rafé, but that's not why I'm smiling."

"No?" he asked, confused.

"I'm smiling because you make being carefree and happy easy. I can't seem to stop grinning when I'm around you, Coop."

"Oh." He stopped, a wide smile breaking out on his face. "I, uh, yeah." Coop blushed, full-on blushed, his cheeks turning bright red as he tried to find his words. Reaching up on my tiptoes, I kissed him on the nose, repaying the gesture and then pulled a stunned silent Coop through the door. Chuckling as I entered, I stopped in my tracks as I took in the place.

"Whoa."

"Is this place for real?" Rafé asked, coming to a stop next to us.

"Yep, I just pinched myself, and it hurt, so I'd say I'm definitely not dreaming," Cooper mumbled.

As we stood staring out at the view in front of us, a man walked over, taking in our expressions. "Welcome, I take it this is your first time here?"

Nodding, I noticed everyone else was doing the same. "It's unreal," I whispered.

"It's very real," he confirmed. "I'm assuming you're part of LiveIt?"

"Yes, we are."

"Good, good. Please, come and check-in, and then I'll get you started."

We all numbly walked over, a giddy excitement taking over. When the word jump had been in the clue, I didn't know what to expect. Walking into an adult trampoline course filled with obstacles, zip lines, and javelin that all had to do with chess had apparently struck us all mute.

"I think if this place was clothing optional, it would be

my favorite place in the world," Coop mumbled, causing us all to laugh. The man who'd been grabbing waivers for us to sign stopped, narrowing his eyes at him.

"Clothing is very much required here, boy. Believe me, you don't want to see everyone's private parts bouncing around all over the place. No nilly willy's, got it?"

Jett snorted, breaking his cool facade, and the rest of us followed suit, bursting out in laughter.

"I like you, old man. You're alright," Coop said, wiping his eyes from laughing. "And I promise, I'll keep all my clothes on."

"I'll be watching you just to make sure."

Cooper gave a salute and then led us over to the area the man had pointed to for our belongings. He'd given us special socks with grippers on the bottom to help not slip while jumping.

"So, are we thinking the next clue is somewhere inside?" Rafé asked, getting into it. The more he hung out with us, the more I found him wanting to get involved. Today was the first time he was actively participating.

"Yeah, I think so," Aspen mumbled, looking all around.

"Let's split up into teams since there are 6 of us," Poppy suggested, grabbing my arm. "This one is mine." She tugged me in a different direction, her feet moving quicker than I'd ever seen the woman go before.

"You gotta pee or something, Pop?"

"Nah, I just didn't want them to snatch you from me. I need the scoop, Pen! How's it going wrangling all those dicks? Have you surpassed me and had a foursome yet?"

We climbed up some steps onto one of the trampolines, holding on to one another. We started to jump softly, moving forward a bit. I waited until we had our bearings before I even attempted to say anything.

"Just the brothers so far. Rafé's had his way with my ice cream bar, but hasn't gone full sundae yet."

"Um, say what, now?" she asked, turning. When I bit my lip and shrugged, she laughed, stopping her forward movement. "Full sundae!" she cackled, causing everyone to turn and look. Shushing her, I grabbed her arm and tugged her to keep moving so we didn't get run over by other people jumping.

"What's it been like with the brothers then?" she whispered, leaning close. We were holding onto one another as we jumped now, small little bounces. Hopefully, the guys found the clue because we were not making much forward progress.

"It's been incredible." I held her eyes, a smile on my face. "Once I got everything out of my head, and only heard my voice, I could just let go and be free. I've had more sex this week than I think I did all year dating Walter."

"I'm so proud. I could cry." Poppy pantomimed tears, wiping them from her eyes.

"Oh, hush." Giggling, I dragged her some more, wanting to get off this part and onto the next. Jumping wasn't as fun as I thought.

"Now, it's your turn. How are things going with Jett?"

"I mean, he's a broody fucker. His moods change more than mine. Perhaps, I should offer to give him some meds and mellow him the fuck out."

"Ha, ha. Don't joke about yourself that way, Poppy. You know it's more serious than that."

"I know. But somedays, it feels like the only way to not hate my fucking brain is to laugh about it."

"Yeah, I get that. Just make sure you keep everything in perspective."

"I will. Besides, I have you to remind me when I don't."

"You got that right. But back to the good stuff," I urged, wiggling my eyebrows at her.

"Phew, so good. I think I came like three times this morning. I want to smack his mouth off his face 50% of the time, but he knows how to use it for good too, so I guess I'll let him keep it. He sang to me this morning as we laid naked in bed, and fuck, Pen, I nearly orgasmed from the man's voice alone. That's never happened to me before! I think I'm starting to, like, I dunno, have feelings for him." She turned to me with concern on her face.

"Would that be so bad?" I asked.

"Oh yeah, the worst. I'll never see him after we leave here. I can't be catching feelings for him! In fact, I'm throwing them back." She shook her whole body, dropping my arm, and mimed tossing something over her shoulder. Sighing, she then turned to me, a smile on her face. "There, all gone."

Shaking my head, I laughed as I pulled her along. We made it off the trampoline and now had to get across the next portion by crawling through a tunnel or zipping over a net on a bar with two handles.

"Hmm, the idea of crawling puts me off, but I also know my arm strength is shit, and I'd fall on my face if I tried to hold myself up over that net. Knowing my luck, I'd stop in the middle of the course and then have to crawl anyway."

"Good point," I agreed, moving toward the tunnel. On our way there, we were intercepted, and Aspen stole me, grabbing me around the waist and running off. Laughing, I waved bye to Poppy, who was now left with Jett. She rolled her eyes, but I saw the slight smile as she stuck her butt in his face to start down the tunnel.

"Where we going, Asp?" I asked, looking down at him.

"We're almost there." He placed me on my feet a second later, turning me around. In front of me was a giant slide. I looked over my shoulder at him, my brows raised in shock, as I tried to form a sentence. "You can't be serious."

"Very. We're going together." He wrapped his arms around my waist and sat down with me in his lap. "You ready?"

"No, but I don't think that matters."

Aspen smiled, laying down on the mat and pulling me up more on his chest, so my head was closer to his. "Hold on tight."

He let his feet go, and we started down the slide. Grabbing his arms, I held on tight as we careened in the dark around the curves. It was quite scary, but I did feel safe with Aspen's arms around me. "You doing okay?" he whispered, his breath fanning across my skin.

"Mmhmm."

I felt his chuckle rumble through his body, soothing me. "I got you, Penny." His voice came out strong, and I believed him. He did have me in more ways than just this slide. Relaxing back, I let myself sink into his body and closed my eyes. Just imagining it as a fun ride with him, it didn't seem as scary. The air shifted, the light filtering in, and I opened my eyes right as we exited the shoot and flew across into the empty space before we started to descend, landing on a soft balloon. Or at least it felt like one. We sank down, rising up slowly as the air around us returned from its disbursement.

Laughing, I rolled over, smiling at Aspen. "That wasn't too horrible, but I hope I never have to do it again."

"Fair, but it was fun. Thank you for trusting me."

"Of course." Leaning down, I kissed him quickly before rolling off. I knew if I stayed, we'd take it too far, our lust for one another at an all time high. When I sat up, I found a grinning Coop waiting for me with a hand outstretched for me to grab. Taking it, he lifted me up, bringing me closer to him.

"Thanks, Coop. I'm guessing it's your turn now?"

"You know it. Come on, Freckles. I think the clue is in the next part." I waved at Aspen, who was climbing out of the area. Rafé was leaning against the wall and winked at me as I passed. I blew him a kiss, feeling flirty. He caught it, the gesture cheesy, but it made my heart soar, and I knew I was in trouble when it came to matters of the heart, but I found it hard to care about the inevitable pain at the moment.

"What's the next part, Coop?"

"The Knight's ball."

"That sounds very unhygienic," I snorted.

Cooper laughed but shook his head. "Nah, we're good. I believe the clue is taped to a ball, though, so we're gonna have to look through them. You ready?"

"Uh, yeah, I guess." He picked me up and tossed me into the pit, and I realized I needed to start asking more questions. Plastic balls clicked together as my body made contact, and I attempted to use my non-existent core muscles to lift myself. Coop dove headfirst into the pit, just a big kid at heart, it seemed.

Once I was sitting, I started to look through the balls, remembering something about the sun, so I decided to check the red ones. Wading through them, I tossed the ones I'd checked over my shoulder, not realizing someone was behind me until I heard an "ow."

Spinning, I found a kid glaring at me. "Oops, sorry."

He moved over but kept his eyes on me the rest of the time. I turned back to the task at hand, hoping to get out of here soon. Coop's arm rose up out of the pit a few seconds later, a red ball in his hand. His head followed a few seconds later, a smile of victory on his face.

"I got it!"

He stood, his arm raised as balls fell around him, a massive grin on his face, the dimple shining at me. Coop bent down, his free arm wrapping around me, and pulled me up, out of the balls, into his chest.

"You make everything fun, Penny."

"That's funny because I thought the same about you."

"Well, maybe we just let each other be who we're meant to be."

"Maybe," I agreed, smiling. "Now, let's find the others so we can read this clue. I kind of want to win this."

He dropped a kiss on my lips before spinning and pulling me along as he high-stepped it out of the ball pit. Coop looked like a giant as he stepped out, the balls like ping pong balls compared to his large frame. The kids in there dove out of the way, not wanting to get hit with any of the flying plastic.

When he got to the edge, he lifted me up, sitting me on

the border, and then lifted himself out. His biceps bulged, the muscles practically winking at me in the process.

"You got some drool there, Freckles."

"Probably," I admitted, making Coop laugh. He leaned closer, about to kiss me, when a plastic ball hit him in the face. Turning, I spotted the kid I'd hit wearing a smug look, sticking his tongue out at us. Sputtering, I got up, pulling a stunned Cooper to his feet.

"Did that kid just hit me?"

"Yeah, don't ask. I was kind of owed."

"I, just…"

We found the rest of the group waiting at the exit, apprehension on their faces. Coop held the ball high again, lofting his hard-earned trophy into the air. Everyone started whooping and dancing in celebration as we neared.

"Fuck yeah!" Poppy shouted, earning looks from some parents. Grabbing her arm, we all gathered around the ball to read the next clue.

"It moves at the speed of many feet. The more you drank, the more you rank, and to win this clue, you must cross the line before the buzzer."

Looking up, I wasn't the only one who had no idea. "What the what?"

Rafé was biting his lip but looked at me, almost like he was deciding something. His phone buzzed, and he looked at it briefly before shoving it in his pocket. "I might have an idea."

Nodding, we all stepped closer, not wanting to miss what he said.

"Follow me." He pivoted, grabbing his shoes from the

cubby and putting them on as he made his way over to the door. Rafé stopped when none of us had moved to follow.

"It's outside. I think I have to show you for it to make sense. I could be wrong, but," he stopped, swallowing, "I have a good guess."

Shrugging, I walked over, the others following, and we all grabbed our shoes and made our way out of the trampoline center. Shouts rang out behind us, and I turned to find Jemma. She winked, and I knew we needed to hurry. Pushing the others out the door, we followed Rafé as he led us around a few streets until we stopped in front of a green and yellow wagon. Or, well, it was more like a six-person bike with a bar in the middle.

Repeating the clues, it made sense, except for the rank part. The attendant looked at us, waiting to see if we were going to get on.

"A bicycle bar?" Coop asked.

"Yeah, many feet, drinking, and well, there happens to be a drunk race today."

"It's true," the man at the bike bar said. "It starts soon if you want to enter."

Everyone looked at me for some reason, but I didn't have any other answers, so I shrugged, walking up to the man and shaking his hand. "Let's do this!"

Climbing up, I found myself next to Rafé and Aspen, Cooper, Jett, and Poppy across from me.

"Put your feet on the pedals below you. You can choose any of the choices in front of you to drink. The more you drink, the faster you will go because you will decrease your weight. I'll be your guide, steering you. All you have to worry about is turning those pedals and drinking. You guys ready?"

"Yeah! Ginger Nuts on three," Coop shouted. "1, 2, 3."

"Ginger Nuts!"

Laughing, we started to pedal and began to pour ourselves drinks. Turning to the two men next to me, I raised my glass. "Cheers!"

Taking a sip, I hoped this time drinking ended better. Though, in the grand scheme of things, that vibrator karaoke was beginning to seem less like a bad mistake and the turning point in my life.

"Bottoms up!"

CHAPTER
TWENTY

JETT

THE GANG LAUGHED AROUND ME, AND I WANTED TO JOIN IN, allow myself to express what I was feeling for once. We were peddling down some street, a few other carts around us as we made our way through the city.

"This is a fantastic way to tour the area!" Penny exclaimed, looking around with wide eyes. I wanted to hate the ever-optimistic redhead with a tough underbelly, but I couldn't find it in me.

"The question is, little gangsta, whether or not you're able to walk when we cross the finish line?" I taunted, smirking.

She narrowed her eyes at me, and I couldn't help but smile wider. Something in me couldn't help but push her buttons. It wasn't a sexual feeling, something I found strange, but more of a friendly, protective vibe. Penny made me want to tease her while at the same time hurt any of these baboons if they hurt her. It was odd, and I didn't know how to take it.

"I'll be able to walk better than you." She stuck out her tongue, giggling, and I sat up, concerned she'd had too much. I shifted my eyes to Aspen, giving him a look. Years of friendship gave us the knowledge to know what the other was saying without saying it. He nodded, and I relaxed, knowing he wouldn't let her have any more beer.

Poppy leaned closer, her breath tickling my neck as she spoke. "You know, if you hadn't just finger fucked me up against a wall, I'd be concerned you liked my friend."

Turning, I kept my face blank as I raked my eyes over her. Poppy was the most gorgeous woman I'd ever met, and every part of me yearned to be near her, on her, and in her. A need and desire I'd been riding at every opportunity since I've been here. Which, of course, scared the fuck out of me and made me be a dick when I wasn't getting dicked.

Leaning close, I whispered, "Red, you know damn well there's nothing to worry about, or do I need to remind you by shoving my dick down your throat at our next stop?"

Poppy sucked in a breath, licking her lips, and I watched as she rubbed her hand between her thighs, rubbing her pussy. Smirking, I leaned back, knowing I'd won that battle, but it wouldn't be the last, not with Poppy. The reality that I looked forward to it, shocked me.

I was used to life slapping me upside the head when I thought I had it figured out. What I wasn't used to, the slapping being because of a woman.

My life had made sense two weeks ago. I got up, wrote a bit, sang some songs, worked out, showered, ate, and repeated. There was the occasional hookup after a show when the adrenaline was riding me, but for the most part, women and the occasional man, had been a means to an end. I didn't think about them after our time together. It was one night, and then I moved on. It helped that our tour bus did the actual leaving, making it easy to fuck and forget.

I wouldn't admit it was a lonely life, because what did I have to complain about?

A rising career? Check.

Good friends? Check.

Getting to play music as my job? Check.

A supportive adoptive family? Check.

And yet, it felt empty, not as satisfying as I'd dreamed. I'd always believed if I just got to the point where I could put my music out into the world, be recognized for my genius, and be appreciated for my creativity… *then* I'd feel complete.

But I didn't. In fact, recently, I felt more lost than ever before.

It was what had begun my search for my biological family. Perhaps if I knew where I came from, why my parents gave me up for adoption, then I'd have the answer to the gaping wound in my chest.

The very wound I stuffed with witty banter, broody songs, and damsels in distress. And Poppy was rearranging it all. She wasn't a damsel and the fact she didn't need me both scared and thrilled me. A nudge from my other side had me turning to find Cooper watching me.

"You okay, man? You seem a bit deep in thought."

"Hmm, yeah, I'm good. Didn't get much sleep, if you know what I mean?" I joked, falling back into the playboy

I was known as, forgetting momentarily who I was talking to.

Cooper was one of my oldest friends. When he moved to our hometown and his mom married Aspen's dad, he slid into our group with ease. The thing I appreciated about Coop was he didn't bullshit. He called things how they were and didn't let you off the hook just because you wanted to be.

He lifted an eyebrow, not buying my excuse, and I shifted closer to him. "I uh, got that call I've been waiting on, but now I'm not sure what to do about it."

Coop smiled wide, a question on his lips as to why when Poppy's laugh rang out, and his eyes shifted over my head to her. A realization fell over him, and he nodded.

"Ah. I mean, that's awesome, and I'm sure quite terrifying at the same time. If you were to talk with her about it, I'm sure she'd understand."

Lifting my eyebrow now, I gave him a look. Poppy was a lot of things, but I didn't know any girl who'd be fine with me ditching them to go meet another woman, especially when I couldn't tell them who she was. Poppy would hear I was leaving and assume I didn't want to be with her.

And that was where I was stuck.

Typically, I'd jump on the chance to escape and have a ready-made excuse to ditch. But Poppy made me question everything. She made me feel like maybe I didn't need to pull this string, that perhaps I could be enough on my own. Poppy was the type of woman who made you feel ten feet tall with the ability to defeat all the dragons who tried to burn your world to the ground.

It was the type of thing I'd been searching for my whole life.

But I didn't know how to trust it.

The fear that it wasn't real and only in my head made me want to pull back, put up my walls and protect the fragile thing in my chest masquerading as my heart.

My phone buzzed again, the reminder I had a choice to make soon. Poppy laughed at the three across from us, little gangsta making some funny face as she retold a story about how Poppy got her detention in the fifth grade.

I love how she leaned into me, her body always touching mine like gravity couldn't even keep us apart. Her smell of apples and tulips filled my nostrils, and my cock instantly started to harden. I wondered if I'd ever be able to eat the fruit again without thinking of her. Her hand slid up my thigh casually, naturally finding its way there as she talked.

If Poppy was the one who set my soul on fire, should I forget about this search and focus on the direction my life was headed? Or, in order to get the life I wanted, did I need to do this now, so I didn't have any regrets?

That was the question that had been plaguing me since I'd gotten the call.

Did I stay, or did I go?

Either way, it was going to hurt, but which one was more preferable?

I could only hope she'd be there at the end in either situation.

CHAPTER
TWENTY-ONE

"Drink, Drink, Drink!"

Gulping down the last of the beer, I laughed as I wiped away the foam. Smiling wide, I looked at Jett, who'd been increasingly quiet as the day went on. I kept trying to distance myself from him in return, but he always sensed it, pulling me right back.

I didn't know what I was doing, but I hoped it wouldn't bite me in the ass later.

"Alright, folks, you're coming up to the last stretch. There are two carts in front of you. It's time to drink and pedal and see if we can catch them!" the driver stated, his straw hat tilting to the side as he steered the monstrous beer cart over a millimeter.

"Let's do it, guys, come on! Fresh glasses for all, except Penny. I think she's had enough," I said, looking pointedly at my best friend.

She stuck her tongue out at me but didn't deny the fact

that after two beers, she was already a little glassy-eyed. Penny was great at a lot of things, holding her liquor, not one of them. Something I admired about her, actually. She didn't use alcohol to solve her problems or to hide. I couldn't always say the same, and I was the one who needed to watch it the most.

Which only made me want to drink more.

Call it rebelliousness or 'me perpetuating the cycle' as one of my therapists told me, I couldn't seem to stop drinking. It wasn't something I had to do, but I enjoyed the freedom it gave me. It was one of the few times I could shut the thoughts off, dull the anxiety, and just be without worrying.

Which I knew was all relative, the alcohol only adding to the issues I had, but it was what I had at the moment, so I went with it.

"Go! Go!" Cooper shouted, cheering on the driver as we skirted around one cart, leaving only one more ahead of us. They were far off, though, and I doubted we could drink that much beer to make a difference.

Smiling, I looked over at Jett, catching him watching me. For a second, I let myself get lost in his eyes, fantasizing about love and happily ever after. He was the first guy I wanted to envision something with beyond one night.

And I didn't know what to do with that. My usual MO was to retreat, and yet, it didn't work with Jett when he constantly pulled me in with the power of his dick.

I had dreams that didn't include being tied down. But maybe, our goals could be combined together?

I typically steered clear of musicians, our need for attention and eccentricities too much for one relationship.

Jett pushed me to be better, though. He didn't hinder or steal the spotlight but made me want to shine even more. Being near him was a drug I greedily inhaled. He didn't just have that charisma on the stage, but everything about him felt bigger and more. He had the 'it' factor, and I knew it was only a matter of time before he hit it big.

"Red, do I even want to ask what is going through your head right now? You seem too quiet. I think you're plotting something."

Snorting, I shook my head. "I'm not the plotter. That's Pen over there. I see something, I do. I'm simple like that."

Jett leaned closer, whispering, "There's nothing simple about you, Poppy. Don't sell yourself short."

My insides heated, my vagina taking notice and ready to party again as my clit began to throb with need. Sucking my lip between my teeth, I watched as his eyes became hooded. This was the danger with us. We were both so hot for one another, it was hard to do anything other than fuck.

Our fire and passion called to the other, exploding into epic bangfests, and I wanted to believe it could move beyond the bedroom. He'd taken care of me that first day, showing me a nurturing side I hadn't thought he'd possess, making me wonder if it could be more.

He fit all the boxes I denied having—passionate, great cock, good with his tongue, and didn't shy away from the scary shit.

But…

There was always that *but.*

Could *I* give my heart to someone? I'd done that once and been epically rejected, so much so, I hadn't even confessed it to Penny, too embarrassed to admit it. Then there was the incident with Huxley at school, the last guy I'd called my boyfriend. After that disaster, I made a vow to never let a guy distract me from my goals and always put myself first.

So there was a but.

But what if our goals aligned, was I letting a guy distract me this time?

But wasn't Jett different?

But hadn't that vow been from a broken-hearted, naive fool?

But could I trust my judgment?

But. But. But.

Was it my own doing in a sense of self-preservation? Or were my fears and buts valid? I didn't know, and that was the part that had me spinning out.

Cheers rang out, and I tossed my hands in the air as we crossed the line. "Wahoo! We did it! 2nd place bitches!"

"That was more fun than I thought it would be," Penny said, beaming at the two guys next to her. Seeing her embrace the things she wanted made me a proud mama, and it encouraged me to do the same.

"Congrats, Ginger Nuts. For completing the race and coming in second, I have your last clue along with a bonus." The driver handed the envelope to Cooper, hopping off his seat as he walked over to one of the other drivers, leaving us on the drink cart.

"Oooh! What does it say?" Penny asked, clasping her hands together happily.

I felt Jett shift against me, pulling his phone out of his pocket. I'd felt it vibrate several times as we pedaled. Now that I thought about it, he'd been avoiding it all night and morning, but it had been going off several times.

I watched as he rechecked it, sighing as he opened it. He looked over, and I noticed some fear and regret in his eyes. It was all I needed to know he was about to hurt me. Locking up my feelings, I shoved them down.

But he was just another guy, like all the others.

In the end, I could never get past the but.

CHAPTER
TWENTY-TWO

PENNY

Stumbling off the pedal bar, Aspen clutched my arm, helping to keep me steady. Smiling, I took his hand as we gathered with our group to read the clue together. Cooper opened the envelope, pulling out two pieces of paper. Unfolding the first clue, he looked up at all of us after he read it.

"You'll probably use me for fights in the summer. If I leak in your house, call the plumber!"

"I have no clue what that means," I mumbled.

"What's the other one say?" Rafé prodded.

Cooper handed the paper to Jett, so he could open the next one. He looked up, an odd expression on his face. "It just says, 'duck.'"

"Duck?"

"Wait!" Poppy shouted, snapping her fingers together. She spun around in a circle, her hair flying out behind her, and pointed to a park across the street. "There's a duck pond there. I read it on the map, and the answer to the other one is water."

The guys looked at her in shock, but I shrugged, used to her random bits of weird info.

"Look at you smarty pants! Let's go."

She stuck her tongue out at me, but I took off, ready to win this thing, my desire to be the best surging forward. Power walking, I hurried myself over to the park and straight toward the pond. A large fountain was in the middle, and that was when I saw them. The guys seemed to piece it together simultaneously, rushing forward to grab the water guns out of the plastic tub that was sitting there.

"Now what?" Coop asked, looking around him.

Almost in answer to his question, a loud chime went off, echoing out the speakers I spotted through the park.

"Welcome LiveIt competitors! If you've made it here, then you're at the last stage of your scavenger/obstacle course. To win this one, you'll need to make it to the other end of the park. Your water guns are filled with a colored liquid. You'll earn points for each contestant you hit who wears your team color, as well as having the least amount of color at the end. Have fun, and remember, if you're not on LiveIt, then you're dead! It's time to get drenched!"

"I really don't like the sound of that," I muttered, looking around.

"When do we start?" Aspen asked right before a loud buzzer rang out causing me to jump.

"Okay, that's just getting creepy!" I shouted, the others laughing at me.

"Come on, Freckles! Let's go." Cooper pulled me along, and I followed, not the best with directions or strategies when it came to things like this.

"It'd be nice if we knew how many teams were here," Aspen commented, looking over his shoulder.

Rafé pulled out his phone, his brows creasing as he typed in a message before shoving it back into his pocket. He scrubbed his hand over his face and exhaled, a breath leaving him before he turned to us. When he saw I was watching, he cringed.

"Sorry, work."

"Everything okay?" I asked.

"My boss isn't happy I'm not answering."

"Dude, life's too short to have a bitchy boss. There's always another job out there."

"Yeah, I guess," Rafé replied, dismissing Cooper, but Coop wasn't one to be ignored. He stopped, turning toward Rafé, a serious look on his face this time.

"No, seriously. Do you like your job?"

"Not really."

"What would you want to do?"

"I don't know. That's the problem. I've always liked too many things that I've never been great at anything."

"That's not true. You're great at making people feel comfortable. Even when I was laying on top of you for an obscene amount of time, you never called me out for it," I teased.

"Well, do you have an opening for a body pillow?" he quipped back, a smile returning to his face.

"Actually, I just might!" Chuckling, I bumped his shoulder.

"That would be great, but I think you'd get bored of me eventually."

Coop pushed me behind a tree, putting his finger to his lips for a second before we heard people rushing by. The part of the park we were in was a maze of trees, providing good cover to hide. When they'd passed, Coop let go and motioned for us to walk. I looked around, realizing the other three were no longer with us.

"What did you want to be when you were a kid?" Cooper asked as he ducked behind trees, rolling around like he was in combat.

Rafé blew out a breath, looking to the sky. "I guess before I understood how jobs worked, I wanted to make movies or at least things that made people feel something. I remember watching them with my grandparents and laughing, or even being moved to tears and the power there was in a good story. But that dream died when I realized how hard it was to make it as a director."

Shrieks of laughter rang out ahead of us, and we stopped to listen. Footsteps sounded from behind, and I looked at the guys in shock. Coop grabbed Rafé and I, pushing us in the direction we needed to go. "Run!"

We took off as he started shooting his water gun behind us. He caught up when he needed to repump, and I handed him mine, taking his.

"Thanks, Freckles."

Nodding, I smiled as I tried to get the water gun ready. Rafé and I ducked down behind a bench as we watched a few other people engaged in a battle ahead of us.

"Oh, look! There's Jemma!"

She heard me, because like a dummy, I hadn't kept my voice low, and she grinned wide, stalking toward us, her gun pointed at me. Falling back on my butt, I crawled as fast as possible until I remembered I could run. Getting up, I took off, laughing as I ducked and wove around trees as I tried to escape Jemma.

Taking a chance, I ducked behind a tree and listened for footsteps. I'd left the guys to their own devices, figuring Jemma was someone I could manage. When I heard a noise, I lifted the gun up, and the moment they stepped around the tree, I pushed the trigger, letting the stream of red water fly.

A grunt sounded as the liquid hit a chest, and I looked up, not realizing I'd closed my eyes. Instead of Jemma, I found Keelan staring at me, a grimace on his face.

"Oops." Taking off running, I laughed as I ran from the quiet giant, hoping he wouldn't kill me in my sleep. Looking back, I checked to see if he was following and collided with a body.

"Oof!" Landing on the grass, I found a smiling Rafé under me.

"Well, like I said, you make a good landing spot." Laughing, I rolled off him, pulling him to sitting.

"I'd be your safe spot all day long if I could, you know." He leaned into me, and my heart swelled. Turning my head, I peered up, my eyelashes fluttering closed as I pressed my lips to his. The kiss was sweet, our lips barely able to open before I was hit with cold liquid. Sputtering, I pulled apart from him and found Keelan and Jemma standing in front of us. Smiling, I shrugged. It was fair play.

"Gotcha!" Jemma sang. "And well done, snatching a couple of men while you're here. I thought I was the only one." She winked, turning to go but stopped. "Though, you're braver than I, knocking boots with a producer. That's so G.O.A.T!" She took Keelan's hand, sauntering off, ready to find her next target, no doubt.

Waving them bye, I smiled, despite not understanding what she meant. Turning to ask Rafé, I watched his face pale as he turned to me, an apology on his lips.

"I was going to tell you."

"Tell her what?" Aspen asked, jogging toward us, out of breath.

"He's apparently a producer. I'm just not sure of what," I answered, pulling away slightly. Aspen lifted his head, confusion on his face as well. Rafé sighed, hanging his head. He took a few deep breaths before he looked up, sincerity shining in his eyes.

"Let's finish this, and I'll tell you everything. All of you," he added, looking over to Aspen.

Nodding, I stood, shaking off the grass. My shirt now had blue on it from Jemma's water gun, and I sighed, hoping it would come out. Anxiety started to rise as I thought about the stain, not wanting to appear disorderly. I could already hear the criticism from my mother.

What did you expect, Penny? You can't keep one man here; why did you think you could keep three?

If you'd tried harder, you'd get more attention.

You're a dirty, poor representation of your sister.

No one will want you when they're around Poppy. You're not doing yourself any favors being friends with her.

I kept trying to wipe the dye off my hands, the blue a representation of all my failures, all my delusions of grandeur, all my catastrophic misgivings. What was I even doing here? I should be home doing everything I could to get my job back. I should be forming a new parent committee for the next school year, organizing the bake sales, and keeping to my crafts. Those were the things I was good at, the things I could manage. This wasn't me. This was just me playing dress-up and trying to be someone I wasn't. It was better I knew that before I fell too far down the hole and lost everything but my dignity.

"Penny!"

Sucking in a breath, I stopped my aimless walking and looked up into Aspen's hazel eyes. Mine tracked his back and forth, searching for something. I kept rubbing my hands, pushing off the stain, hoping if it wasn't there, then no one could see all my sins.

"Penny!" This time when I looked up, I found Poppy standing there, her hands braced on my shoulders. "What happened, Pen?"

"It won't come off, Poppy. I'm a screw up, and I shouldn't be here. I need to go."

"Ssh, come on. I'll help you. Let's go." She pulled me under her arm, and I followed, feeling better now that Poppy was here. Poppy always fixed everything.

I felt water hitting my hands, and I jolted a little, blinking my eyes, and I discovered Poppy smoothing soap over my hands. Looking up into the mirror, I found her watching me. "What happened?"

Shrugging, I hung my head back. I didn't want to admit I'd freaked out and fell into a brief panic episode.

"I think it was my fault," Rafé said, and I turned, spotting him standing in the doorway with a look of remorse on his face. Aspen stood in front of him, his arms crossed, not letting him enter.

I smiled softly, shaking my head. "No, it wasn't. Not really." Looking back at my hands, I found they were no longer blue. Dropping Poppy's, I turned off the water and dried them on the paper towel she handed me. Tossing it into the trash, I pulled her into a hug, needing her comfort for a moment.

"Thanks, PJ."

"Anytime, PB." A watery laugh left me, and I pulled back, wiping my eyes. When I turned fully, I spotted Cooper and Jett also watched me with concern.

Smiling, I raised a shoulder and dropped it. "Sorry, I'm kind of a mess. It's why I try not to drink. It makes it come out more, it seems. But I think we all have some things to discuss?" I asked, looking at Rafé. Clearing my throat, I waited for him to respond.

"Yes, I'd like the chance to explain."

"My reaction wasn't because of you. I just want you to know that. I would like to hear what you have to say, but I don't feel you owe me anything. We've just met, and it's not like you deceived me. It was just shocking to hear it from Jemma, but it doesn't change how I feel."

"Really?" he asked, relief rolling through his body as he sagged against the door.

"Yes. I'd like to hear more about your job if you're up for it, but I'm not mad at you."

"Okay."

"Let's head back to the bungalow then, grab some food, and we can all have a conversation without all the noise around us," Jett suggested, and I found myself smiling at him in relief.

"That sounds perfect."

Cooper held out his hand, and I took it with a smile. My mind had been lying to me in a moment of panic, allowing the doubts to enter, but I didn't have to let them take root. In fact, I wasn't going to. This was my chance to choose differently. If I wanted things in my life to change, to be different, then it started right here at this moment.

Letting out a slow breath, I envisioned shedding my chameleon skin and stepping into the unknown, ready to take on the world—mistakes and all.

CHAPTER
TWENTY-THREE

RAFÉ

Everyone stared at me, their expressions blank as I dropped my baggage on them. I'd been dreading this, knowing it would change everything, but something in me was ready to face the firing squad. It felt as if, for the first time ever, the pain of this truth would be worth it in the end, a cleansing fire, refining my edges.

"So, you were spying on us?" Cooper asked, a hurt look crossing his face.

"No!" I shouted, practically lurching forward as my body attempted to soothe them. "I promise. Meeting Penny and all of you was completely coincidental and natural. Everything has been real and genuine, and I haven't reported anything to the show."

"Then," Cooper stated, looking around at everyone else, "I don't understand the issue here." His face scrunched up; his brow creased.

"Same," Aspen agreed, rubbing his jaw in thought. "I

mean, it's a little weird you never told us your job, even when you had to run off to work, but it wasn't ever a big deal to me. If you hadn't known who we were, we might've not gotten to our jobs yet." He stopped, shrugging his shoulder. "Because, that's all it is, a job. It's not who you are. If you say you haven't lied to us or used anything to get a story, then I have no issue with you. I think you're a cool dude and part of our little group."

I relaxed slightly but looked over at the person who held my heart. It was her reaction I cared the most about. Penny smiled, her face a brilliant ray of sunshine she kept beaming into my life, illuminating all the shadows and making the monsters that lurked there run away.

"If that's what all the hubbub was about, then what happened with you, little gangsta?" Jett asked, staring over at her. He leaned back in a chair, his foot propped up on one, his arm draped over the back of another. It was the epitome of the cool guy pose, and I snickered as I took him in. Years of working on these gigs, I could spot a facade a mile away. I just wasn't sure what his was about yet.

"Oh, that… past stuff," Penny said, dropping her eyes and waving us off. She began to shift uncomfortably, fidgeting as she looked everywhere but at him.

"Bullshit," he began, but when Poppy leveled him with a deadly gaze, he dropped his feet to the floor, sighing. "Listen, I'm not trying to be an asshole, but you've wormed your annoying self into my life, and I care about you. I don't show it much, but I hold on to the people who make it past my barriers for dear life. Just ask these fuckers. They haven't been able to escape me over the years." He smiled at her, his tone soft as he conveyed his message.

Penny blew out a breath, her hair moving slightly

from the force. Poppy squeezed her hand, and not for the first time, I was envious of their bond. I'd never had a friend like that, and I hoped nothing ever came between them. It was rare and special and should be preserved at all costs.

"Before we came here, I broke up with my boyfriend and practically lost my job within twenty-four hours. This trip has been a chance to let go of all the things that held me back my entire life. Some days, I've been able to do that, and others, the weight of my parents' disappointment presses down on me, and I spiral." She shrugged, picking a piece of lint and flicking it. "It might sound pathetic, but I made a personal DIY list to help me not fall into that version of myself," she said, chuckling, "but I don't think I've been great at following it."

Jett stared at her, and I wondered for a second if he liked her too. He seemed to be into Poppy, but I knew how hard Penny's presence was to ignore, so I wouldn't put it past him. Though, as I watched, it wasn't a look of heat that filled his eyes, but one of protectiveness, almost like an older brother.

"What's on the list?" Aspen asked, sitting up in curiosity.

"Oh, well, for starters, stop changing myself to fit others' needs."

"Do you think you've been doing that with us?" Coop asked, motioning to everyone around the circle. We'd all gathered in the guys' bungalow and were spread out between the couches, table, and island. Penny was on the sofa with Poppy on one side and Cooper on the other. He was turned so he could look at her.

Penny thought about it for a second before shaking her

head. "No, I don't think so." She turned her head to Poppy, looking at her. "What do you think?"

"You've been one hundred percent Penelope Anne Baxter." She smiled before a loud chuckle left her. "Oh my God, why hadn't I ever thought of this before! If you'd stayed with Walter, do you know what your last name would've been?"

Penny stared at her for a moment before her mouth hung open, and she covered it, shaking her head violently. "Oh, God! Nope! I must've repressed that. Not to mention, my initials would've been PAP. I would've been a vaginal screening! Probably the only attention my vagina would've gotten in that marriage." The girls burst out laughing, clutching one another as we looked confused.

"Um, care to share? I'm dying to know now what the joke is," Coop asked.

"Yeah, so, Walter's last name… it's Pennington."

We all stayed quiet for a second before we got it, bursting out into laughter with them. When we'd laughed for a while, Aspen wiped his eyes, shaking his head. "No, I don't think I can see you as Penny Pennington. Imagine anyone trying to say your name without laughing the rest of your life. I think you managed to dodge a bullet, and not just because I'm glad you're single."

"Thanks, Asp. I agree."

"So, back to your list," Coop teased, shaking the hand he was holding.

"Oh, yeah," she giggled, "well, the next was to figure out what set my soul on fire, which I still haven't. The third was to do something purely for myself, which, I think I've definitely done." She blushed, hiding her face for a moment while she smiled. Clearing her throat, she began again. "Don't laugh, P, but another one was to remind myself that it's okay to lose and to try something I suck at."

Poppy didn't even make it two seconds before she had one booming out of her. "Well, I think you did that with the dance-a-thon. You sucked so hard at that one."

"Thanks," Penny said, pushing Poppy's shoulder in protest. "Next was to say no every once in a while. I don't think I've had to say no to anything yet," she mused before moving on. "And the last two were to quit apologizing for things, and that it's okay to ask for help. I think I've done those two fairly well, so all in all, I guess I've done better with my list than I thought." She sat back, a satisfied smirk on her face.

"You know what this means then?" I asked. Penny looked at me, shaking her head. "We can help each other figure out what, how did you say it, 'something that sets our souls on fire'? Yeah, that. I think meeting all of you was the push I needed to quit doing a job I hate. I guess it's time I adopted some of the items from your list myself."

"I like that. Figuring it out together doesn't sound as scary either."

"This calls for a celebration. Do we have any activities tonight?" Aspen asked.

"No," I offered, knowing the schedule. "There's a gathering to go over the scavenger hunt, so I guess if you want to go to that."

"I'm guessing we didn't win with my freak out?" she asked, biting her lip.

"I'm pretty sure Jemma's team won this one, but we were technically disqualified," Coop admitted. "Someone reported we had six players." His eyes glanced over to me, and I cringed, not having thought of that. "Though, you were the only one to hit Keelan, so props to you," he said to Penny.

We all laughed as she retold how she accidentally sprayed him, thinking he was Jemma. I spent the rest of the night ignoring my phone and getting to know Ginger Nuts with no barriers. I found myself relaxing into the group, the fear of being hurt and abandoned leaving me with each minute. They even all helped me create a list of possible things I could do instead once the show ended. Some of them were creative alternatives I never would've considered. It was amazing how opening your eyes, stepping outside yourself, and allowing others into your bubble could change the course of your life so drastically.

But I guess when things were meant to be, you just had to be brave enough to grab hold of them and take what you wanted.

CHAPTER
TWENTY-FOUR

COOPER

"You have one hour to complete your mission. You may now begin."

The bell rang, signaling it was go-time, and Ginger Nuts jumped toward the workbench. Aspen dove for the instructions first, and the rest of us looked over the items spread out. The beach was set up with several workstations under tents, and each group had its own area. Based on the items splayed out, I had a feeling this was going to be oriented toward Penny's skill set. I was looking forward to seeing her in action.

"Guys, come here," Aspen said, motioning us over. We huddled together as we read over the details, and Penny became more animated by the second with each word uncovered.

"Oh, this is going to be great. I can't wait," Penny said, clapping her hands. I smiled at her, lifting my eyes from the paper. She was so cute when she was excited. Since the paintball incident, I'd noticed how freer she'd been. Penny wasn't worried about impressing others or doing the wrong thing as much. She'd taken her list to heart and was running with it.

"So, it sounds like we need to create a scene using the items provided to showcase our time here."

"It's like they took sandcastles and gingerbread houses and shoved them together," Poppy said, snorting.

"But it will be fun! What do we think our theme should be?" Penny asked, organizing the materials. She had sand, popsicle sticks, shells, and bits of a palm leaf on one side. Glue, tape, paper, and string to another, with glitter, tiny accessories, and random odds and ends to the front.

"What are your sections?" I asked, moving closer. I leaned into her, enjoying the feel of her body against mine. She smelled of coconuts today, and I knew she'd put on more sunscreen since we'd be out on the beach. I didn't mind it, though, the smell quickly becoming associated with her.

"Binding, decorating, and foundation," she said, pointing at the three.

"Smart." I bumped her hip, and she looked up, smiling. Leaning down, I captured her lips in a brief kiss, careful to remember there were cameras everywhere.

"Okay, so, what do we think our theme should focus on?" Aspen asked, pulling us back toward him. He'd said it to all of us, but based on his attention to Penny, it was clear he meant it mostly for her. I think we all knew this was her strong suit and needed to leave it up to her to decide for us.

"I was thinking we could do a fairy garden," she said, not missing a beat. "They're small, and it's more unique than a house that I feel the others will do. We can add all the things that have meant something to us this trip. Does it say we can only use these items?" she asked, knowing Aspen would've memorized rules by this point.

He shook his head. "Just that it has to be things you naturally find. You can't go and buy anything, but if you find a different shell, or have something on your person, then it's fair game."

"Perfect. Okay, here are my thoughts." Penny pulled us close, going over what she needed, sending people to retrieve a few things that weren't given to us. When she turned to me, I was eager to hear my task.

"Yes, sunshine?" I asked.

"Can you see if you can find one of those pineapple drinks you had the first day?" She bit her lip as she waited, and I had to focus on not ravaging her.

"I thought you said I couldn't buy something?" I remembered when the lust cleared a little.

"I did. I said, 'find.'" Her fingers came up to do air quotes. "If you find one discarded, it's free game." She shrugged, a blush coming to her cheeks.

"On it!" I kissed her cheek, skipping off to find a pineapple. If it meant that much to her, our first encounter, I'd have one tattooed on me just so I could see that blush every time she looked at it.

It only took me a few minutes to find the bar where I'd gotten the drink. Unfortunately, I didn't find any pineapple drinks, and I didn't fancy digging through the trash.

"Think, Coop, think." Spinning in circles, I spotted the bar where the garnishes were. The cup of umbrellas and fruit were a beacon, pulling me to them.

"What can I get you?" the bartender asked, spotting me leaning against the counter.

"I was wondering if the umbrella and fruit were free?"

"Um, yeah, I suppose so." He eyed me strangely, but I didn't feel like explaining myself to him, so I grabbed a cup and picked one of each, and then added five umbrellas.

"Thanks!" I smiled wide, not caring if I looked like an idiot.

"Yeah, sure." He dismissed me, going back to his paying customers, and I hightailed it back to the contest area.

"So, bad news, no discarded pineapples at 11 a.m., but good news, I improvised." I presented the cup with a flourish, Penny's eyes beaming as she took it in.

"It's perfect, Coop." She took the cup, setting it next to an ice cream cone, a guitar pick, and a tiny little jump rope. Picking it up, I turned to her.

"Did you make this?" I asked, turning it over in my hand.

"Uh, yeah. It's just a bit of rope and glue. It's nothing." She shrugged, turning back to the table. I didn't miss her cheeks tinting again, and the warmth of knowing she cared about me filled me.

"It's something to me."

She glanced over, a retort on her tongue, but when she saw my face, she stopped. "Thank you." I watched as Penny swallowed, working through something. "I'm so used to dismissing what I do that it's hard to stop. But yes, thank you. I need to learn to accept compliments, especially when they're from people I know who care and aren't just saying it to win favor."

Pulling her close, I nuzzled her neck, whispering in her ear. "I plan to compliment you every day from here on out. I want you to wake up each morning excited to hear what I'll say, accepting it as truth." I heard her sharp inhale, but I didn't pull back until I kissed the space below her ear. Penny took a few minutes to orient herself, but once she did, she laser-focused on her task.

"Okay, gang! Let's do it." She handed out the orders, and everyone began to work on things. Aspen focused on the foundation, Poppy and Jett worked on the binding, and Penny and I worked on setting up the space. We were making good progress when the announcer came on.

"This is your thirty-minute warning."

"Is that enough?" I asked, watching as Penny tensed. Everyone looked up, waiting for her direction. I loved that she was getting to take charge, and we all were following her lead.

"Yeah, I think so. We just need to get this area completed." She pointed to a section that hadn't been developed yet, and I switched what I was doing to help her. Together, our team worked diligently to put all the pieces of our time on this island. With only seconds to spare, we stepped back, eyeing our creation.

"Whoa, it looks so cool," Poppy cheered, hugging Penny. "You did it, girl!"

The diorama consisted of a beach, volleyball net, and pool with a swim-up bar. In the sand were toothpick people with fruit heads with items on beach towels that represented us all. There was a guitar pick for Aspen, and the jump rope for me. Penny's had an ice cream cone hat, and Poppy's was a tiny microphone made out of foil. The best, though, was Jett's. I laughed, waiting to see if he noticed. He squinted, leaning forward.

"Is that a Hershey kiss on my head?"

Penny nodded, laughing. She covered her mouth, mumbling her words, "Sorry, I thought it was funny. You're sweet now, I guess."

Jett rolled his eyes but smiled, knocking her shoulder. "It's kind of funny, little gangsta. I was a shithead at first." We all laughed, enjoying the moment as our team bonded. Poppy took a picture of us all and then our design, streaming it for the app.

"Please bring your carts over to the judging station," the voice bellowed, and we jumped, pushing our carts to get in line. Thankfully, we weren't the last ones. I positioned ours under our team's name, backing away carefully. Stepping back, a shout had me looking up.

"Look out!"

Somehow, I managed to dive for the sand, missing the cart that was headed toward me. Spitting out the grainy substance, I looked around to see if the cart had hit anyone. Penny ran to me, helping me dust off the sand. "Are you okay?" she asked, looking me over critically. Aspen kneeled beside her, looking me over as well.

"Yeah, I'm fine." I stood up, dusting off more sand when I realized where the cart would've hit because it missed me.

"I'm scared to turn around," I admitted, looking at their faces.

"It doesn't matter," Penny said, brushing off sand. Her hands were getting close to my nether regions, and I grasped them, not wanting to hide a boner in front of all these people.

"I'm good, sunshine. I appreciate your help, but if you keep checking me over, we're gonna have a different situation on our hands."

"Oh, sorry, I was just worried you'd hurt yourself and then wouldn't be able to jump rope anymore."

"I'm okay. Promise." I looked over at Aspen, and he relaxed at my words too. "So, our entry?"

"Ruined," Jett sighed, walking over to us. "Red is going off on the team whose cart ran into ours. She's saying it was on purpose. It's the team right behind us."

"It doesn't matter," Penny said, grabbing mine and Aspen's hands. "I'm just glad we're okay. Can we just leave? I don't want to be here anymore."

I looked over her head at my brother, and he had a worried expression on his face as well.

"Absolutely, Penny. Maybe we could stop by the ice cream place and try some more flavors?"

"Yeah, sure." Her voice was flat, but she let us lead her there. Poppy and Jett stayed back to deal with the competition. Pulling out my phone, I hoped Rafé would be able to get away.

ME: Emergency. Ice cream bar.

It didn't take him long to respond, and I sighed in relief when his reply came through.

Rafé: I saw. Already on my way.

Silently, we walked through the bar, and we watched as she carefully added flavors to her bowl. It looked like a candy mixture, and I wondered if today's flavor was just comfort. By the time we got to the checkout, Rafé walked in and headed for us.

"They're going to use the video footage as your entry since yours was destroyed before the judges could see it."

"Okay," she mumbled, taking a bite.

"What's wrong, Penny? What can we do?" Aspen asked, his need to fix it riding him hard. I was surprised he'd lasted this long.

"It's fine."

"Penny." I turned her head toward me, taking her head between my hands. "Someone once told me that fine is just the cowardly way of saying you needed help. You're not a coward. So, tell us what's going through that beautiful mind of yours."

She bit her lip, her eyes searching mine before she closed them, exhaling. "I'm just used to things I work on getting destroyed, so I'm not surprised. That's all."

"Hey, I think you need to add something new to the list."

"What?" she asked, opening her eyes.

"Yeah," Aspen agreed, capturing her attention.

"Mmhmm," Rafé said too.

"I don't know if I like you three ganging up on me."

Smiling, I tucked a strand of her red hair behind her ear. "Too bad, sweet cheeks. You're stuck with us now. I speak for the three of us when I say that you need to add 'believing in the good.' Don't count out the good just because something happened. It doesn't make everything else we've done lose its value. At the end of the day, this is just a two-week competition. But the important thing is that we all met and found one another."

"You're right. I'm sorry. I just worked so hard, and then

to see it fall to pieces, it made me feel like everything I touch is tainted."

"Well, that's not true. We're all still here, and you've touched us in lots of places," I teased.

Penny's face reddened, and I smiled wider, looking over at the other guys. "How about we make this ice cream to go and head back to the bungalow? I think we could use a chill night."

"You read my mind, brother!"

"I have to head back to work, but I'll drop by later if that's okay?" Rafé asked, looking at Penny.

"Of course. I'm sorry you got pulled away for my stupid stuff."

"Nonsense. I wanted to be here. You're what's important to me. Don't forget that." He leaned in and kissed her briefly, tearing himself away to head out the doors.

Arm in arm, Penny walked back to our hut, a smile on her face, and I knew that this could work. The four of us together were a team, and it was one I wanted to be part of.

CHAPTER
TWENTY-FIVE

PENNY

Laughing, I laid my head on Aspen's shoulder, and he pulled me closer to him. Cooper regaled us with stories of their misspent youth while he painted my toenails. Every so often, he'd stop, give me a look, and threaten to paint my whole foot if I didn't stop moving.

"Stop being so funny, then!" I said, blowing him a kiss.

"I didn't choose the funny life; the funny life chose me, sweet cheeks." He lifted his head, winking. "Good thing I'm almost done then, huh?"

"Coop, tell her about the time we forked Old Mr. Winter's place."

"What does that even mean?" I asked, looking around with a laugh.

"Oh, it was classic. So, we took a box of plastic forks and then stuck them all in his yard. It's like the most ridiculous and least invasive prank. Not a mess to pick up like toilet paper or shaving cream, but funny to wake up and see hundreds of tiny forks sticking out of your lawn."

Trying to hold in my chuckle, I tilted my head into Aspen more, hoping the muffling would help control the movement. A hand grabbed my foot, shaking it, and I peeked back out.

"There! Perfection even if you're the worst staying-still-person there ever was."

"I don't think that's a thing." I smiled, biting my lip to hold in another laugh. Earlier, I'd thought my life was falling back into a pattern where I tried hard, failed, and then would spiral into a place where it felt like nothing mattered because I wasn't good enough to begin with. Somehow, three guys I'd just met managed to show me it didn't matter.

Cooper, Aspen, and Rafé were changing my life, and they didn't even know how much.

"You know, I don't think I've said thank you for making me not dwell on what happened."

"No need, Penelope." Aspen kissed my nose and stood, and I realized he heard the door before us and was going to open it.

"He's right, Pen-Pen."

"Are you going to call me everything under the sun?"

"Yep." He leaned forward, kissing my nose. "Until I find one that sticks."

"Surprisingly, I'm okay with this game."

"Look who I found," Aspen chirped, walking back in.

Rafé stood behind him, a few bags held in his hands. "Hey, guys! I figured I'd bring food to us tonight."

"You're officially my favorite person," Coop said, hopping up to see what all he brought.

I turned, leaning on the back of the couch as I watched the three of them sort through the bags. When I realized I was the one sighing happily, I pinched myself just to make sure I wasn't dreaming.

"Ouch." Laughing, I stood up and walked over to them, joining them in uncovering the lids of the food items.

"I brought a little of everything."

When I looked around at the items, I knew he wasn't kidding. Spaghetti, burgers, steak, pasta, and tacos spilled over the table, along with several side items.

"Wow, this all looks yummy." My stomach growled, and I chuckled, patting it. "My stomach agrees." Rafé handed me a plate, kissing my cheek as he walked over to the bar to grab utensils. Once we had our plates full, we opted to dine outside on the deck. It was a lovely night with the breeze off the water an excellent relief from the heat. The sun was also beginning to set, giving us the perfect backdrop to our dinner.

"This is the best," I said, sighing as I took a bite.

"Who knew she liked macaroni and cheese so much," Aspen joked.

"Ha, ha! Yes, this is good, but I meant eating out here with all of you. It's nice just getting to spend time without the competition and away from everyone else."

"Agreed. I can't believe our time is almost over," Coop said, his voice going softer at the end.

"Yeah. I don't want to think about it ending yet. Let's just focus on right now."

The others nodded, but I could see it was on everyone's mind, so I decided to change the subject. "We should watch a movie after this or go night swimming." I waggled my eyebrows, hoping to convey my true intentions.

Rafé cleared his throat, looking between the three of us. But it was Cooper who spoke up.

"Actually, I need to call my trainer and go over some scheduling things, and Aspen needs to practice his guitar." He elbowed his brother, who nodded, clutching his stomach.

"Yup, sure do. In fact, we should probably head out now."

"Yeah, good call. I don't want to keep Jeremy waiting. He gets feisty when he's impatient."

I blinked, not understanding what was happening. They both kissed me on the cheek, taking containers with them as they hurried out of my hut.

"Um, what just happened?" I asked, looking at the last person left.

"They just said." Rafé blinked, looking at me like I hadn't witnessed the last few seconds.

"Um, yes, I heard them, but why did they do that. Felt a little out of the blue."

"I don't know what you mean, but I guess it's just us tonight." His face tinged red, and I realized what was happening finally as the light bulb flicked on.

"Oh." I smiled and willed my cheeks to not turn red. It was a losing battle. "That, um, sounds perfect."

His shoulders relaxed, and I realized that Rafé must've felt out of the loop at times with all of us being around one another more. Getting up, I walked over and pushed his chair back some so I could sit in his lap.

"Hi."

"Hey, Pen."

"I'm glad you're here. I miss you throughout the day when you're working."

"You do?" he asked.

"Yeah." Cupping his jaw, I pulled his face down, bringing his lips to mine. "I do."

The kiss started off slow, but soon we were battling one another as his tongue twirled with mine. Rafé's hands moved up my legs, gripping my thighs. Running my fingers through his hair, we made out as the sun set, nothing but the ocean and sounds of the night around us.

"God, I love kissing you," he said, breaking for air as he trailed his lips over my neck, sucking in small bouts.

"Yeah? You're really great at it." My voice came out raspy, and I knew I needed more. Twisting my body around, I straddled him, bringing my center in direct contact with his. I knew what I wanted to do, and we'd gotten close a couple of times, but Rafé had always seemed to hold himself back. Holding his head between my hands, I peered deep into his eyes, searching for the answer.

"I don't want to push you further than you're ready, but if you were waiting on a green light from me, then I'm ready. I'm one hundred percent on board with taking our relationship to the next level."

He chuckled, and he smoothed some of my hair down. "I want that. Before, I couldn't let myself go there with you until you knew the truth about who I was. Now that you know, nothing is holding me back."

Rafé planted a kiss on my lips and stood at the same time. Wrapping my arms and legs around him, I held on for dear life, trusting he had me. He managed to make it inside and I pointed toward my room, figuring that was his destination.

He laid me down on the bed, and we both stopped for a second to remove our clothes, no longer wanting them in between us. It was challenging to focus on getting my own off when he distracted me. Bronze skin, delectable muscles, and a V stared at me. Licking my lips, I found myself nodding as I leaned up on my knees, pulling the last of my clothes off me.

"Fuck, you're beautiful," Rafé said, pulling my attention up to his face. The heat in his eyes could've started an inferno. Sucking in a breath, I reached out for him, pulling him with me as I fell back to the bed.

"I want you so fucking much," I whispered against his lips.

Our bodies started to move, needing the friction as much as we did. I felt him reach over, grabbing the condom and rolling it on in quick succession. Lifting my leg, he positioned himself at my center, looked up to meet my eyes, and then thrust in. My back arched off the bed, a gasp leaving me as I felt his fullness.

"God, yes," I moaned. Reaching up, I pulled him down closer, wanting to feel his body against mine. Slowly, he began to move, wrapping his arms around me as he pushed in more. The movements were small, but with each hip roll, I felt him deeper than I'd ever felt anyone before.

Rolling to the side, he hooked his arm under my knee, wrenching it up to his and providing him more leverage. Reaching down, I clasped his butt cheeks, wanting to push him farther in. Together, we rolled, and I found myself on top.

"Oh, hello," I teased. "My turn."

He placed his hands behind his head, smiling up at me. Rolling my hips forward, I braced down on his chest as I found my rhythm. Using my position, I picked up the pace, my clit hitting his pelvis with each thrust forward. One hand reached up to grab my breast, tweaking my nipple as I rode his dick. His other hand moved to my clit, rubbing my button, perfectly synchronizing with my movements.

"Shit, you're good at that," I wheezed, my breaths coming out uneven.

"You look like a Goddess riding me. I think this is my new favorite thing."

His words were endearing and made me feel powerful, pushing me to ride him harder as I rocked. Leaning back, I braced my hands on his thighs, hitting a new angle.

"Oh yes, oh fuck." Thrusting forward, I found my release as I orgasmed all over his hard cock. The muscles tightened in my thighs, convulsing as my walls hugged him.

"Shit. That felt good," he said huskily.

"Your turn, stud." Winking, I rolled us over, letting him lead this time. Smoothing his hand over my face, he peered down with utter adoration.

"I'm so glad I met you. You've changed my life, Penny." Pressing his lips to mine, he kissed me like it was the secret to everything, not letting go as his thrusts quickened, and I found myself holding onto him with everything I had. Sensations coursed through me, and I knew I was close again. When I felt him quickly thrust forward, I arched up, hitting a spot I thought was a myth. As he stilled in me, twitching as he came, I fell apart around him.

Pulling back, we both panted as we attempted to catch our breaths. "I don't know if I'm an idiot for waiting so long or a genius because it made it better waiting."

"Definitely a genius." Giggling, I kissed his nose.

Together, we cleaned up, took a quick shower, and then snuggled over the covers with dessert and a feel-good movie.

Each time his phone buzzed, I felt him growing tenser, and I worried his job would eventually come between us. I didn't want to be the reason he got fired.

"If you need to go back to work, I'm okay," I finally said after the tenth time he'd ignored the caller.

"No. I'm here with you. That can all wait. I promise."

"I just feel like you're sacrificing a lot to be with me."

"I'm sacrificing nothing, Pen." His eyes held mine, and I knew he was being sincere.

Kissing him softly, I curled back in his arms, the final piece of what I'd needed holding me tight.

CHAPTER
TWENTY-SIX

RAFÉ

Waking up this morning, I felt excited about my day and the prospects in front of me. I just needed to quit my job first and find a way to tell my mom. I wanted to finish this show, feeling the need to follow through and not let others down. It was probably something to work more on later, but currently, I was still me, and I couldn't change my whole personality overnight.

Though, Georgina was testing that commitment.

She had me running all over the place, sending me numerous messages and requests to keep me busy after not reaching me last night. It almost seemed like she was on to my feelings of wanting to quit, or perhaps she had a radar for when others got happy, and she stepped in to ruin it. At this point, it wouldn't surprise me. Georgina seemed to only be satisfied when she was ruining other people's lives.

As I stared down at the last message she'd sent, bile

rose to the surface as I blinked, wishing it would disappear. I couldn't do it. I'd finally hit my limit. The imaginary line I'd been moving back inch by inch over the past few years had finally stopped. I guess I could let go of my fear of disappointing some people when it meant devastating another.

And I wouldn't do this.

I wouldn't ruin Penny's life or make a spectacle out of her or the other guys. I guess I had morals after all. Though a voice whispered, "would you care if it was anyone else?" I'd like to think I would. No one should be used this way. No one.

And yet, wasn't that what I'd done daily for the past five years?

The phone in my hand rang, and I jumped, almost dropping it in the process as I debated on not answering. Her internal radar had finally gone off, my wavering sending her to amp up the forceful persuasion.

"I'm not doing it," I said in lieu of a greeting.

"Tiff, tiff, Rafé. I think the correct response is, 'why yes, Georgina, I'll be right on that.' None of this can't, Rafé. It's unbecoming."

Rolling my eyes, I dropped my head back, staring at the ceiling as I pondered how to deal with this. Scraping my hand down my face, I knew what I wanted to do; the question was if I could.

"… And that is why you'll set this into motion and reveal it. There's a huge story here, Rafé! Think of the ratings!"

"Don't you think there's more to life than ratings, Georgina? What about integrity? Respect? Being able to sleep at night?"

"Pfft. Those things exist for poor people to hold on to. I'd much rather follow power, build prestige, and have more money than I know what to do with. And I sleep very well at night on my 1000 thread count sheets, thank you very much. This is the life, Rafé! You do this story, and you'll be able to do whatever you want from here. I know you've thought about directing before or even writing your own show. This will open all the doors. LiveIt hired us to produce this for them and make it successful, and the network wants to go all out for this. It will be huge! Your name will be plastered everywhere! Think about how this will help your family."

And there it was.

The ace of spades she used whenever she felt me wavering. Georgina knew of my father's condition and how I was the primary source of income for them. In the past, it had been enough to keep me in line, but it wasn't anymore. I'd find another way, one where I didn't sell my soul each day to do a job.

Penny had shown me what it felt like to hope. Even in the short time I'd known her, I'd felt more alive, more like myself, than I had in years. So much so, I'd forgotten who that person was, the one who'd started out in Hollywood with a dream. Even "Casper" had made me realize how much I'd missed having friends. In show business, there was no such thing as friends. You were either a source to use or competition.

I had to trust my family would want me to be happy as well. Success had been ingrained in me, but so had family.

"I am," I said, my voice strong for once.

Georgina scoffed, and I could practically hear her eyes

roll. "If you've decided to grow a conscience now, don't forget that I own you."

"I don't care. There's nothing you can do to me that hasn't already been done. Don't you get it, Georgina? I'm done. I'm so done."

She laughed, and I braced myself as I prepared for the backlash. "Fine. But don't say I didn't warn you. Now that you're not an employee, you're fair game."

She hung up, and a cold fear filled me, but I'd meant what I said—I didn't care. A life lived in fear wasn't a life lived.

I wanted to start living; I needed it, actually. And it began with Penny.

After packing up my belongings, I wasn't surprised to find one of the other producers waiting for me. I'd expected it, and why I'd gone to grab my things first before they had the chance to go through them or toss any of my stuff out. I'd conveniently hidden the image she'd sent, hoping to buy some time. I knew it wasn't a permanent solution, but hopefully, at least a way to buy time to figure out a solution. I was taking a page out of Penny's book and using her list—asking for help.

"You finally did it?" my ex-coworker asked, a shocked expression on his face.

"Yeah, I did."

"Good on you."

"Thanks, man."

He nodded, and I continued on my way. The contestants had a 'capture the flag' type game today, and I hoped I could find Ginger Nuts. I'd taken a brief look at the cameras but hadn't seen them, so I was going to have to take the chance of where I thought they'd be and hope it paid off. But first, I had to make a phone call.

"Hello, Mamá."

"Mijo! How are you?"

"I'm good, really good, actually, but there are some things I need to tell you. Are you sitting down?"

"Yes. Is everything okay?"

"Yeah, I think it's going to be, but there will be some changes."

Coming clean to my mother about everything was the best medicine. After she spent fifteen minutes cursing me in Spanish about how she and Papi had worked hard so we'd have better lives, and that didn't mean working jobs we hated. Then she spent ten minutes crying and saying how sorry she was to place the burden on me and that had never been her intention. Once I admitted I just wanted to make her proud, she told me she already was, always had been.

"Mijo, can I ask what has brought about this change? What is responsible for allowing my son to be open and honest with me?"

Blowing out a breath, I smiled. "Ah, well, a culmination of things. After Rebecca left me at the altar, I dove into work, thinking it was the answer, but the only good thing my job did was provide for Papi and lead me here, where I met someone who changed my perspective on what life was meant to be like."

"Would this someone happen to be of the female variety?"

"Um, pardon?" I blushed, rubbing the back of my head.

"No lying to your mother, Mijo! You see what that caused?" she joked.

"You're right, Mamá. And yes, the someone does happen to be a girl."

Another twenty minutes later, I finally got my mother off the phone after filling her in about Penny and promising to visit soon. It'd felt nice, to be honest, to clear the air. She promised they'd be fine and had been putting most of what I'd sent into savings. Apparently, one of my pregnant sisters had been taking courses online and had a knack for investing, and my parents had been fine for a while now. Mamá hadn't wanted to appear ungrateful, putting what I sent aside for future grandchildren or in case of an emergency. It seemed we'd both avoided talking about it and only made the issue worse in the process.

Pocketing my phone, I felt like a different man, and almost like 100 pounds had been lifted off me over the past two days. With a gleeful jaunt in my step, I set off, excited to find the people who'd helped me see life could be different.

CHAPTER
TWENTY-SEVEN

PENNY

Heavy breathing sounded around me, and not in a fun way. I was out of shape, but at least Aspen and Poppy seemed to be as bad off. The three of us had run on the beach, the sand not helping our ability. Detouring by the pool, we hunkered down behind some lounge chairs, a few palm trees over our heads for a break.

"Shit," Poppy wheezed, "I'm so… out of… breath."

"Same." I didn't try for more. I knew if I did, I'd either vomit or pass out from lack of oxygen. Sweat pebbled on my skin, and my face throbbed in rhythm with my heart, undoubtedly a deep red shade. My shoulders were a bit tender, too, and I knew I needed to apply more sunscreen. After about five minutes, we all seemed to have caught our breath, and Poppy sat up from her lounged position, kicking my leg.

"Hmm?"

"You're pinking. Need more sunscreen."

I looked at my arms, even though I'd already come to the same conclusion. It was one of those inevitable things, like when someone said not to look, you couldn't help but to still look.

"Yeah, I know. We can head back to the hut and grab it. Surely, Cooper's either captured someone else's flag, or Jett's lost ours."

"I've never wished for Jett to lose at something so hard," Aspen said, laughing.

Nodding, I crouched down to peek around the chairs to see if the coast was clear. When I looked back over my shoulder, I found Aspen staring at my ass while Poppy snickered into her hand.

"What? Did I sit on something?"

"Um, no," Aspen said, lifting his eyes to mine. "It's just that, are those llamas on your underwear?"

I peered back more, again, not knowing why since I knew what was on my underwear. Still, I played it off like I was just discovering it. "Huh, I guess so. I wondered if these shorts were see-through, and now, I know." I shrugged, standing and brushing my hands off.

Poppy was used to me not caring about things other people worried about and just held out her hand for me to pull her up. Aspen looked befuddled as he stood, a crease between his brows. "Are you not embarrassed or worried others will stare?"

"No," I snorted. Poppy locked her arm through mine, and we began our walk back, avoiding the sun as much as possible. Aspen still looked confused when I glanced over at him. Taking pity on him, I reached out with my free hand, taking hold of his hand. "Things like that don't bother me. I'm weird, okay?"

"No, you're not. I mean, okay, maybe a little, but not in a bad way." Laughing, I squeezed his hand, not even put out by that description.

"When Poppy and I were younger, her parents always made her go to a camp each summer, and of course, she had to drag me along. Well, for a while there, Poppy wanted to be an actress, imagine that!" Aspen smiled while Poppy just listened, her head on my shoulder, lost in her thoughts. "Well, I sucked at acting, but what the camp did teach me was not to be embarrassed. I guess I grew a tolerance to it, and it's helped me do things I'd normally avoid. Things that do embarrass me?" I huffed, smiling as I squeezed his hand. "Making a fool of myself in front of a cute guy after arguing I was right, and I guess sending out my secret shame to the entire school, including my kids' parents. That was pretty mortifying."

"I actually get that. It's how I'm able to sing in front of others. For the most part, I don't care what they think, it's only when it calls into question my ability to write songs that I get embarrassed singing. I'm guessing it's kind of like that?"

Thinking it over, I nodded. "Yeah, I guess that does explain it. My underwear? Not going to worry about it because who cares? They're cute! If they're looking at my ass, then that's their problem. Looking like a drunk fool in front of my student's parents? Now, that's a bit cringy. But after some separation, I'm not as embarrassed about it as I was. I think it was more about the worry they'd think of me differently and question whether I could do my job."

"With Penny, it's more about competency. She's not afraid to make a fool of herself, and most days she's the first one to laugh. But tell her she's dumb, and she'll stay up all night working on something to prove you wrong."

"Yeah, that's bad, isn't it? I should probably work on not needing the approval of others so much when it comes to stuff like that."

Aspen knocked my shoulder, gaining my attention. "We've all got things to work on, babe. Besides, it just means you're not perfect. I kind of like that."

Smiling like a loon, I let go of his hand when we neared our hut and opened the door. It was silent inside our place, and I made my way to the counter where I'd left the extra bottle of sunscreen. I was surprised to find Jett on our deck, pacing as he talked on the phone. Picking up the sunscreen, I walked over to tell him we were here when I heard part of his conversation come through the open door.

"Yeah, I'm looking forward to meeting you too. It may sound weird, but I feel like I've been waiting my whole life to meet you."

I stopped in my tracks, not sure what I'd just heard. I looked over my shoulder, hoping Poppy hadn't overheard it, but the pained look on her face told me she had. She turned, walking out, and I followed. Aspen had waited outside for us, the plan to head back to their place once we had the sunscreen. I wasn't sure what Jett was doing here.

He looked up from his phone when he saw us. "Good news, Coop stole your roommate's flag, so we can head back now."

"Awesome." I might have said it overly cheery, my smile trying to erupt off my face to smooth over the weirdness. Had Jett been talking to another woman? It sure sounded like it. Poppy already had her shields up, her sunglasses in place as she crossed her arms.

"Wonderful. You know what, I think I'm going to see what Jemma's up to for a while. You guys have a good afternoon. Maybe I'll see you later?"

She'd already started in the other direction, but I nodded, letting her go. I knew Poppy needed time to deal with it before she'd want to talk or wallow. Aspen gave me a look of concern for her, but I waved him off, grabbing his hand. Before we made it all the way back, Cooper intercepted us. He was bouncing all around, excited about his victory. He gave us a very animated play-by-play when Rafé jogged down the dock, catching us.

"Guys, there you are. I've been looking for you."

"What's up?"

"Good news? I quit my job. Bad news? They have pictures of the three of you… naked."

Cold dread filled me, the panic wanting to rise. If the show leaked that, I would definitely lose my job. The school's ears must've been burning because my phone started to ring with a video call from my principal.

"Fuck!" With shaky hands, I jogged the rest of the way but stopped when I couldn't open the door. "Can someone open this, please! It's my boss."

Cooper rushed forward, unlocking the door, and I rushed in, looking around for a perfect place to take the call. When it rang again, I jumped and sat down in the first seat I came to. Holding the phone up, I smiled in an attempt to remain calm, my future on the line. The principal's face filled the screen, and he moved back to show a conference room full of people. I recognized some parents, other teachers, and members of the school board gathered around the table.

"Ms. Baxter, I'm glad we were able to get a hold of you. When we hadn't heard back from you via email, we worried something had happened," he said. I didn't buy it for a minute, though. He was one of those people who made you feel guilty for doing anything other than eat, sleep, teach.

"My apologies, Principal Allen. I'm currently out of the country on vacation and haven't read it yet."

I heard someone mutter, "How important could her job be if she was out of the country?"

I couldn't place who said it, but I wouldn't put it past being Samantha. Most of the faces around the table were smiling, nodding to me when I made eye contact. The principal shuffled, dismissing my comment when he didn't shame me and focused back on what he'd called for.

"Well, there's been a slight change since we last spoke." He cleared his throat, loosening his tie. I noticed how a few people were glaring at him now, and I was curious what had happened. "It seems I was a bit hasty in your dismissal, and as your fellow teachers, along with numerous parents, have told me, they consider you an integral part of our school. Meeting with the school board and several concerned parents, it's been decided to consider your last two days as your consequence served, and fully reinstated for the fall semester."

Shock slammed into me, and I quickly flattened my expression as I formulated a response in my head. "Oh, wow, that's very unexpected. I am, of course, delighted to hear I'm valued at Maple Ridge Elementary."

A noise to my left had me looking up, and I met Cooper's eyes. The champagne color soothed me, encouraging me to take back my job. But I didn't miss the hint of sadness there as well. My words stopped as I looked over at Aspen and Rafé as well. All three guys wore pleased expressions as they smiled at me, but their eyes all conveyed the same thing—disappointment.

Some of the ideas we'd tossed around last night had been about traveling with the band and doing virtual jobs as we went. I guess they'd been more excited about the idea than they'd let on, about the prospect of our relationship continuing beyond these fourteen days.

Focusing back at the room on camera, I looked around at all my coworkers, parents of former students, and the administration. It was right then I realized something significant. When I heard Principal Allen say those words I'd been wanting to hear since I left his office, I hadn't felt relief like I'd believed I would. Instead, I felt dread.

"Ms. Baxter, you were saying?"

Blinking, I focused back on the man, and I knew exactly how to complete the list I'd set out for myself. "Sorry, but I'm afraid I can't accept."

The man sputtered, his face growing purple as he tried to hold in the hatred he wanted to spew at me. I noticed one of the teachers I was friends with nod, giving me a smile of encouragement, and I squared my shoulders, holding the phone up higher as I stared right back at them all.

"I appreciate everyone gathering to support me. It means the world to me to know I impacted your child's life or yours during my stint as a teacher. And while the incident that landed me in this mess is still quite humiliating and something I wished I'd thought through more before it occurred, I can't help but be thankful for the push it gave me. You see, I haven't just been out of the country on vacation. I've been part of a social experiment LiveIt is holding this summer, and while I'm probably not supposed to tell you that, it's been instrumental in changing me. LiveIt's taught me to embrace the quirky, the silly, and to go out and live life to the fullest. I used to think social media was a way for people to just show off, but it's more than that. Yes, there are dangers, but there's also a huge community of people willing to support you if you step out of your comfort zone and ask. I've learned more about myself in the past two weeks than I think I have my whole life. I'm not the same person who left Somerville, and I won't be the same one who returns there when I do."

I looked up, hoping I'd guessed right, and found all three men smiling broadly at me this time, filling me with the courage I needed to continue.

"I think it's time for me to spread my wings, and to do that, I can't return to my job as a teacher at Maple Ridge. So, thank you for the opportunity, but I cannot accept it. I have to say no."

Before the principal could retort back, Mrs. Jeffries smiled wide at me, a proud look on her face. "We hate to see you go, Ms. Baxter. You've been a valued part of our staff, and we will miss you terribly. Please stop by when you're back in town so we can wish you a proper farewell. Good luck."

She clicked off the camera, stopping whatever vitriol

the principal might've said, and I sagged back on the couch, lowering the phone to my lap. A sense of relief, giddy excitement, and a small ounce of terror filled me. The sofa dipped next to me, and someone took my hand, grounding me enough to look over. "Do you really mean it, Pen?" Aspen asked.

"Yeah, I do." I nodded, pushing away the fear. This would be good for me. "I'd like to broaden my horizons and see what else is out there. Plus, I'm not ready to say goodbye to whatever this is. I know it started as something fun, a vacation fling, but I hope I'm not alone in saying it feels bigger than that."

"No!" Cooper shouted, hopping over the couch, landing on my other side. Laughing at his exuberance, I clutched him with my other hand. "I feel it too, Freckles."

"I do as well," Aspen confirmed, pulling my focus back to him. Rafé walked over, crouching down in front of me.

"Same for me, and I'm kind of in the same boat, adrift at sea and trying to figure out which direction to go. I guess the photo isn't as big of a deal now either."

"Wait, give me the details and I'll send it over to our agent. She'll squash it. I don't know about you, but Jett and I definitely signed things stating we get approval on all media releases if it were to put anything about our career in a negative light. It'll be dead before tomorrow. Your boss doesn't have anything," Aspen stated proudly.

"You're right. I forgot about that. Georgina was prob-ably hoping she could leak it before LiveIt realized it and make them pay any fines. I'll let Cynthia know too so she can keep an eye out."

"Cynthia?" the three of us asked.

"Yeah, the woman in charge of everything here." Rafé tilted his head, looking at us all oddly.

"Do you mean, clipboard lady?" I questioned, scrunching my nose as I tried to make the connection.

He huffed a laugh. "Yeah, I guess so."

Smiling, I looped my arms around all of them, bringing them in for a four-person hug. Our heads knocked together some, making us all laugh.

"Sorry, I guess we'll have to get used to figuring out dynamics and how to fit together."

"Speaking of," Cooper began, wagging his eyebrows seductively, but was interrupted when Jett returned. He had the largest smile on his face that I'd ever seen, happiness and hope exuding out of him.

"Guys, I have some news to share." He looked around the room, noticing Poppy wasn't there. "Where's Red? I have to tell you all at once."

"Um, she's probably singing some bad karaoke at the bar."

Jett frowned but shook it off. "Well, okay, let's go grab her. I don't have much time."

We all stood, and I grabbed the bottle of sunscreen, remembering to apply it as we walked back to the resort. Sure enough, when we entered one of the cabanas, Poppy was on stage singing a song—a heartbreaking one about cheaters and being left. She had her eyes closed, her whole body into the music, and every single person in the audience was captivated by her performance.

"Wow. I never realized she could sing like that," Jett whispered in awe. I didn't know what to think about him. He seemed to really like Poppy, and surely he wouldn't be that excited about including her in his news if he was getting together with someone else. But the phone call we'd overheard had made it seem like he was. I hoped whatever he had to share would clear it up.

The song ended, and Poppy opened her eyes. They immediately landed on Jett, and I watched as she first smiled, excited to see him, but then it was like she remembered the pain, and her wall slammed up. When she started off the stage, her gaze zeroed in on someone, and I knew it was going to be bad.

"Oh no." I started forward to stop her, but Jett stopped me, his jaw clenched tight, and he shook his head. Just as her arms wrapped around some guy's neck and her head leaned down to kiss him, he stalked away. Sighing, I looked at the guys, not knowing what to do. Aspen gave my shoulder a squeeze, comforting me that I didn't have to do it all on my own.

"I'll take Jett; you get Poppy."

Nodding, I dragged Cooper with me, feeling the need for some muscle. "Pop," I said when we got closer, but she kept kissing the guy ignoring me.

"Poppy." Still nothing.

"Poppy, I quit my job, and I'm going on tour with the band."

That did it. She yanked her lips off the guy, pushing his face away as she backed away, turning to me.

"You did what?" Her face was a mix of pain and glee, and I wanted to comfort and solve the problem for her.

"I quit. They offered me my position back, but I told them no. I did it, Pop. I said no."

She smiled, inching toward me for a hug when she remembered the other half. Crossing her arms, she stopped. "So, you're going to shack up with some guys you've met after two weeks and tour around with them? That doesn't seem like you."

Her words stung, and I felt my eyes start to tear up at the corners. This was different than before. This wasn't her upset I was trying to help; this was something else, this was personal. Before I could say anything to her, Cooper stepped in.

"Whoa, Poppy, not cool. I don't know what your beef with Jett is right now, but it's not fair to take it out on Penny. You should be proud of her. She stood up to them, and you know what she has with us is more than some fling. Don't degrade our connection because you're upset."

I was stunned, and a little turned on, if I was honest, by Cooper's words. Poppy apparently was just as shocked, her mouth falling open as she regarded him. Snapping it closed, she turned to me, looking me over from head to toe in a way I'd never seen her do before. She dropped her arms, leaning back on the balls of her feet.

"He's right, and I'm sorry. It actually makes what I have to share with you easier, too."

"Oh?" I didn't hug her, yet something still felt off.

"Yeah." Poppy put her hands in her pockets, stepping forward, and I realized she'd iced me out for a second, lumping me with everyone. The realization hurt, but I shoved it away, focusing on the now.

"After I sang my first song, someone from the show approached me and said a label was interested in me. I'm going to leave in a few weeks to record an album. I'm going to get to do it, Pen."

Happiness filled me, and I reached out, hugging her. "Oh my goodness, Pop! That's amazing! I'm so proud of you." Stepping back, I smiled wide, shaking her arms in excitement. "I guess we both are leaving this place changed."

"Yeah, we are. But hey, listen, I'm going to hang out here for a bit. Jemma said she'd stop by, and I just need to sing it out, you know. You guys go back and enjoy your last night here, and I'll meet you at the bungalow in the morning, packed and ready to go!"

"Okay, sure, I guess that works if you're sure you're okay?"

"Totally. I'm perfect. Couldn't be happier, in fact." She smiled wide, but I wasn't buying it, but there wasn't any use in trying to get her to be vulnerable here. I'd have to wait until we were back home.

"Okay, PB&J forever, though. Don't forget me once you become all famous."

"Never." She kissed my cheek before she sauntered back to the stage, telling the sound person what she wanted to sing next.

I leaned into Cooper, and he wrapped his arm around me. We watched her for a few seconds, but when it became clear she meant what she said about singing it out, I pulled him along, back to our place. We found Rafé and Aspen walking toward us before we made it all the way there.

"How's Jett?"

"Well, he's gone; caught an earlier flight. Said he was meeting someone special but didn't want to elaborate. I told him about your plans, and he said he was fine with it, but to be ready in a week because the bus didn't wait for anyone."

"That sounds like Jett."

"Yeah," he agreed, smiling. "So, any luck with Poppy?

What happened between them? They were fine this morning."

"I uh, well, we overheard something, so I'm sure that's what Poppy is dealing with, and she's apparently going to make an album. Someone approached her while she was singing."

"Huh, that's cool. Sucks for us though, I know Jett had pitched her opening for us to our agent."

That surprised me, and the thought of all of us together sounded terrific, but I let it go, knowing it was just a pipe dream.

"Well, regardless, I'm excited. I guess we should start packing and say our goodbyes to people. I know my flight is early in the morning."

"Yeah, same," the brothers agreed.

"Can I crash with someone tonight? I kind of lost my room when I quit my job?" Rafé admitted, laughing.

"Of course, in fact, Jett's room is open now, so you can take it unless we want to do a massive sleepover?" Cooper suggested, giving me his bedroom eyes.

"As fun as that sounds, we'd never make our flights, and I don't know about you, but I'm looking forward to what's next for us."

The guys pouted but eventually agreed, and we spent the evening packing and saying goodbye to the place we'd all come to know and love. It was no surprise that Jemma's team, Aces, won after our disqualification, but second place wasn't too shabby either. I never thought I'd be grateful for an app, but I found myself giving a whispered thanks to LiveIt as we left the resort the following day. As my plane took off, headed back for my hometown, I felt different than I'd imagined I would on the journey here.

When I arrived, I thought I'd lost everything, no longer sure of who I was, what I was going to do, or who I would be. On this island, in the span of two weeks, I found myself and three men who helped me see it was okay not to have it all together. In fact, they showed me I was allowed to want more than stability, and that sometimes, our greatest mistakes were our biggest opportunities.

And I owed it all to my hot pink vibrator.

CHAPTER
TWENTY-EIGHT

POPPY

WE'D BEEN BACK IN SOMERVILLE FOR TWO WEEKS, AND MY mood had done nothing but grow crabbier by the day. I'd attempted to hold it together for Penny, but I was a raging bull about to run for the roses, not caring who I trampled in my path.

She was so happy, though. I couldn't begrudge her this.

So, I kept silent and helped her pack up her apartment, finding room to put her plants at my place. She was dropping off the last of them before they hit the road. She was trying to convince the guys to let her take her pet gerbil, but so far, that hadn't gone over well.

Though, the epic battle had been with her parents. Duke and Debra had not been happy with me when they'd learned I'd taken Penny to a foreign country. They were now convinced I'd tainted her, talking her into dating three guys and going on tour. Seriously, the way her mother spoke about me, you'd think I had magical powers of bewitching.

If that was the case, I wouldn't be grumpy as hell, bloated, and single.

Jett hadn't reached out to me once since he stormed out of the cabana lounge, and I didn't blame him. I'd overreacted like usual and made a mess of things. Aspen swore there wasn't another woman involved, dismissing whatever Penny and I'd overheard.

Which meant it had to be something else, but it didn't matter. I'd screwed it up by kissing another guy, and he'd already forgotten me. His silence communicated as such.

Leaning against the entryway, I watched my best friend with her lover boys.

"No, Penny. I think you're adorable, but I don't want a stinky furball on the bus. It's cramped enough already. He would be miserable, and so would we. Please, don't make me the bad guy because I'm the only one thinking logically here."

Cooper and Penny pouted as they stood in front of Aspen, his papa-bear face holding strong. Sighing, I walked out into the living room that had become Penny's temporary room after subletting her apartment.

"Just leave the hideous thing here. If I can't watch him, I'm sure Liam can. He seems to have a soft spot for the thing."

"Ssh," she hissed, covering the ears of the thing in question. "He can hear you!"

"And? He's an animal. He has no idea what I'm saying. On second thought, you better get Liam. You're already putting a great deal of faith in me to keep your plants alive. I'm barely able to keep myself fed and watered. I'm going to make a horrible plant mom."

"You'll be fine." Penny hopped over, her happiness bubbling over. "But you're right. I better call Liam. Can I use your phone? Mine's still charging."

"Yeah, it's in the bedroom."

"Thanks."

I watched her go, eyeing the two guys in my apartment. Rafé had come home with her for the first week but was now spending some time with his parents. He would meet up with them on their second stop. Cooper was traveling to a few cities along with them until he had to do some appearances for his jump rope thing. I'd honestly quit listening when they started to talk about the logistics, only focusing on the parts where Jett's name was mentioned. I knew every city they would be in. Every city where he would be, singing to some other girl who wasn't me.

Fuck, I hated the fact I missed his broody ass.

Penny bounced back out of my room, a smile on her face. "Liam said to call him later, and he'll stop by and grab Chester." She held the gerbil up to her mouth, kissing the furball.

"I'll miss you, Chester. You be good for Liam. I'll see you real soon."

"Who's this Liam guy, and why is he willing to watch your pet?" Coop asked, crossing his arms.

"Down boy, he's my brother's best friend. Penny and I grew up with him. He's always hovering about. He's the protective type."

"Also known as Poppy's unrequited first love," Penny sang, swooning.

"Unrequited being the keyword. Besides, that was middle school, I've let Liam go. We're friends now, nothing more."

"Sure." Coop smiled, joining in with Penny now that he knew he wasn't a threat.

Rolling my eyes, I threw the magazine I hadn't been reading down and stomped to my room in annoyance. Once I was clear of them, I bolted to the bathroom, barely making it to the toilet before I hurled everything I'd managed to get down.

Sitting back on my ass, I wiped my mouth with the back of my hand, sighing as I tried to regain some composure. I needed to get up and put on my game face. As much as I lamented that I no longer cared about Liam, he had been my first heartbreak, and the one who'd set me on a course of never wanting to settle down. Somehow, he'd become integral to my life, and I couldn't imagine it without him, the same as Pen, but it didn't mean I still didn't pine for him.

Heaving myself up, I rinsed my mouth, looking into the mirror. Fuck, I looked horrible. This bug had been hitting me harder than I realized. I hadn't told Penny, too worried she'd read into it as me needing her to stay and try to take care of me. I could do that just fine, despite what she believed. Splashing water on my face, I went about applying makeup to help cover up my ghostly pallor and the dark circles that seemed to have lived on my face the past week. Sleep hadn't been easy either, dreams of broody men keeping me awake.

I never thought I had a type other than willing, but I was starting to see a pattern forming for the difficult ones. I was sure my therapist would say it was because I either didn't feel worthy of love, choosing the most unreliable candidate, or I self-sabotaged any chance by picking someone who wouldn't treat me with respect back.

Either way you sliced it; I was fucked up when it came to relationships. Another reason why I shouldn't be left in charge of a living thing. I'd find a way to screw that gerbil up too if it was left here.

Feeling more human, I grabbed my favorite t-shirt, a pair of cut-off shorts, and threw a hat on over my hair. There was no amount of product that would tame the beast today. Slipping on some converse, I walked out into the living room as they were finishing up the rules of gerbil care with Liam.

He looked up when I entered, his blue eyes searing me, and my clit immediately throbbed in response. The damn man was too hot for his own good, and I was useless to resist him. Liam watched each step I took, ignoring Penny as she went on and on about her gerbil like he hadn't watched the thing for the past two weeks.

"Well, I think that's all. Thanks so much, Liam."

"It's fine, Pen. You know Sarah loves to take care of her."

"Oh, I'm going to miss your niece. Give her a hug for me, okay?"

He nodded, his eyes back on me. "You eaten anything today? You look pale."

"Yes, I'm fine. Quit mothering me."

I rolled my eyes, not wanting to like how much his care warmed me, even if I did hate it to a small degree. He felt responsible for me, always had, some bro code he'd made with my brother. I just wish it was because he cared about me.

Slouching against the couch, my energy waned as I tried to keep the bile that wanted to rise up again down. Penny rushed over, throwing her arms around me, and I hugged her tight, not sure how I felt about missing her just yet.

"I'm going to miss you so much, Pop," she cried into my neck.

"I'm going to miss you so much, Pen." Laughing, we pulled away, wiping each other's tears.

"PB&J forever, though."

"Forever."

She hooked her pinky with mine, and I pulled her in once more for a hug. "Be good and keep living your list. You're gonna kill it, okay?"

"Yeah. It's just going to be weird without you," she whispered back.

"It will be fine. You have the guys. You'll barely even miss me with all the sex you'll be having."

She blushed at the thought, and I laughed. My bestie was growing up.

"Oh! Speaking of, I took the last of the tampons. I didn't have time to go out and get some. Sorry, I know your period is right about now too. Hey! Maybe we'll get out of sync now that we're not together twenty-four-seven."

"Yeah, maybe," I mumbled. Something about what she just said hitting me.

She hugged me tight, kissing my cheek before she pulled away and walked over to the guys. I seared them both with a look, making sure they took notice. "I'm leaving her in your hands. Do nothing to hurt her or I will bury you. Penny has her ways; well, I have mine. And I can guarantee, they're not as fun." I narrowed my eyes, pointing fingers.

"No worries, Pop. We've got her. Come and visit us on the road at some point. I know we can figure something out," Aspen offered, sincerity ringing through.

"Yeah, maybe. It just depends on how busy I am." I deflected his invite, not wanting to admit I'd made up the whole thing about the record label, and the thought of seeing Jett kissing another girl made me want to hurl. He nodded, taking Penny's hand, and I watched, staying back as they gathered the last few bags she had. Penny stopped at the door, turning to look at me.

One second she was there, the next she was in my arms and I hugged my friend, both of us crying.

"I'll call you every day. So much, you'll be tired of me."

"Not possible," I said, sniffling. "I'm going to miss you but go and be the awesome Penny I know you to be. I'll be fine. I promise."

"I love you, Pop."

"I love you, Pen."

"Thanks for dragging me to the Caribbean. Once again, you saved me and changed my life."

"Nah, I just changed your scenery, you did the rest. Now, go, before I decide to climb into your suitcase and surgically glue myself to you. That would be awkward." I grimaced, and she laughed, wiping her eyes.

"Yeah, okay. I'll talk to you soon."

We let go of another and she walked out, and I knew, without a shadow of a doubt that we'd be okay. We were best friends, and that was a bond that lasted forever.

The End…. For now.

Want more of PB&J?
Join Penny as she goes on tour with Shadows of Mayhem
in part two of her story this fall.
And Poppy, well, she's got a story to tell as well.
Join my newsletter to stay up to date on all book related
information and releases.

PENNY'S DIY-ING LIST

1) Stop changing yourself to fit what others needed—no more chameleoning
2) Figure out what makes your soul catch fire and do that, even if it was no longer teaching
3) Do something purely for you
4) It's okay to lose—it builds character. Try something you suck at, and just have fun.
5) Say no every once in a while. You don't have to do things for people to like you.
6) Quit apologizing for things you have no control over
7) It's okay to ask for help every now and then

FROM THE AUTHOR

Thank you for reading Vibing. This story was meant to be part of a vacation rom-com anthology, but that fell through and was canceled as things happen at times. I loved this story too much to let it go, so I decided to publish it independently.

Penny and Poppy have an amazing friendship, one I hope you have in your life. We all need a PB&J friendship. This story will have a second part to finish out Penny's arc and start Poppy's, and then Poppy will have a book. That girl has a great story to tell, and I can't wait to write it.

It will intersect with Lennox and her guys in Open Road, so grab that series if you haven't. You just know fun will be had when all of those characters get together. The timeline on these books will vary as they are more passion projects for me that I write in between other things. If you've looked at my schedule the past few months, it's been crammed full of stories, so they've been shelved for now. Make sure to subscribe to my newsletter or join my reader group so you can stay up to date on all things PB&J!

As with any book, it can't be written without a lot of other people. My alpha readers for this book, Emma, Kayla, and Amber, thank you for putting forth the time and love. To my beta divas who read this over Christmas,

Megan, Lindsay, Shawna, and Michelle, thank you for loving this book and laughing. To all my arckies and streeties, you guys are the best. Thank you for spreading the love of Ginger Nuts.

ALSO BY KRIS BUTLER

For the most up to date info on release dates, check out my website:
www.authorkrisbutler.com

CRUEL STEPS

#football #stepbrother #MFM #danceteam #plus size FMC

2 guys, no MM

Cruel Steps

BEAUTY AND THE CLEATS

#baseball #standalone series #heartfelt

The Cleat Retreat (Blake's prequel)

The Pitch Slap (Blake's book, MMFMM)

No Balking Way (Bryce's book, MMF)

Whiff it Real Good (Ledger's book, MM)

LUX BRUMALIS (COMPLETED)

#hockey #girlboss #nonbinary sibling

3 guys, no MM

Penalty Box

Dead Lift

Breakaway

THE COUNCIL SERIES (COMPLETED)

#figure skating #secret past #dark elements

7 guys, lots of MM with bi-awakening

Damaged Dreams

Shattered Secrets

Fractured Futures

Bosh Bells & Epic Fails

The Council Boxset

THE ORDER DUET (COUNCIL SPINOFF)

#secret agency #spy + hacker games #fashionista

4 guys, light MM (in book 2 at the end, and bonus)

Stiletto Sins

Lipstick Lies

The Order Duet Omnibus

DRESSED TO KILL SHARED WORLD (STANDALONE)

#female assassin #quirky & curvy #twins

4 guys, no MM

Raven

F*CK STEAL KILL (STANDALONE)

#morally gray #bestie unalivers #sassy

3 guys, biawakening, (FF in Joy's chapter)

F*ck Steal Kill

DARK CONFESSIONS (COMPLETED)

#mafia #therapist #foster kids + dogs #tattoos

5 guys with MM

Dangerous Truths

Dangerous Lies

Dangerous Vows

Reckless (Cami's Novella)

Relentless (Nat's Novella)

Dangerous Love

Truth Lies Vows Love: The Complete Series

TATTOOED HEARTS DUET (COMPLETED)

#tattoos #penpals #music #curvy fmc

3 guys with MM

Riddled Deceit (Part 1)

Smudged Lines (Part 2)

Open Road (Road trip Novella)

Tattooed Hearts Completed Duet

MUSIC CITY DIARIES (TATTOOED HEARTS SPIN-OFF)

#motorcycle club #age gap #TW #cam girl

4 guys, no MM

Beautiful Agony

Beautiful Envy

Beautiful Unity

Music City Diaries: The Complete Series

VACATION ROMCOM

#romcom #social media experiment #besties

3 guys, no MM

Vibing

THE COMPANION LOVE TRAP

#30 yo FMC #plus size FMC #MMFM #cruise #fake dating

3 guys, MM

The Companion Love Trap

CAGED HEAT

#mfm #40yoFMC #age-gap (younger guy / older guy) #cage fighting

Caged Heat

SINNERS FAIRYTALES (STANDALONE)

#Rapunzel retelling #dance #TW

3 guys, no MM

Pride

ABOUT THE AUTHOR

Kris Butler writes under a pen name to have some separation from her everyday life. Writing has become her second love, providing a safe place to normalize mental health through her characters. Kris enjoys writing emotional books with flawed characters, sassy heroines, and all the book boyfriends she loves to drool over. You can find her at home most nights reading with her husband and furbaby, trying to maintain her nerdy sock collection, or playing tabletop games with her friends. Kris loves to talk with readers about her books, even if it's just them yelling at her for that cliffhanger. If you enjoyed her book, please consider leaving a review. You can find her in her reader group or on social media.

Join my newsletter
Join my reader group
Check out my website